MURDER ON THE MEDITERRANEAN

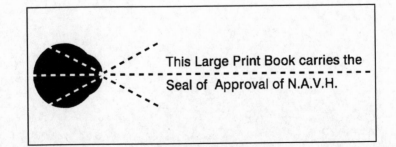
This Large Print Book carries the Seal of Approval of N.A.V.H.

A CAPUCINE CULINARY MYSTERY

MURDER ON THE
MEDITERRANEAN

ALEXANDER CAMPION

THORNDIKE PRESS
A part of Gale, Cengage Learning

Farmington Hills, Mich • San Francisco • New York • Waterville, Maine
Meriden, Conn • Mason, Ohio • Chicago

GALE
CENGAGE Learning®

LIBRARY OF CONGRESS CATALOGING-IN-PUBLICATION DATA

Campion, Alexander.
    Murder on the Mediterranean / by Alexander Campion. — Large print
edition.
        pages ; cm. — (A Capucine culinary mystery) (Thorndike Press large print
mystery)
    ISBN 978-1-4104-7107-9 (hardcover) — ISBN 1-4104-7107-1 (hardcover)
    1. Le Tellier, Capucine (Fictitious character)—Fiction. 2. Murder—
Investigation—Fiction. 3. Western Mediterranean—Fiction. 4. Large type
books. I. Title.
PS3603.A4848M87 2014
813'.6—dc23   2014025671

Published in 2014 by arrangement with Kensington Books, an imprint
of Kensington Publishing Corp.

As always, this one is dedicated to T. Without her support and insight there would have been no book. In addition, without her strength buoying the author through a seemingly eternal stretch of bad health, there would have been no author either.

The book is also dedicated to the Toronto General Hospital Lung Transplant Team who tirelessly applied their infinite skills to ensure that all the moving parts continue to hum and tick as intended.

CHAPTER 1

The cramps seared without mercy. On the lee side of the cockpit she contorted into a fetal twist, feet tight against buttocks, knees hard under chin. Like synchronized dancers, the twin wheels of the helm gyrated back and forth in the grip of the autopilot. Two women sat huddled on the other side of the cockpit, ostracizing her with their whispers. She glared at them, as if their rudeness was the source of her pain.

Another spasm wrenched her lower abdomen in a vise grip. She grunted. On the horizon a static of lightning was followed by a dull bowling-ball rumble of thunder. Greasy, fat drops of rain began to fall out of the sooty sky. She stood up, grabbed a foul-weather jacket from a heap at the foot of the settee, slipped it on, and inched across the sloping deck toward the bow.

Another spasm stunned her. A torrent buckled down, aimed only at her, soaking her to the skin. She couldn't manage to pull the jacket closed. Drenched, her T-shirt stuck to her breasts and stomach. Shuddering, she continued to fumble with the jacket. It wasn't hers. She must have picked up one of the women's. *Great.* Now, on top of everything else, she was going to get an earful when she got back to the cockpit. Even in the downpour, those rich bitches would get their noses all out of joint if one of them had to wear her taped-up, oil-stained piece of shit.

A violent spasm heaved at her bowels. Only one thing mattered, getting to the bow before it was too late. Doubled over, she shuffled along the heaving, sloping nonslip surface of the deck, her bare feet skating through the cascading water. The pain intensified. She wasn't going to make it to the bow.

The top of her head rammed into the wire cable of the forestay. She gasped a sob of pain and relief. The surprise loosened her grip on her muscles, and she felt the contractions of unstoppable peristalsis take charge. She ripped off the foul-weather jacket, threw it down on the deck, shrugged her shoulders out of the elastic suspenders of her foul-weather pants, pushed them down to her knees with the panties inside, gripped the forestay with both hands, swung herself out over the bow pulpit railing. The action unleashed the full force of the eruption. She was sure the explosion of her intestines could be heard in the cockpit, forty-five feet away, despite the din of the storm.

The relief lasted only seconds. She convulsed in pain again. And once again. And yet again. A figure emerged from the sticky darkness. Bound to be one of the two bitches, who'd come to see what was wrong. For a brief second, her embarrassment overrode the anguish of her gut. Hoping to keep from being seen in her mortifying position, she bleated out, "It's nothing. I'll be back in a second. Don't worry about me." Another spasm. Another spurt.

But it wasn't a woman. *Oh God, not now.* He was back. This was absolutely too much. She hurled insults. Strong hands grabbed her naked ankles and shook her legs. Her colon pumped out a weak but satisfying spurt. She relaxed her grip on the forestay, felt herself shoved hard forward, toppled off the bow pulpit, fell butt first into the sea.

She tried to tread water, but the pants around her ankles held fast. As she squirmed to kick off the foulie pants, she felt the slick hull of the boat rub against her arm. She scrabbled, grabbing for a handhold on the slick gel-coated side of the boat. In an instant the boat was gone, its tiny white stern light no more than a pinprick in the blackness.

She thrashed, but the bagging pants dragged her deeper and deeper the more she struggled. She swallowed a mouthful of salt water, gagged, coughed, swallowed more.

Her last thought was that drowning was supposed to be the most peaceful of deaths. How could everyone have been so wrong about that?

CHAPTER 2

"Capucine, I don't know how I let you talk me into this escapade. The thought of tossing helplessly over the waves of the open sea in your tiny walnut shell has been keeping me awake for days."

Police Judiciaire *commissaire* Capucine Le Tellier smiled at her erstwhile boss, *Juge d'Instruction* Inès Maistre, from under mischievous eyebrows and tilted her head back to swallow the sugary dregs of her demitasse of *café express.*

"The *Diomede* is hardly a nutshell, and she's definitely not mine. She's a bareboat charter. A fifty-five-foot Dufour with four cabins and all the room in the world. Much bigger than my first apartment after I graduated from Sciences Po. Look, you can see her over there."

Capucine pointed at a substantial yacht docked on the other side of the marina. The mainsail furled on its boom was sheathed in a navy-blue cover lettered MEDITERRANEAN ANCHORAGE YACHTS.

Inès peered at the boats over reading glasses perched on the tip of her nose, shrugged her shoulders in Gallic resignation. With an effort Capucine twisted her frown into a smile. The women were almost the same age, still south of their midthirties, and had worked together often in the antediluvian era, a few years prior, when Capucine was still a reluctant hotshot in the fiscal brigade. Capucine had never been entirely at ease with Inès. Her neurotic obsession with putting corporate criminals behind bars was as unsettling as it was captivating.

Capucine had blurted out her invitation two weeks earlier, when an unexpected surge of camaraderie had washed over her during a luncheon meeting. Inès wanted Capucine to work with her on a case. Even though Capucine now had her hands full with her own brigade in the tough working-class Twentieth Arrondissement, the thought of lending a hand on an intricate financial problem had produced a thrill.

A waiter — an eighteen-year-old who was obviously paying for his summer in the sun by working tables — came up with menus. He had a hard time tearing his eyes away from Capucine's décolleté. She concluded she might just have gone one button too far with her white linen shirt.

"Any news on your suspect?" Capucine asked Inès.

"He's a bit more than a suspect. He's guilty as hell. All we have to do is prove it."

"Would you like me to explain about the dishes?" the young waiter asked, eyes still glued to Capucine. Capucine ignored him as if she hadn't heard.

"And he was released two days ago, but that was only to be expected."

The situation was straightforward. The guilty-as-hell man in question was the young grandson of the chairman of a venerable family-owned Paris investment bank, Tottinguer & Cie. The house was so ancient, the name was pronounced differently from the way it was spelled. Nevertheless, Inès was convinced the bank's management, including the grandson, were inveterate financial miscreants. She had been after them for years and had never been able to produce even the slightest simulacrum of a case.

But now she might have found a chink in their armour. André Tottinguer, the grandson, a *gérant* of the bank and also a known philanderer, had been arrested for assault-

13

ing his wife. Inès had explained that Tottinguer had arrived home, returning from a tryst, at four in the morning to find his wife pressing the barrels of his Purdey shotgun up against his nose, her finger white tight on the trigger. Fortunately, the silly woman had left the safety on. He grabbed the gun, chased her down the stairwell, fired one shot into the ceiling and another through the lobby's interior glass door after she'd run out. The wife, in her bathrobe and pajamas, managed to find a cab and get to her sister's. The concierge of the building called the police, who arrested Tottinguer.

"And why did the police let him go?"

"That was my idea. No prosecutor would have even tried to present a case of attempted manslaughter. Charges might have been brought for *tapage nocturne,* creating a disturbance in the night, but all you get for that is a fine.

"No, I want to use this incident for an investigation of domestic violence. With your experience in the Twentieth, you're an expert. Once I have him solidly behind bars, the wife will cooperate with me and get me all the fuel I need for the financial prosecution of the whole family."

Capucine didn't know what to say. She twisted her mouth in the tight French frown that could mean either assent or incredulity.

"Capucine, I'm going to get him this time. Believe me. He'll go up for twenty years. And the rest of the family will follow right after. Just watch me." Inès gripped the edge of the table so hard, her knuckles paled.

There was an awkward silence. The tintinnabulation of steel halyards rattling against aluminum masts became audible.

Inès made a valiant attempt to put the conversation back on an even keel.

"Tell me more about this boat trip of yours."

"We leave on the morning tide tomorrow morning and sail straight for Bonifacio. You'll love it. It's the most beautiful town in Corsica, built high up on a white cliff so eroded by the sea that the town overhangs the water and looks like it might collapse at any moment. Then we spend a few days exploring the east coast of Sardinia and sail straight back here."

"And who else is there going to be?"

"There'll be nine of us in all. Six others besides you and me and my husband, Alexandre. My cousin Jacques — he's with the Ministry of the Interior — is coming, too. And one of Alexandre's cronies, Serge Monnot, who owns a number of very popular bars in the Marais, will be the skipper. He's an avid sailor, and he's the one who chartered the boat. Then there's Angélique Berthier and her husband, Dominique. Angélique was a classmate of mine at Sciences Po. She's doing very well as a partner in a head-hunting firm. Actually, we've drifted a bit apart since school, but we used to be very close friends. Her husband, Dominique, is wonderful, a charming marine watercolorist. And there's a woman I don't know, Florence Henriot. She's a friend of Serge's and is in charge of one of the imprints at Hachette. She used to be a famous professional racing sailor. Twice she won the Route du Rhum single-handed yacht race to Guadeloupe."

Inès grimaced and shuddered histrionically. "How could anyone want to do that? God knows how long she was alone on a boat without really sleeping or having a proper bath." She looked up sharply at Capucine. "There are bathrooms on this boat, aren't there?"

"Of course. There's one attached en suite to each of the cabins. Except on a boat they're called heads, not bathrooms."

Inès snorted and shook her head slightly. "That only makes eight people. Who's the ninth?"

"The professional crew member Serge

16

hired. A young girl, apparently. She's on board to cook and clean and help him when he maneuvers the boat, so all we have to do is lie around in the sun and eat delicious meals."

"Good. We'll put the time to good use. We need to brainstorm about Tottinguer."

"And unwind a little. Let's not forget about that part. You're going to be enchanted by Bonifacio, and the Costa Smeralda in Sardinia is the most beautiful coast in the Mediterranean."

"Maybe, but my main objective is to keep you fully in my sights until you're formally assigned to me. If need be, I'll handcuff our wrists together."

Capucine laughed over politely at the joke.

Inès frowned at Capucine over her reading glasses. "Capucine, I need to get this man. Without the quality of the police work you can bring to my team, I'm dead. Just dead."

CHAPTER 3

Five miles away in Saint-Tropez, Alexandre also sat at a restaurant table overlooking the inimitable azure of the Mediterranean. He had asked for the check, and the maître d' had arrived with thimble-size glasses of *liqueur de framboise* and the assurance that the honor of Monsieur de Huguelet's presence at the restaurant Pétrus was far more compensation than the establishment deserved. He was, after all, the undisputed doyen of restaurant critics.

"When was the last time you actually paid for a meal in a restaurant, *mon cousin?*" Jacques asked with a smirk.

Despite himself, Alexandre was invariably amused by Jacques, the son of Capucine's father's brother. The two had grown up together as brother and sister. Jacques never tired of hinting that there might have been something a bit more than purely fraternal to the relationship. Jacques also took unrestrained joy in the fact that he held an ill-defined, but apparently exalted, post with the DGSE, France's intelligence service, which occasionally cast him in the role of éminence grise in Capucine's cases.

Alexandre sipped his bone-chilling *alcool.* He would not allow himself to be baited. The meal had been excellent. They had both had Mediterranean spiny lobster. Jacques had chosen less well and had ordered his sautéed on a door-size teppanyaki grill, while Alexandre had chosen his presented in delicate fresh pasta *ravioles* with a creamy sauce of liquefied fennel bulbs, shallots, mustard, and just a hint of orange juice. Far more than satisfactory.

The restaurant Pétrus had recently opened at the north end of Saint-Tropez's fabled quai Jean Jaurès and was fast making a name for itself not only as a fashionable, *dans le vent* restaurant, but also as the purveyor of reference of prepared meals to the mega yachts that populated the quai. Alexandre decided he would write something upbeat about the Pétrus in his blog on *Le Figaro*'s website.

The framboise downed, hands shaken, promises to return made, favorable mentions in the press hinted at, Alexandre and Jacques set out on their postprandial stroll down the quai Jean Jaurès.

The Saint-Tropez port was immutable, crammed with wide, porch-size fantail decks of gigantic yachts berthed stern to quai, invariably decorated with an ornate vase of flowers on a table, swarming with young, tanned, obsequious, athletic crew in shorts and T-shirt uniforms.

"We have only one boat slave, it seems," Jacques said languidly, aping a disappointed moue. "I hope she makes up in pulchritude what we lack in quantity."

Alexandre harrumphed. "The last thing we need on this cruise is a boat girl. Florence is a world-champion sailor. Serge is very competent. Capucine knows her way around boats. If you ask me, Serge took one look at that coffin-size forepeak cabin and decided it would be perfect for some minion he could boss around like Captain Bligh."

At this point in their *flânocherie,* as Alexandre called it, they reached Sénéquier, the fabled café epicenter of the Riviera. Considering that the vacation ideal of every French person under the age of thirty-five was to spend the month of August with elbows propped up on one of Sénéquier's red, triangular tables, it was not surprising that there were no seats available on the terrace.

Two girls, their long legs at the apricot

beginnings of their summer tans, stood up to leave. Jacques pirouetted into a canvas director's chair with the finesse of a dancer, and Alexandre followed suit by spilling into his. A waiter arrived, imperiously flicking his side towel in irritation. There was a queue inside, and he had already received copious tips in exchange for a table. Jacques looked blandly at the man, straightening the crease in his Lanvin white-linen trousers, revealing creamy soft, baby-blue suede Tod's driving shoes. The waiter checked and respectfully stood up straight. Then he caught sight of Alexandre, felt he should recognize him, stood up straighter still.

"Messieurs?" he asked with exaggerated politeness.

"Pastis," Alexandre ordered, glancing at Jacques, who nodded.

When the drinks came, they both fell silent, admiring the high-school chemistry trick of the clear golden pastis turning milky white when water was added.

"Actually," Alexandre said after his first sip, "I really am in a pet about this boat girl of Serge's. I'd planned on doing the cooking myself. Working on those tiny boat stoves is an exciting challenge. I have a whole folder of recipes and a carrier bag filled with basic necessities . . . tins of pâté

21

de foie gras and a few jars of truffles and . . ."

Alexandre had failed to attract Jacques's attention. Alexandre searched the terrace for the source of Jacques's fascination. Jacques seemed captivated by some creature in the very depths of the terrace. This was unexpected, since Jacques never looked at women. A fact that, when combined with his immoderate interest in clothes, made the family wonder if he wasn't, well, just possibly a soupçon fey. Then Alexandre focused on the woman, a translucent beauty with alabaster skin, silken pale blond hair, and ice-blue eyes. Even a woolly mammoth would have stared.

Alexandre caught sight of her companion and jumped up.

"Régis!" he exclaimed happily. "*Toi ici!* You're the very last person I expected to run into in this crass temple of see and be seen. What on earth are you doing here?"

It was the work of a moment to whisk two chairs away from an adjoining table and make introductions. Régis de la Rochelle was a food photographer, well known for his commercials and his illustrations of pricey coffee-table cookbooks; the seraphic creature was called Aude Thevenoux and was, apparently, some sort of lawyer.

"Having an absolutely miserable time," Aude answered for him. Her face revealed not the slightest trace of expression when she spoke. It was almost as if she were a life-size porcelain doll of exquisite delicacy equipped with a sound system operated by a third party.

"The plan was to come down here and charter a boat and go somewhere," Régis said, "but everything is rented, so we're stuck in our drab little hotel room up in the hills."

"And the traffic jams are so bad, it's an hour cab ride to drive the two miles into town," Aude contributed with no more than a ventriloquist's movement of her lips.

"I have the perfect solution," Jacques said. "We have a boat chartered in Port Grimaud. We're leaving for Corsica in the morning. Why don't you come with us? We have plenty of room."

Alexandre hiked his eyebrows. This was a whole new Jacques.

"We could put you up on the settee in the main salon," Jacques said. "It can turn into a double bed. We're going to do an overnight crossing straight to Bonifacio. We could drop you off there, and you could have your vacation away from the crowds, or at least the worst of them."

Aude looked into Jacques's eyes, mute. Even though not a word had been exchanged, the bargain was sealed.

More pastis was ordered.

Régis chatted at Alexandre about his current project as one of the photographers on Alain Ducasse's latest tome. Jacques and Aude looked into each other's eyes.

Lubricated by a series of pastises, they became steeped in conversations as the radiant sunshine bore through the umbrella over the table and the afternoon wore on. When the shadows lengthened, Alexandre's thoughts turned to dinner. It was high time to find a cab and make their way back to Port Grimaud to hatch a plan for the evening meal with Capucine and that odd juge d'instruction friend of hers. He called for the bill, waving away any attempt from Régis to share. As they rose, Aude looked into Jacques's eyes.

"*A demain,*" she said. Alexandre had a strong sense of their complicity.

"We're at the Mediterranean Anchorage Yachts Marina in Port Grimaud," Jacques said. "Our skipper wants to get going by ten tomorrow morning."

Aude said nothing. She shook Alexandre's hand and leaned forward to allow Jacques to kiss her cheeks.

CHAPTER 4

"You let Jacques do *what?*" Capucine glared at Alexandre, her spoon dinging loudly as she stirred her café au lait on the tiny terrace of their hotel room overlooking one of the myriad canals that had been constructed to provide Port Grimaud with a veneer of antiquity. The contrived mix of burnt siennas and red ochers intending to create the look of "the Venice of France" exacerbated Capucine's irritation.

Alexandre was still partially enveloped in the arms of Morpheus. For him, seven thirty was hardly the hour for a levee. Left to his own devices, he would have begun his day at ten at the earliest. He looked balefully at Capucine from under lids three-quarters closed. It was clear that he would remain mute until he had taken the first sip from the split of champagne he had ordered, further escalating Capucine's ire.

"All right, I admit I made a mistake, too,"

Capucine said. "Inviting Inès was an impulse. I confess she intimidates me. And, yes, she may be a little too, well, intense, and, well . . ." Capucine lowered her voice. "Maybe just a bit too plebeian for this crowd." Her volume returned to normal. "But still, we talked it over with Serge, and he had absolutely no problems with her. Remember? But inviting on the spur of the moment not one, but two, people you ran into at a café, and proposing that they sleep on the sofa of an already overcrowded boat, without even thinking of consulting anyone, well, my dear, that's frankly quite over the top."

Capucine's tirade was interrupted by the arrival of room service.

The restorative power of the good monk Dom Pérignon's sparkling wine on Alexandre was never anything less than astonishing. Halfway through his flute Alexandre's ebullient bonhomie was fully restored.

He favored Capucine with his most fulsome smile. Capucine thawed, but only around the edges.

"Serge will be over the moon when he sees Aude. Trust me. And Régis is a good buddy and an excellent cook. Between the two of us our victuals alone will make the trip worthwhile."

"That remains to be seen."

Nearly an hour late — after all, the physical elements of post-squabble reconciliations are not to be rushed — Capucine and Alexandre stood at the end of a long floating dock, facing the ample stern of a generously proportioned sailboat. Their friend Serge, transformed from his Paris persona, stood sixty-five feet away at the bow of the boat. In the City of Light, in trim Italian suits worn tieless, with the top two buttons of his silk shirts left undone, he seemed always prepared for a paparazzo to snap him for the lifestyle pages of the glossies, which seemed never to tire of him. Now he had recast himself into a Mediterranean sailing bum. Clad only in shorts and boat shoes, he was already deeply tanned, his cheeks stubbled, his hard, flat chest adorned with a luminescent jade juju hanging from his neck on a leather thong. He stood next to a fresh-faced young man in a blue polo shirt marked MEDITERRANEAN ANCHORAGE YACHTS. Both peered intently at a clipboard, checking off the boat's inventory. Serge's bubble of self-importance was palpable even from the dock.

Capucine and Alexandre greeted Inès, who hovered twenty feet from the stern.

Exchanging inanities about the glory of the weather, the trio waited to be invited on board once the inventory was complete. A couple clanked down the aluminum ramp leading to the dock, their shrill argument far louder than the ringing of the metal plates under their feet.

"I saw the way you were hitting on that waitress! You've reached the point where you don't even wait for lunch. You're on the prowl even at breakfast. And you have the effrontery to do it right in front of me!"

It was hard to detect even a vestige of the sensitive Sciences Po Angélique in her current headhunter manifestation. The Modigliani face and shock of chestnut hair were still there, but her earlier delicacy had been overlaid by the intransient hardness of a top-of-the-line headhunter. On the other hand, Dominique, dreamy and placid in the storm of the harangue, remained the quintessential artist, concerned only with adjusting the knot of his fuchsia Liberty Print neck scarf.

Catching sight of Capucine, Angélique doused her rage. The females air kissed loudly, while the males thumped backs robustly. As this display of affection went on, a tall, wiry woman, face sunbaked brown as a saddle, clanked down the ramp with no more luggage than a diminutive backpack slung over one shoulder. Florence Henriot's face was unforgettable. It had been plastered over every Saturday supplement for decades when she was the queen of the daring single-handed transoceanic yacht races that so captivated the imagination of the country. She seemed not to have aged a bit. Capucine supposed that was the result of having had her face embalmed by the sun as a teenager.

Puffed up as a blowfish, Serge appeared at the head of two-foot gangway connecting the boat to the dock.

"Hey, there's no need to hang out down there. Come on board. I was just signing the inventory with the man from the charter company. Skipper stuff. You're going to love this boat. She's a total honey."

On board there was a cocktail party scurry of introductions. As the commotion died down, all eyes turned to the dock, where Régis and Aude had arrived, Régis wreathed in winsome smiles, an expensive-looking camera hanging around his neck, Aude statuesque, her beauty even more ethereal than the day before.

Beaming, Alexandre waved them on board. The second round of introductions was interrupted by yet another loud clattering down the ramp. A muscular young woman in very abbreviated, oil-stained cutoff jean shorts, a man's denim shirt tied in a loose knot under her breasts, and none-too-clean bare feet struggled with a grocery cart brimming with primary-colored packaged food products. Régis went to the rail and busily snapped pictures.

"That's our *marin,* Nathalie," Serge said. "I sent her out to buy provisions."

Solicitous of all matters comestible, Alexandre hurtled down the dock to help Nathalie.

Capucine's cousin Jacques had been one the first to arrive on the boat. As Capucine eyed the recent arrival with misgivings, Jacques whispered in her ear, "Not to worry. I understand that she's to be chained in her forepeak dungeon, gnawing on bones, until she's needed. Serge felt that the clanking of her fetters would add an erotic piquantness to the trip."

By their side Dominique examined Nathalie with a knowing eye, clearly mentally removing her few garments. Angélique scowled and spat out an inaudible comment. Serge's lips tightened. Capucine wondered if it was dismay at strife among his crew even before they set off or if he was jealous.

With a shrug of irritation Serge led the group below deck for a tour, leaving Nathalie to cope with her groceries as best she could. Régis brought up the rear guard, the clunk of his camera continuous.

"Do you always take pictures of everything?" Florence asked him.

"Good lord, no. This is for my blog. I'm avid blogger. I usually just post food pictures — I'm a food photographer by trade — but I have a special section for our summer vacation. I'm going to cover our progress day by day. It's my summer treat to myself."

He took a quick snap of Florence, who smiled tolerantly at him, and then wheeled and took one of Aude, hoping to catch her off guard. But she was as composed and expressionless as ever.

The boat's salon was as large as a small living room. There was a sofa to port and a banquette wrapped around a table and two chairs screwed into the floor to starboard. Toward the stern was a large, well-equipped galley screened off from the main area by a long counter. Opposite was a navigation desk flanked by a row of switches and screens that would have been at home on a jumbo jet.

Serge explained it all in enough detail to make their eyes glaze over.

31

Next, they trooped single file to visit each of the four cabins, all roughly the same size and each with a tiny bathroom, which Serge made a point of calling a head. Once the stateroom doors were closed, the units became cozy dollhouse-size flats.

Back in the salon, they spread out, steeling themselves for Serge's inevitable lecture. He boosted himself up on the galley counter, took a deep breath, and looked around the room to make sure all eyes were on him.

"Before we shove off, I want to lay out some ground rules," Serge said in an authoritarian tone. Sensing that he had started out on the wrong foot, he attempted a charming smile, which came out as a forced rictus.

Still pedaling for the right note, he asked, "How many of you have been on a long cruise before?" All the hands went up with the exception of Aude's, Inès's, and Florence's. They clearly felt the question was not worth dignifying with a reply.

"Great. We have lots of experienced talent. Let me tell you how I've allocated the cabins." He checked himself again. "I mean, how I'd suggest we divvy them up."

A frost settled over the group.

"I thought we could put Angélique and

Dominique and Capucine and Alexandre in the two stern cabins, which have double beds, while Florence and Inès and Jacques and I can bunk down in the two forward cabins, which have two single bunks. Régis and Aude will bunk in the salon. Does that work for everyone?"

There were nods and murmurs of lukewarm assent. Capucine noticed that Angélique and Dominique held hands and winked at each other as their cabin was mentioned.

"Good. Now that that's out of the way, let's talk about our cruise. We're going to put to sea in an hour and head straight for Bonifacio. We will have a good, solid twenty-knot westerly all the way down and should make landfall in the early morning, by lunchtime at the latest. We'll spend a day or two there, and when we've had enough of it, we'll head south to Sardinia. We'll map out our plan of attack for Sardinia while we're in Bonifacio. How does that sound?" Serge asked with the enthusiasm of someone who expected a round of applause.

"Does that mean we'll be sailing all night, in the dark?" Inès asked.

"Of course. It's a straight shot from here. We crank in one fifty on the autopilot and tool on down. No problem." He shot Florence a slightly nervous look, searching for approval.

This time the murmurs of agreement were more animated. The prospect of being in Bonifacio the next day was a pleasant one.

Reassured, Serge went on. "Good. We're going to have watches of three hours each all the way down. The wind isn't expected to change direction, so we won't even have to tack and the boat will sail itself on autopilot. If we have to trim the sails at any point, Nathalie and I will handle it. It'll be a piece of cake." Serge smiled condescendingly at Inès.

"Now let's get to the ticklish subject of the Achilles heel of all boats, the heads." Looking at Aude, he explained, "This boat has the latest technology. The head and the shower are in the same cubicle. Make sure you flip the toilet seat down when you use the shower. Otherwise, you could fill up the holding tank. The heads themselves have two cycles. You pump water, throw a lever, and pump it out. There is a plate screwed to the bulkhead with very clear instructions. But the system can be a bit temperamental, and our rule is going to be 'Never put anything in the head that you haven't eaten first.' " Serge gave a snort of TV comedian's laughter that invited the audience to join in.

All he got was polite smiles and shuffling feet. It was a beautiful morning, and they were about to embark on an adventure. No one wanted to be cooped up below deck, listening to a pep talk about sewage.

The mood was broken when Nathalie thumped down the four steps of the companionway in her grubby bare feet with an armload of groceries. Alexandre and Régis jumped to help.

"Ah, yes," Serge said. "Let me introduce Nathalie. She's going to be our best friend for the next ten days, cooking our meals, cleaning up our boat, and giving me a hand on deck if she has any spare time." He smiled at her with the tolerant affection people gave to scruffy old family dogs that had just wandered in with muddy paws. Nathalie ignored him.

"Nathalie bunks down in the forepeak cabin. The only way you can get to it is through the glass hatch at the bow." He smiled at Nathalie again. Capucine was sure she saw a healthy dollop of lust folded into his patronizing smile.

The group dispersed, Serge and Florence to examine the rigging and the working of the sails, while the others chatted in the sunshine on deck.

Ten minutes later Serge was engrossed in

35

explaining the complexities of the self-furling jib to Capucine, Inès, and Aude. Alexandre, with Régis in his wake, approached Serge with the grim solemnity of a parent about to tell his spouse that he has discovered their child engaged in an act of particularly bizarre self-abuse. Serge looked up in alarm.

"Your boat girl is depraved," Alexandre said.

"Depraved?"

"Either that or she owns stock in the Panzani corporation. In any event, she plans to feed us the full range of their canned pastas." Alexandre paused to let the full gravity of his statement sink in. Serge stared at him, slightly openmouthed. Capucine looked out over the bow pulpit, her back twitching from suppressed giggles.

"Canned pasta every day?" Serge asked lamely.

Régis chimed in. "Worse. Her menus are brightened up with Bolinos." A guffaw eructed from between Capucine's lips.

"Bolinos?"

"They're little plastic cups," Régis explained. "You pull the foil lid halfway back, fill the cup up to the mark with boiling water, wait three minutes, and stir with a spoon. Your dinner is ready. They come in

36

four varieties."

The explanation was greeted with silence.

"We just tried the shepherd's pie. It was far worse than you can imagine," Régis said.

"But there's good news. Nathalie hung on to the receipt. Régis and I are going to the supermarket to return all that swill. We'll be back in an hour. An hour and a half at the most. Since it will be lunchtime by the time we return, we'll serve a light collation, and then you can shove off," Alexandre said.

Serge nodded meekly, his skipper persona usurped in a bloodless palace revolution.

CHAPTER 5

Capucine couldn't help but feel sorry for Serge. He moped on the stern rail, waiting for Alexandre and Régis's return, mournfully scrutinizing the sun's inexorable climb to its zenith. Finally, a good two and a half hours after they had left, Alexandre and Régis arrived, clattering two shopping carts piled high with produce. Alexandre smiled up at Capucine triumphantly, a returning knight paladin who had saved the village from dire perdition.

Serge sprang into action, dispatching his crew to collect the groceries, turned the ignition on, let it shriek its warning for a full minute while the cylinder heads heated, jabbed at the starter button, ordered Nathalie and Florence to cast off the mooring lines, and gently eased the boat out of the marina, while Alexandre and Régis went below to stow their bounty. The notion of a quai-side wait for a "light collation" had volatilized.

To the beat of the throbbing motor, Serge eased through the postcard emerald greens and Tyrian purples of the coastal waters and in fifteen minutes reached the ink–dark blue of the open sea. Capucine sat on the bow pulpit with Inès, smiling at the early afternoon tropical sun. Inès, unnerved even by the gentle rocking of the boat as it glided across the glass-flat sea, clutched the pulpit rails with both hands.

Far behind them, at the stern, Serge, skipper once again, ordered Nathalie to take the helm and Florence to raise the mainsail. As Florence began to crank the halyard winch on the side of the mast, Alexandre stuck his head out of the hatchway like a jack-in-the box, blinking from the brightness of the sea sun.

"*Pas si vite, mon ami.* Not just yet, my friend," Alexandre said, his voice heavy with authority. "Lunch first, and then you can play with your boat to your heart's content."

Clenching his teeth, Serge forced a smile as Florence dropped the six inches of mainsail she had raised and clipped three shock cords to secure the sail in place on the boom.

Alexandre emerged from the hatch with a tray, followed by Régis, bearing another one.

Serge's smile climbed up his face and lit up his eyes. He went below and emerged with two bottles of chilled Tempier rosé and a stack of flimsy plastic glasses adorned with the charter company's florid monogram. He was clearly far more at home in the persona of a host than that of a skipper.

"Look what Alexandre's brought us. We're in for a treat," Serge said.

"Three different bruschette," Régis said, striving for stage center. "One is made with fresh plums, Serrano ham, and ricotta. Another with sautéed chicken covered with yellow and red cherry tomatoes sliced in half, topped with slices of fontina, and then grilled. And a third is made with onions, carrots, zucchini, red beans, baby spinach leaves, sprinkled with *herbes de Provence* and coated with a spinach pesto sauce."

Régis produced his camera and snapped pictures of the trays. Serge filled and distributed glasses. Forgetting he was intended to serve lunch, Régis rearranged the serving dishes, creating an expressionist tableau of summer colors.

"Do we have to wait until you've completely reclothed the model before we can partake?" Jacques asked. There were three beats of shocked silence before the cockpit rippled with laughter.

The wings of the table in the middle of the cockpit were raised, converting it into a cozy restaurant booth. The group scuttled around like schoolchildren gathering for their three o'clock *gouter.* Aude wound up at the stern end of the cockpit, inches away from Nathalie, at the helm. Angélique and Inès squatted, legs folded, on the sill of the hatch. The volume of chatter increased as the wine circulated. The contretemps of the morning evaporated as quickly as summer dew. The bruschette were perfect: light, flavorful, estival. As the serving dishes passed from hand to hand, Aude pivoted and glared at Nathalie's feet, directly behind her, gray with the grime of Port Grimaud's streets.

Elegant as a prima ballerina rising from a plié, Aude stood up, stepped onto the deck, and repositioned herself on the sliding cover of the hatch, towering over the group, a princess with her subjects assembled respectfully before her.

Solicitous of every crew member, topping up every glass when it was half full, serving every nearly filled plate with additional bruschetta, Serge was in his element. Capucine knew from Alexandre that Serge's success with his restaurant-bar business stemmed from his ability to simultaneously animate

41

the front of the house of five different restaurants, and not from his business acumen.

When Serge bent over Inès to pour wine, she fingered at his shirt.

"I couldn't find a life preserver in my cabin. Isn't it dangerous not having one? Shouldn't there be one?"

As she spoke, her pluck on his shirt escalated into a crumpling grip. Alexandre felt the calm of the afternoon percolate away in an unpleasant sea change. High time for Inès to have the conversation nudged back ashore.

"Do you know, Inès, that we have a movie auteur on board so skillful, he could have made our mouths water even for the canned Panzani slop we so barely escaped?"

"Régis? I thought he was in advertising."

"I hardly think of it as advertising," Régis said, affronted. "I'm a *table* director, not a *movie* director. Trust me, that's where the real skill is required. I work only with food. Take that TV ad for Charolais Allô that came out yesterday — you know, the one with the steam rising from a succulent *pavé de bœuf* and fries that look like they would melt in your mouth. It took me a whole week to pull it off."

"Inès," Dominique said, wresting the attention back, "there's nothing to worry about. These boats are unsinkable. But I'm sure if you think you'd feel safer with a life vest on while you're on watch, Serge would be happy to issue you one."

He showed Alexandre and Capucine the sketch he had been working on. In the drawing the dumped mainsail had been morphed into something organic, perhaps the disemboweled colon of an animal. A blond woman, naked from the waist up, sat in the cockpit, contemplating the sail. All that could be seen of her was a shapely back, hair done up in a ballerina bun, a long and sinuous neck.

Angélique peered down at the sketch and screeched, "That's not my breast. My breasts are larger." She pressed her index finger hard into the pencil drawing, smudging the side of the torso, where the shadow of a breast might, or might not, have appeared. "And I know exactly who it is! It's that filthy boat girl. Serge, if I'd known you were going to hire people like that, I'd never have come." She pushed by her neighbors, stalked down the companionway, and slammed the cabin door.

Unperturbed, Dominique restored the offending breast with a few pencil strokes. Jacques made the merest moue at Aude and hiked his eyebrows microscopically. Aude produced the hint of a smile back at him. Capucine was sure she saw that.

His confidence restored, his belly full, Serge took over the helm and, with a sweep of his hand, motioned Nathalie to clear the dishes. With a plastic clatter she piled them up, stuffing the remains of half-eaten bruschetta into her mouth. The cockpit was quickly vacated.

The sails went up with a rattle of halyard winches, the boat heeled over, the engine stopped, and the sounds of the sea lapping at the hull became audible.

Capucine, Aude, and Angélique slipped below to put on bathing suits and reappeared on deck, Angélique with a pile of art magazines, Capucine with the latest Fred Vargas mystery, Aude with a slim volume of poetry. The women spread out on deck, removed the tops to their bathing suits, and lathered themselves with suntan oil.

Angélique sat at the masthead with Dominique, flipping through the pages of art magazines, as he observed the mandatory ritual of oiling his wife's naked back. Alexandre joined Capucine on the bow. They sat, legs dangling over the side, heads ducked under the top wire of the lifeline to keep themselves vertical, admiring the receding coast. This was pure bliss, Capucine told herself. Why hadn't they ever gone on a long cruise before? Capucine smirked when she caught Alexandre scrutinizing the breasts of the two women. Men and their inexplicable breast fetish. How odd it was. Aude, with her sculptured alabaster breasts, was indifferent, but Angélique caught Alexandre's glimpse and arched her back, making her full breasts even larger.

Of course, women were even more caught up in the fetish than men were. Proud as she was of showing off her mammaries on deck, Angélique would be mortified if one of the males on board had come across her topless below deck. And all this over instruments the Maker had intended merely for the nourishment of offspring.

Half an hour later, just as Alexandre and Capucine were contemplating a short siesta in their cabin, Régis appeared on deck with a large pitcher and another stack of plastic glasses.

"Negronis," he said. "My own variety. I make them with gin, Campari, Martini & Rossi, a healthy splash of Prosecco, and a wedge of orange. Since we're heading for Italy, we may as well italianate ourselves." The bubbly Negronis elevated the afternoon into something significant, possibly even transcendent.

Away from the land, the breeze stiffened to the promised twenty knots and backed to the south. Serge trimmed the sails flat and hard as iron, and the brave *Diomede* heeled well over, crashing aggressively into the intensifying chop. Sleek as the Dufour looked at her berth, Capucine realized that she really was a heavy bathtub of a boat, built stiff to make an inexperienced crew feel secure. She came alive only in a strong wind, and even then she was still unyielding, hanging on to the vertical with all her might, plowing through the waves instead of soaring.

Inès groaned and rolled her eyes. Serge motioned Angélique to the helm and went below. There was no doubt Angélique was a master at the wheel. Capucine snuggled under Alexandre's arm and rejoiced in the afternoon. They were definitely going to go cruising more often.

A good bit later Alexandre went below to begin some culinary complexity that apparently was the sine qua non of dinner. Capucine gave the large deck a cursory look for Inès but didn't see her. Just as she concluded that Inès had gone below to nurse her seasickness in her bunk, Capucine heard a retching sound and saw Inès's skinny buttocks, clad in olive-drab shorts, peek out from under the taut genoa.

Capucine went forward to the bow and swung around the luff of the jib. Inès was kneeled over the lifeline, pathetically making an offering of Alexandre's bruschetta to the sea. Capucine commiserated. There was no despair deeper than wrenching seasickness.

Her hand loosely around the lifeline, Capucine inched down the deck to join Inès, who looked up and smiled bleakly. Hidden behind the luminous backdrop of the enormous genoa, they were isolated in a magical world, sandwiched between the rushing sea and the glowing white expanse of Dacron.

A strong gust heeled the boat over more, putting the rail under water. Capucine clutched the lifeline as the water rose to her knees. Inès was slammed hard into one of the vertical stainless-steel lifeline stanchions and then began to slip under the lowest wire. She was inches away from being washed overboard. Capucine pushed through the water, folded one arm around Inès's torso, locked the other around the lifeline, clenched her muscles.

The Dacron of the genoa crashed down

on them like a falling brick wall. Capucine stretched, put her arm around the lifeline until her hands could clasp onto opposing wrists, locking Inès in her grasp. Capucine hung on for all she was worth. They both went under water for eternal seconds. The sail scraped roughly over their backs, tearing at their clothes until the boat's angle of heel lessened. Capucine and Inès coughed and sputtered. Florence crossed the deck in long, sure-footed strides, picked them both up by the collars, dumped them none too gently onto the cushions of the cockpit. They sat in lumps, still gasping for breath, salt water streaming from their bedraggled hair.

Ignoring them, Florence went to the port-side wheel, unscrewed a knob, and jockeyed the helm, looking sternly at the rigging and the sea. Like a rambunctious dog subjugated by the return of its master, the boat sailed placidly on through the brilliant afternoon, guided only by Florence's two fingers lightly on the top of the giant wheel.

A drowned rat, Inès sputtered, wet strands of colorless hair covering her eyes. Her glasses were gone. Capucine smiled at her. "Why, you're beautiful without your glasses." She giggled. Inès giggled with her. It was the first time Capucine had ever seen her laugh.

People poured through the hatchway like circus clowns bursting out of a miniature car. Angélique was furious. She shouted at Capucine and Inès, stabbing at them with her index finger. She had been at the helm, doing quite a good job with such a big boat, when Serge had abandoned her to go below. The boat had been hit by a violent squall. Frightened as she was, she had had the presence of mind to do the right thing. She had edged the helm downwind and had eased the sails to reduce the list. She'd had no idea two people were sitting on the lee rail. How could she have? They should have told her. It was their fault, not hers. And she had been brave enough to stay at the helm until she had been relieved by Florence. No one appreciated her.

As Alexandre led Capucine below to the comforts of towels, hair dryer, fresh clothes, and a hot rum toddy, Dominique emerged on deck to the harridan shrieks of Angélique. "You had the nerve to leave me alone on deck while you were panting after that grubby, hussy boat girl, and just look what happened. Your incessant skirt chasing nearly killed two people."

Chapter 6

When the sun set with a kaleidoscopic show of brilliant reds and pinks spread out over the slate-blue sea, Capucine told herself the ultimate proof of the Dear's divinity was His ability to keep such a garish show from being vulgar.

Most of the group was still on deck, chatting. A ship's bell clanged. Régis stuck his head out of the hatchway.

"*Allez. Allez, les amis.* Dinner's ready. Do you want to eat up here or down below?"

"It's such a beautiful evening. Let's eat on dec—" Dominique started to say.

He was cut off by Angélique, who sat at the bow with Capucine and Inès.

"Below, definitely, Régis. It's starting to get cold."

Régis gave Dominique a conspiratorial smile.

Without the horizon as a reference, the heel of the boat was far more apparent below deck. Capucine let the slope of the deck propel her to the galley console. Alexandre was at his diminutive stove, in the midst of one his cooking epiphanies. The stove, set on gimbals, was the only horizontal surface in the salon. Alexandre had found a wide strap that hooked into the counter at the sides of the stove, allowing the cook to lean back in complete comfort against the boat's heel. On one burner he was making some sort of sauce; on another he was sautéing something that could have been miniature rugby balls. The salon smelled pleasantly of garlic.

At his side, Régis was enthusiastically taking pictures of Alexandre *à l'œuvre.*

"Our first real meal on the boat," he announced at large. "My blog entry is going to be fabulous. I'm going to write it right after dinner."

With a flourish Alexandre wrapped a side towel around the handle of the metal skillet and put it in the oven. He undid one of the clips of the strap and climbed up the incline into Capucine's arms.

"I'm so in love with youuu," he sang. "And also so in love with this little stove," he continued in his normal voice. "Cooking on that toy-size thing is a challenge. But you know what they say. The test of a deep-sea sailor is the ability to make perfect profiteroles in a gale-force storm. And I intend to pass that test before this cruise is over."

Behind them, Régis laid a damp cloth on the table to prevent the dishes from sliding and then proceeded to lay the table. He tucked the knives and forks wrapped in paper napkins on the uphill sides of the plates and tested everything with his finger to see if it was secure against the list.

Six of the group inched their way up the hill onto the settees, those in the center sitting back as if in reclining chairs. Serge sat at one end and squeezed over to make room for Aude, who sat perfectly erect without any effort or apparent means of support.

Capucine sat in one of the three swivel chairs screwed into the floor and leaned far forward, bracing herself on the table with her elbows. The damp from the tablecloth was clammy and unpleasant on her elbows. The boat hammered through the chop with loud banging resonating through it from the bow. Still, Capucine told herself, the discomfort was part and parcel of the thing, more a testimony to adventure than a trial. They really were deep at sea, in their own private universe. The feeling could not be equaled.

With a flourish, Régis placed a large Plexiglas bowl filled with dark primary colors in front of Angélique. He shuffled downhill back to the galley area and returned with a small metal pot containing a dark liquid, which he poured with great care over the dish. He handed Angélique a Plexiglas salad knife-and-fork set and dropped back a few feet, his camera poised.

"Can you toss this and then serve, Angélique? It seems we have to eat it while the sauce it still hot." The second Angélique's implements touched the bowl, a bright flash and then two more dazed the diners. "Great shot," Régis announced. "Now give me some action, Angélique. I want to see some real tossing. I need drama."

Turning to face Alexandre, who had removed his little rugby balls from the oven and was covering them with aluminum foil, Régis asked, "What do you call this again?"

Alexandre pushed his way up the incline, smiling the proud grin of a three-star chef emerging from his kitchen. Capucine was sure he imagined himself in a foot-high, immaculate white chef's toque.

"*Bagna cauda*. It's a Niçois classic. Potatoes, baby beets, baby leeks, baby carrots, spring onions, radishes, bell peppers, endive, and many other things, but most importantly, properly trimmed baby artichokes.

The sauce is made with anchovies and garlic in olive oil. But the point of the thing is that it has to be eaten hot. Hence the name."

As always, Alexandre's food had a mesmerizing effect. No one spoke for thirty seconds. The anchovies gave the delicate baby vegetables a piquancy that elevated them to the ethereal. Dishes like this never surprised Capucine when Alexandre made them on his enormous La Cornue stove in their apartment, but the fact that he was able to pull it off on a tiny stove on a heaving sea impressed her. She hoped they might have a serious storm so he could attempt profiteroles.

Capucine looked over at Inès to see how she was coping with her first in-cabin meal. She seemed to be relishing the bagna cauda.

"So tell us, Serge," Angélique said with exaggerated cheerfulness, "all about Bonifacio. What time are we going to get there, and what's it going to look like?"

Serge puffed out his chest like a carrier pigeon. "Bonifacio is one of the great natural harbors of the world. It's at the end of a narrow gorge nearly half a mile long and cut into the rock. And high up on the rock, above the harbor, there's a small town —"

Florence cut him off. "There are places

where you can have lunch and lean out the window as far as you can and still not see where the sea meets the bottom of the cliff. I always move my chair very carefully."

Serge jockeyed to regain the microphone. "We'll arrive in the middle of the morning. We're going to have a hard sail tonight, and so I'm going to tell you how I want to assign the crew —"

"Voilà," Alexandre said, arriving with a platter, leaning forward against the incline. Régis's incessant flashes lit up the room like a nightclub.

The main course was beautifully browned squid, bloated with a stuffing of crab, the squid's chopped tentacles, onions, green peppers, red bell peppers, and a bit of garlic; seasoned with curry and hot mustard powder; and sprinkled with lime. It was accompanied by an elegant *tian* of thin slices of tomatoes and eggplant, topped with little pieces of fresh goat cheese, covered with the Midi's ubiquitous herbes de Provence and a latticework of a truly excellent olive oil Alexandre had unearthed on his shopping foray. This all was served with an unctuous, round, honey-noted Ott rosé.

There was another moment of silence as the first bites were tasted. From her seat Capucine could see Nathalie scowling at them from her position at the helm. Even though the sun had set nearly an hour before, the dusk was still rosy bright.

Florence followed Capucine's gaze.

"Serge," Florence said. "Whose head is Nathalie going to use?"

"I, er, hadn't —"

"It's going to take more than a bathroom to scrape the filth off that girl's feet," Angélique said. "Someone needs to put a pressure hose to her."

She glanced at Aude, hoping for an agreeing comment, but Aude just looked back, her porcelain face expressionless. Angélique smirked self-righteously, as if Aude had agreed with her vigorously. Capucine noted, not for the first time, that Aude's blank face had a Rorschach quality of reflecting the mood and opinion of the person talking to her. It must be those all-knowing, preternaturally blue eyes.

Jacques also stared at Aude, the top half of his face deadly serious, but the bottom twisted into a wry smirk. "I wouldn't be too quick with that pressure hose. Nothing is more erotic than a big-breasted wench seasoned with the soil of the earth. Think Tom Jones." He shrieked his donkey bray, ear piercingly loud in the confines of the salon.

Obviously embarrassed by the turn the conversation had taken, Régis said, "Florence, tell us about your single-handed races. I just can't imagine anyone sailing a boat as big as this all by herself."

Florence smiled modestly. "Actually, most of the boats I sailed were more than twice as long as this one, and since they were three-hulled trimarans, they were a whole lot wider. Handling the boat is the easy part. You just take everything very, very slowly, very carefully, one step at a time. You win races by being lucky about the weather. The first Route du Rhum I won, I arrived a full day before the others because I took a southerly route and had a nice following wind for three days, while everyone else was stuck in a dead calm."

"Don't you get lonely?"

"No. If you're not terrified in the middle of a storm, you're numb from lack of sleep. It's like being on drugs. Of course, you lose it a little. I can understand why so many of these guys who do the single-handed circumnavigation of the globe wind up nuts."

Florence continued on with tales of loopy single-handed sailors. Capucine lost the thread. She wondered who had really been at the helm when they took their ducking.

With a clatter, Régis cleared the dishes

and put new plates on the table, along with a selection of cheeses from the Midi, a big wedge of pale Moulis, three different goat cheeses, and a large slab of Bleu des Causses, which looked like a thick-crusted Roquefort.

"Be sure to try that," Alexandre said to the group. "It's Roquefort's milder, more elegant cousin."

Florence edged out of her seat and stood up effortlessly, despite the steep list of the floor. "Serge, why don't you have a peek at our position and make sure we don't have a course change? Shout it up to me if you want a new heading. I'm going to spell Nathalie so she can eat."

"Yes, good thinking. I was just about to do that." Serge stood up, limped his way to the navigation desk, and began poking at the electronic instruments and making pencil marks on the chart.

"Florence, we're dead on course. Steady as she goes," he shouted.

Nathalie's bare feet thumped down the companionway steps. She swept the table with a rancorous look. She went to the galley area, where Régis was washing dishes. Two of the squid had been left in the foil-covered frying pan for her. She pulled off the foil and wrinkled her nose in distaste.

The group at the table watched her out of the corner of their eyes.

"Here's how we should divide up the watches," Serge said.

Nathalie picked up one of the squid with her fingers, put it to her nose, sniffed it suspiciously. She made a childish moue of distaste. Alexandre frowned at her.

"The boat will be on autopilot, so there's nothing to do except keep your eyes open and call me if there's a change in wind direction. Is that clear?"

Nathalie took a deep, resigned breath and bit off a third of one of the squid. The stuffing oozed out, sticking to her upper and lower lips as she chewed. She swallowed with a loud gulp, wiped her mouth with the back of her hand, and stuffed in the rest of the squid.

"I'll take the first watch with Alexandre and Aude. Then at midnight Florence will come up with Capucine and Jacques. At four in the morning Nathalie will take over with Angélique and Régis. How that?"

"Perfect," Jacques said sotto voce to Capucine. "Angélique can get to work with her power hose."

Nathalie appeared to approve of the squid. She grabbed the second squid in her fist and took a large bite. A blob of stuffing fell on her dimpled chin. She chewed on, swallowed with a gulp, scraped the stuffing off her chin with two fingers, then put them in her mouth and sucked loudly.

The people at the table made a great show of avoiding the spectacle. Capucine had not the slightest doubt that Nathalie was putting it on intentionally.

"Pure Antonioni," Jacques said sotto voce with his Cheshire cat smile. "Only he fully understood the eroticism of the *belle fauve* — the beautiful savage." He shrieked his high-pitched laugh. Capucine looked at Aude to see how she would react. She had turned her head toward Jacques, and Capucine was sure she saw a faint smile, but when she looked again, she thought she must have imagined it. Aude's lips had remained as immobile, as if they had been cut from white Tuscan marble.

At one in the morning Capucine leaned back in the cockpit, her feet up on the now-folded table and her head resting on the back of a settee cushion, watching the canopy of stars gyrate lazily back and forth as the boat rolled. She thought of Ulysses, who had sailed these very waters in his adventures and misadventures. She thought of how this little sea, when you got right down to it, was the placenta of the Western world's civilizations.

Florence was at the helm, a few feet away, her hand languidly draped over one of the twin wheels, eyes glued to the horizon, throwing an occasional glance at the compass in front of her, which cast a faint, candle-like glow on her mannish features. She had switched the autopilot off. The feel of the boat had immediately softened, the boat itself becoming responsive to the give and take of the sea. On long cruises Capucine was always amazed how, even when you were eyes-shut-tight asleep in your bunk, you could always tell who was at the helm. And you always slept far better with an experienced hand on the wheel.

The sky was solid with stars. There were so many, it seemed almost that the lighted dots occupied more area than the dark spaces. Harking back to her childhood summers on the beach in Brittany, she found the few constellations she could recognize. There was the Big Dipper, guiding her eyes to the North Star. She searched for her father's favorite cluster of stars, the Pleiades, which he always liked to call "a little pâté." Where was it? There it was. Fainter than she remembered, but very much present and accounted for.

Finding the Pleiades had always been her summer nighttime swan song. Her father would sit with her on the beach until they found it and congratulated themselves. Then —

"You know, *cousine,* you should do the wet T-shirt thing more often. You have the perfect *nichons* for it. It's a look that suits you. Your juge chum, not so much. If the best you can muster is a fried egg, you should stay dry."

"I thought you two were asleep," Florence said from above.

Capucine tilted her head back again and took in the heavens. She was rewarded with a small cascade of shooting stars.

"It's on nights like this that you can understand the appeal of single-handed sailing. It must be pure bliss to be able to plug yourself fully into the cosmos."

"Except that you don't. You're always worried about something. You're going to have to hoist yourself up the mast in the morning to find out why the masthead block is making that funny squeak. The air smells like a small sea change that you weren't expecting. You're going to have to get a radio link and download the latest Met report, crappy as they are. You haven't sat on the head in two days, and that's bound to spell trouble. Stargazing is for pleasure cruises."

"So why do you do it?"

"Because I was nuts as a kid. I'm over it. This is the first time I've been on a boat in years."

"But you were famous."

"Famous and poor. Now I'm president of a company, even if it's a very small company, and I have a bank account with actual money in it. That's a very nice thing to have, I've learned."

Capucine sat up straight. "And you really didn't know that Inès was sitting on the lee rail, under the jib?"

"No. I'm sorry if I scared you both. I was a million miles away, in my own world. I had just come up on deck to relieve Angélique, and I made the course adjustment reflexively. Totally without thinking. I really don't know how it happened. I guess I'm just not used to sailing with other people."

CHAPTER 7

Even the grace of the next morning's flat, dark disk of the sea under the cerulean dome of cloudless sky did not come close to dissipating Serge's high dudgeon. They were over three hours behind his schedule. The fact that no one except Serge cared in the slightest considerably exacerbated his despondency. He spent the morning diving down the companionway to his navigation desk, popping back up like a sweaty rabbit, shaking his head in despair. At one o'clock, in the middle of a lunch of *pain bagnat — salade niçoise* soaked into hollowed-out, garlic-scrubbed *tranches* of baguette — prepared by Alexandre and Régis, Serge dived back down his rabbit hole, only to reemerge wreathed in a victorious smile. Landfall off the port bow was apparently imminent. But nothing happened for twenty long minutes, when a gray smudge deigned to appear on the horizon.

"Nathalie, Florence, prepare yourselves. We're about to change course."

Florence poured herself another glass of rosé and dimpled at Serge. "In twenty minutes, *mon ami,* not before. Take it easy. Have some of the pain bagnat. It'll do you a world of good." Nathalie, at the helm, did not even look at him.

Serge disappeared below and popped up again in fifteen minutes. "Now?"

"Not quite yet."

Serge disappeared again.

A few minutes later, Florence drained her glass and stuck her head through the hatch.

"Now, Serge, now. Come on deck."

"Oh-nine-oh," Serge barked in the stentorian tone of a black-and-white war movie.

The boat veered. Florence shook the mainsheet free of its cleat and let the sail out to a forty-five-degree angle, then repeated the maneuver with the jib. The boat righted itself slightly, picked up speed, and seemed to relax once its nose was no longer held hard into the wind.

Within half an hour the white cliffs of Bonifacio were visible. Serge raced up and down the companionway, calling out course changes. The boat veered to the north, sails full out, wallowing in the swell.

Soon they could see the town hanging by

its fingernails to the rock above the cliff, as if in mortal fear of being blown off into the sea.

The rhythm of Serge's dives below increased. Eventually, Florence lost patience, made a moue of annoyance, indicated with a tamping motion of her palm that Serge was to sit still. The boat rolled its way on toward the cliffs.

"Nathalie, come a few degrees to port, please," Florence said. Serge jolted up to adjust the sails. Florence tamped him back into his seat.

A slim breach in the cliffs appeared as if by magic. Serge jumped up. "Nathalie, start the engine and prepare to lower the sails."

"Not yet," Florence said.

They nosed into an endless gorge, the town high above them. Only a miracle forestalled a collapse of the eroded cliffs into the sea.

"Now," Florence said.

Serge leapt up like a jack-in-the-box. The warning shriek of the ignition broke the calm. The sails came down with a loud rumble.

The burping diesel fed them deeper and deeper down the endless rock-faced gorge. After fifteen minutes they reached a village, smeared around the semicircle of the gorge's cul-de-sac. Around the little harbor, the berthed boats were as tightly packed as tinned sardines. At one end, a long row of restaurants, bars, and nightclubs defaced the white façades of timeworn houses.

Inching forward with the engine almost at an idle, Serge circled the marina in search of a berth. He finally chose one in front of a bar that was already animated in the middle of the afternoon. Awkwardly, he lined up the boat stern to quai and attempted to back in at a snail's pace. Crew members from the adjacent boats appeared on their decks to scrutinize the maneuver.

A third of the way into the slip *Diomede* shifted sideways, threatening to ram the vessel on its port side. Serge spun the wheel, accelerated the engine. *Diomede* lurched even more violently at the neighboring boat. A man on deck — in his late fifties, white-fleeced barrel chest sun-toasted nut brown — put one leg over his lifeline and fended *Diomede* off, shaking his head, spitting out disgusted "*Oh là là là*s." Serge jerked the accelerator lever, the engine roared, and the boat fought against the man's leg.

Gently, Florence edged Serge aside with her hip. She threw the engine into forward and eased the boat out of the slip. In an attempt to reinstate Serge's amour propre,

67

Florence explained, "That bar is the hottest spot in Bonifacio. Drunks will be coming out all night, yelling and barfing. Kids love to pass out — or amuse themselves — in the cockpits of boats berthed out in front. We'll sleep much better on the other side of the cove."

She motored over to an empty spot directly opposite, swung the wheel hard right, gunned the engine in sharp bursts. The boat, once again docile and obedient in a master's hands, pivoted in the opposite direction. When the boat was lined up with the slip, Florence put the engine in reverse, waited for the boat to gain speed, killed the engine, walked to the bow, picked up the line attached to the mooring buoy, stopped the boat's movement, cleated off, marched rapidly to the stern, stepped ashore with both stern lines, cleated them off, and hopped back on deck. This was all done in seconds, with no more effort than a man bending over to tie his shoes.

Serge danced a jig halfway between envy and irritation.

Jacques said to Capucine over loudly, "You see, cousine, she learned to do that playing with rubber ducks in her bathtub. I tell you, rubber toys are the key to happiness." His donkey bray was loud enough to echo off the cliff wall.

Serge examined the boat's mooring with great care, retied one of Florence's perfectly cleat hitches, and then collected everyone's passports to deposit them at the *capitainerie du port* and register their arrival.

"The great thing to do in Bonifacio is to climb the steps to the old town and explore. The village's architecture is unspoiled, and the shopping is fabulous," he said. "When I get through with the port captain, I'll join you up there, and we can have an *apéro* in a quaint bar and then move on for dinner. Some of the restaurants have absolutely spectacular sea views." Once again Serge was far more at ease in his mantle of a Club Med vacation animator than in his skipper's cap.

Spontaneously, the crew divided itself into two groups: shoppers and sightseers who wanted to explore the old fort. Capucine went for the shops, and Alexandre for the fort.

The old town, perched high up over the cliffs, was as precious as promised, crooked little streets hardly wide enough to allow the passage of a single car, rickety little houses leaning against one another for support, sparkling with fresh coats of whitewash.

Over the years Bonifacio had entirely given itself over to tourism. Every second shop sold postcards and T-shirts. The little group of shoppers eventually found a boutique that would have been at home in Saint-Germain. Muted, sophisticated techno music throbbed from a high-powered sound system, and anorexic, androgynous salesgirls in abbreviated skirts milled among the customers, murmuring advice. Capucine discovered a pile of fabulous linen T-shirts decorated with a styled wood-block version of the Corsican flag. As she was searching the stack for a powder-blue one in her size, an ecstatic Angélique rushed up, holding a pair of peach-colored espadrilles with long beige satin ribbons.

"Know what these are?" she asked with a radiant smile.

"Lanvin espadrilles," Capucine said. "I'd kill for a pair, but Alexandre would never forgive me. They cost over four hundred euros."

"Not these. They're beautifully done knockoffs, and they're only thirty-five euros." Giggling, Capucine and Angélique rushed off to the corner of the shop where Angélique had found the shoes.

As Capucine ducked her head into a large basket, foraging for a pair in her size in a pale blue that would match her new T-shirt, she heard a squeal of tires and a blaring horn in the street outside the shop. She was surprised to see Angélique at the door. Capucine rushed out just in time to see Florence grab Inès's shirt and haul her off the street into the doorway. There was a flurry of commotion. A small Peugeot with Corsican plates hurtled by, its horn blaring. A swarthy man leaned out the window, clapped his right hand on the crook of his elbow, raised his left forearm in the classic insult, yelled, "*Touristi Francesi, fuora!* French tourists, go home! Leave our island to us! Leave Corsica to the Corsicans." The car rocketed off.

Angélique was on her knees on the narrow sidewalk. She must have been jostled in the attempt to get at Inès.

"Corsican separatists," someone said.

"That brutal Florence shoved me," Angelique wailed. "Capucine, if you'd told me there would be violent dykes on this trip, I'd never have come."

Capucine gently took her arm. "Are you all right?"

"No, I'm very much *not* all right! Look at my knee. It's bleeding. And my skirt is torn. Not that any of you care. And where's my husband when I need him? Don't bother

71

telling me. I know perfectly well what he's up to, that goddamn philandering cad!"

Inès very gently slipped her arm through Angélique's. "There's a pharmacy just at the end of the street. Let's go there and have them put an antiseptic on your knee. The last thing you want is an infection. These streets are probably alive with microbes. . . ." There was a silent sigh of relief as the two walked down the street, Angélique taking great pains to limp theatrically. The fact that it was Inès who had been in danger was quite forgotten.

The group continued to wander and discovered a miniscule restaurant on the ground floor of a two-window-wide house. From the street it was obvious that there was a magnificent view of the sea. Cell phones were put to use to summon the fort explorers, who trooped in, moved all the tables adjacent to the window together, and ordered apéros of fortified wine. A frisson ran through the group when they realized that they were on the overhang, well out over the sea. Drinks in hand, they amused themselves by leaning as far as they could out the window, attempting, in vain, to see the cliff face below them.

Aude, who had been dispatched down the street to let Angélique and Inès know where the group had gone, arrived with her two wards. Simultaneously, the group from the fort became boisterous, anxious to learn about Inès's encounter with the Corsican separatists. When everyone was seated, it was noticed that Serge was at the table, too, as if he had materialized from thin air.

"I ran up all those steps, and it took forever to find you," he said with a sheepish smile.

Ignoring him, Angélique showed off her knee, which was covered in an oversize compress, and summarily instructed the waiter to prepare her a pot of tea from the herbal tea that the pharmacist had given her. With acid cynicism, she asked the group at large, "And, of course, my husband has yet to appear?"

Resuming his Club Med mantle, Serge gushed about the view and, in a confidential whisper, said that he had it on good authority that the food at the restaurant was outstanding.

Alexandre, who had been examining the menu, cocked an eyebrow at him.

The main topic at dinner was the violence of the Corsican separatists, who were famous for blowing up villas owned by the French. Capucine noticed that the waitress was so unnerved by the conversation that she avoided the table. As the main courses were served, Alexandre whispered in Capucine's ear, "It's a shame Nathalie had to boat sit. She would have loved this. The ravioli in marinara sauce are going to be worthy of Chef Boyardee himself."

Serge overheard but misunderstood. "Don't feel sorry for her. I needed her to top up our supply of provisions" — Alexandre winced — "and the boat needed a thorough cleaning." He paused awkwardly. "And don't forget, she's being paid and we're on vacation."

The insipid dinner was served with a particularly muscular Corsican red wine that made up in vigor and alcoholic content what it lacked in quality and subtlety. Halfway through the main courses, vacation hilarity reemerged. At one point, Capucine looked up from Alexandre to discover that Dominique had materialized at the corner of the table, in front of an enormous plate of the Boyardeesque ravioli, their red sauce luminescent under a pile of dusty Parmesan cheese.

The conversation veered to the next port of call. The group quickly formed a consensus that the supposedly magnificent Costa Smeralda of the northeast of Sardinia — which had been lavishly developed by the

Aga Khan and was now the econiche of movie stars and paparazzi — should be bypassed in favor of a more authentic Sardinia to the south.

Serge announced he had a close friend in Tortoli who owned a fabulous villa and who would be overjoyed to feed them dinner after they had swum on his private beach. The decision to embark at the first light of dawn on a ten- to twelve-hour sail directly to Tortoli was made by acclamation. As was a second decision to descend to the port and have a long series of nightcaps at the so-called hot spot that would have kept them all awake had they been imprudent enough to berth the boat in front of it.

CHAPTER 8

Nathalie stood on the second step of the salon companionway and faced forward, looking over the bow, her eyes flush with the top of the deckhouse, a floating crocodile searching for prey. With slow eyes she followed the group as they walked around the cove. She hated them all, and she hated the boat. They were too rich, too pleased with themselves, too full of self-confidence to be interesting. And the boat was also too rich, too plastic, too fat and sluggish.

As the group started up the long sloping steps leading to the old town, Nathalie grabbed the rim of the overhead hatchway and swung herself onto the salon floor. Time to get to work. The brand-new boat already had the musky aroma of too many people sleeping in a confined space. It made her feel more at home, but she knew they couldn't stand it. Even at sea they wanted the scent of lavatory pine. Damn them all to a Formica-coated hell.

On her knees, she rooted through the locker under the sink and found a red plastic bucket, a handful of cleaning cloths, and a bottle of *nettoyant* Carrefour. She mixed a healthy swig of the green liquid with water from the freshwater tap and went into one of the heads to attack the bowl. In the telephone booth–size enclosure the heat was stifling. She thought of turning on the air-conditioning, but it wasn't worth the effort of going up on deck and starting the engine. Instead, she took off the thin checked shirt she had knotted under her breasts and threw it on the cabin bunk.

This was that cop's cabin. She sure didn't look like a cop with her fancy clothes. Still, despite the clothes and the fact that she was a flic, she was not as bad as the others. And her big teddy-bear husband was kind of cute in an odd sort of way. She could see herself with him. She undid the top brass button of her hacked-off jeans and slid her hand down over her belly. She really could see herself with him.

She yanked her hand out, leaving the button undone, and stood up. *I wonder if she has a gun,* she thought. *Flics are supposed to carry even when they're off duty. At least on TV they are.* She rooted though the drawers of Capucine's locker and found two clips of ammunition but no gun. *I wonder where she hides it. Probably in her panties.* She laughed and rubbed her abdomen with four fingers, itching to get under the waistband of her cut-off jeans.

I have to stop doing that. I'm doing it at least three times a day. If my mother was right, I'm going to explode in so many pimples, I'll look like a pizza. What I really need to do is get off this goddamn plastic tub and get a real life.

She heard footsteps coming down the companionway and turned around. It was the painter one. He was probably the worst of all. He couldn't even think of going up on deck without some fancy outfit that included a silk neckerchief knotted around his neck. *What an asshole.* Still, those wiry bodies with their stringy muscles could be good if you played them right.

Dominique — that was his name, wasn't it? — slid around the cabin door and smiled down at her. Even with that stupid thing around his neck, he did have a cute smile.

"They're making you work while they all go off to play? That hardly seems fair, does it?"

"I'm here for the money, not to socialize."

Without answering, Dominique ran his finger through the sweat on her collarbone and put it to his lips. Yeah, there was definitely something usable about this one.

"Everyone needs to socialize now and then, don't you think?"

His finger continued to trace patterns on her upper chest, slowly working down to the gully between her small, hard breasts. She said nothing. He dropped to his knees, and his finger wandered gently downward, past her navel, into the gap left by the undone button of her shorts.

With his other hand he grabbed her wrist, stood up, attempted to lead her to the bunk.

"Not here. Come with me."

They climbed up the companionway, crossed the deck, then dropped down the forepeak hatch into her coffin-size cuddy.

He was like a rangy animal. As she reached up to latch the hatch, he yanked off her shorts, threw her down on the narrow bunk, and was at her like a jaguar. It took less than a minute. No wonder they call it *la petite mort* — the little death. She screamed, the release liberating. The world came back into focus, glorious, filled with sunshine and hope and joy. She sighed happily.

But he was not finished. He pounced on her, rougher than ever. He dragged her off the bunk, flipped her over the spinnaker bag that filled half her coffin-size cabin, her butt at the apex of the pile.

She started to say no — she hated it there; it hurt; it had a terrible impact on her intestines. But it was too late. He was already halfway in. There was a sharp pain. Then she forced herself to relax and felt almost nothing.

It was over in seconds. She felt the liquid ooze within her. He withdrew with a jerk, smirking, proud of himself, leaving her deflated and depressed. She couldn't even muster the energy to get mad.

"All right, you can get the fuck out now. I have to get to work and clean your crappy plastic boat and then go buy provisions so you can get sozzled and eat your delicious meals." The hollowness of her complaint depressed her even further.

Marking his disdain, he touched a finger to his lips and placed it gently between her legs. He stood up, slipped into his clothes, knotted his ridiculous kerchief with ridiculous care, slipped out of the cuddy. She burned with desire to let him experience a spinnaker pole whacked hard upside his ear. Instead, she downed what was left of a quarter bottle of cheap cognac in two gulps, stood up on the bunk, and hurled the empty at the next boat over, gratified by the visible dent it left in the gel coat.

Wouldn't life be perfect without the need for men?

CHAPTER 9

By ten o'clock that night the crew was exultant in the B'52, the bar-nightclub opposite the berth Serge had initially targeted. Even at that early hour, the noise level made conversation all but impossible. There was no doubt it was the town's hottest spot. Hemmed in by writhing, gyrating golden youths, they drank the club's namesake drink, flaming B'52s, claimed to be made with only three painstakingly poured layers of Kahlúa, Baileys Irish Cream, and Grand Marnier, which were then set alight to produce an evanescent blue flame, dramatic in the almost pitch-black room.

With histrionic brio Serge downed his drinks into an open mouth, oblivious to the pain. The only one who showed the slightest interest was Alexandre, who looked quizzical for a moment and then disappeared behind the bar.

When he returned, he whispered in Capucine's ear, "Just as I thought, the bartender pours a layer of well-heated hundred-twenty-proof *rhum agricole* from Guadeloupe on top. That's what produces the extravagant flame."

The evening wore on. Capucine and Angélique were solicited as dance partners. Florence had disappeared from the table and could be seen in the distance, in earnest conversation with the bartender, drinking what looked like chilled Perrier. Aude's glacial inscrutability discouraged invitations. When slow dances came up, Capucine noticed that Angélique folded herself into Dominique's arms. Conversation among the nondancers stalled, degenerating into telegraphic utterances that floated out, hanging limply over the table, defying reply. The only one who seemed to be having fun was Dominique, who danced sensuously with his wife while his eyes ping-ponged back and forth among the coterie of well-tanned nymphets in the club.

At twelve Serge stretched, yawned, and looked at his multi-dialed watch. "There's no hope our crew is going to be bright-eyed and bushy-tailed on deck at five a.m. tomorrow morning," he said at large. "The only thing to do is shove off now. Good thing I collected our passports from the capitainerie this afternoon. Let's have one more drink and get going."

Twenty minutes later, Serge was doing his best to steer the boat through the narrow gorge by the light of a powerful flashlight he had found in the tool kit after spilling the contents over the salon floor. Even though he was more or less drunk, he had the good sense to drive the boat at a slow speed. One white cliff would appear in the beam of his light, and he would rectify his course, but in no time the opposing wall would appear just as threateningly.

After one particularly close encounter, Florence elbowed Serge away from the wheel, snapped off his light, took the helm, and let the light of the full moon guide her. "Why don't you all go to bed? I'll call you if I need anything."

Serge stretched out on the cockpit settee and fell asleep instantly.

As they went below one by one on unsteady legs, the motor accelerated to cruise speed and the boat became rock hard on a steady course. After a few minutes, those few who were still awake noticed the irritating throb of the engine cease, heard the rattle of the sails going up, felt the boat assume its normal heel, and sensed the natural rhythm of the sea taking over. They were at sea under sail.

At three in the morning Capucine was dragged into a nightmare. She was in a Chinese dungeon, being interrogated by a sinister Fu Manchu–like character with mustaches dangling well below his chin, grinning evilly as he adjusted a device that dripped water on her forehead. She squinted her eyes shut tight. She would never talk, never, never, ever.

"Capucine, wake up." Water dripped on her face from the hood of Florence's foul-weather jacket. "I need you on deck. Nathalie's replacing me, and I want you and Inès on watch with her. You don't have to do anything. Just keep the conversation going so no one goes to sleep. There are squalls coming. Nathalie can handle herself, but if you think you need me, just come and get me."

Capucine shook herself awake and bumped into Inès in the salon. They both had foul-weather jackets in their hands.

On deck, the tangy salt of the sea breeze was a tonic. It blew the last of the alcohol out of their systems. Capucine and Inès stood for a moment, breathing deeply, admiring the phosphorescent glow of the bow waves.

Nathalie, at the helm, shot them a bel-

85

ligerent look. The squall had passed through, and the plastic leather of the cockpit settee was slick with water. Both Capucine and Inès spread out their foul-weather jackets over the banquette and sat face-to-face, their legs touching.

The night wore on with the rhythmic swaying of the boat and glimpses of the extravagant panoply of stars through holes in the black clouds. They spoke disjointedly, straining to see if Nathalie was listening. Once she was sure Nathalie was in her own world, Inès launched into a sotto voce plan of attack for Tottinguer, tapping Capucine's knee point by point for emphasis. As Inès gesticulated, her jacket fell on the deck at the foot of the settee.

Nathalie groaned to herself. *Goddamn that fucker.* I knew this would happen. She clutched at her lower abdomen and moaned again. *I've been in the head the whole fucking afternoon. And for what?* She flicked a switch on the column of the wheel, activating the autopilot, doubled over at the waist, cursed one more time. The boat steered itself, both wheels jerking back and forth like a vaudeville song and dance number. Heavy drops of rain fell.

Nathalie groaned a deep lament, half moan and half wail. "I told that fucker I didn't want to do it, but do they ever listen?" she asked herself rhetorically. More drops of rain fell.

Lurching, she picked up Inès's jacket, shrugged it on, flipped the collar up, and turned her torso to face Capucine. Thunder crackled in the distance. "I'll be back in a sec. Don't worry. The boat will take care of herself." She ran across the deck and disappeared into the dark.

Five minutes later Inès began to fidget. "Where is she?"

"She went up there to have a pee. She's probably communing with nature. She'll be back. Don't worry," Capucine replied.

But after another five minutes, Capucine had lost the strength of her conviction. "Stay here for a moment," she said to Inès. "I'm going to see if I can find her." It began to rain in earnest. She slipped on a jacket and inched forward. Thunder cracked so near the boat, it made Capucine jump. A second later, lightning lit up the boat as brightly as a theater stage. The deck was completely deserted. There could be no doubt about that.

Capucine ran back to the stern and extracted the yellow horseshoe life buoy from its cradle on the rail, along with the attached dan buoy, a six-foot pole with a red flag on top set in a float. Once out of its rack, the life buoy gave off the strong stench of human urine, overpowering the clean ozone smell of the storm. A good number of beer-soaked males must have peed over the stern, hanging on to the whiplike pole for support. As soon as the dan buoy hit the water, a pulsing strobe began to wink. In a few seconds it vanished into the oily black night.

Capucine went below and opened the door to Serge's cabin, half expecting that somehow Nathalie had teleported herself there and was vigorously disporting herself. But Serge lay flat on his back, clad only in the tan shorts he had been wearing in the bar, legs wide apart, mouth slack open, the cabin reeking of stale alcohol.

She shook him awake. "We may have a person overboard."

He shook his head violently to clear it. "Who?"

"Nathalie."

Serge jumped out of his berth, pushed Capucine aside, and made for Florence's cabin, only to discover that Florence was already on her feet at the navigation console. She flicked some switches and raced up the companionway. By the time Capucine returned on deck, it was brilliant with masthead lights and even more conspicuously empty than it had been in the strobe flashes of lightning.

Chapter 10

The deck lights went out. Purple retinal images danced in Capucine's field of vision, leaving her disoriented. It took long minutes for the splotches to disappear and her night vision to reemerge. Finally, she was able to discern the line between the greater darkness of the sea and the lesser darkness of the sky. The storm had passed through, leaving a clean sea smell. Far over the horizon, episodic, soundless flashes of lightning flared.

The sails had been dropped into drunken, disordered piles, as if the boat had broken. Standing tall, her eyes sweeping the middle distance, Florence manned the helm. Next to her, like a little boy yammering for his mother's attention, Serge sputtered, "We need to turn around, do the 'man overboard' drill, come up into the wind, jibe around, reach the position where she went overboard. Hurry. Hurry."

Florence ignored him.

"We've already turned around and are heading back over our course, and the sails are down," Capucine said.

They came up to the pulsing dan buoy and took it on board. They motored on, staring sightlessly into the inky black. There was no sign of Nathalie. There was no sign of anything.

"We have no idea when she went over the side," Capucine said. "The best thing you can do now is to try to contact the nearest port and see if there's any way to put up a search helicopter."

Energized, Serge bustled below.

In less than a minute he returned with the gravitas of a heroic naval officer who had serious news to share. "I was unable to raise anyone with the VHF on channel sixteen. Also, there's no signal on my cell phone. But the good news is that we are only thirty-five miles off Porto Cervo. If we steer two-six-oh, we could be there in less than four hours."

Before he had finished speaking, Florence spun the wheel and the boat heeled in slightly as it made a sharp turn to starboard. "Serge, I need you to get the sails back up," Florence said curtly. "We don't have enough gas to make port on the engine."

Serge set to work cranking the main halyard while Aude held the limp sheet, waiting for the sail to fill. Régis, looking a little dazed, took flash pictures of the deck. He went to the bow and continued snapping.

Serge barked at him, "Régis, this is no time for your blog. Get the jib up as fast as you can. We don't have a second to lose."

But Régis hesitated, taking several pictures of the bow area, even kneeling down to put the bow pulpit in dramatic perspective, before he came back to the jib halyard winch in the cockpit.

Three hours later Serge was able to raise the port captain's office in Porto Cervo on channel sixteen, the international distress frequency. The conversation reverberated loudly across the salon.

"Porto Cervo? This is *Diomede.* Mayday. Mayday. Mayday," Serge said in English, imitating Humphrey Bogart in one of his seagoing films.

"*Diomede.* Isa you sinka?" said a young voice with the sleepy calm of someone who had heard it all before, too many times.

"No, Porto Cervo. We're not sinking. We think someone has gone overboard."

"*Va bene.* That's a not a Mayday. That's a *pan.* You coma inna port and tell me alla about it. I see what I canna do for you."

"Copied, Porto Cervo. We're six miles out. We'll be with you in less than an hour. Over and out!"

They reached Porto Cervo as dawn broke. Even though the little harbor seemed as lifeless as if the world had ended, the port captain's office in Porto Cervo was easy enough to find by the GUARDIA COSTIERA sign high over a steep vertical wall at the very end of a long marina filled with the largest boats Capucine had ever seen. The problem was that there were no empty berths.

While Serge fretted, Florence tied the boat up next to the bottom step of a stone stairway leading up the vertical wall. Capucine and Serge walked up the mossy steps and discovered a new-looking white stucco building with a factory-made pine door. Serge opened it imperiously and strode in. Inside, a very young man in white trousers and a white short-sleeved shirt with black epaulets with one slim silver band sipped coffee from a thick demitasse. He looked up, unimpressed, caught sight of Capucine, and sprang to his feet.

"I'm the skipper of *Diomede*. I radioed you. Remember?" Serge asked.

The man smiled lazily, his eyes never leaving Capucine's breasts. "The Maydaya. You surviva. *Benissimo.*" He eased around the desk and moved a chair two inches to indicate that Capucine should sit. He ignored Serge.

"Ensign," Capucine said, producing her Police Judiciaire ID wallet, "I'm Commissaire Le Tellier of the French Police Judiciaire. We think a woman fell overboard thirty miles out at sea and would like you to send up a helicopter in the hopes that she may still be found."

Butting in, Serge handed the man a slip of paper with latitude and longitude coordinates. "This is as close as I can reckon to where she went over. I'm the skipper."

It was as if the ensign had only just understood the situation. He sat up straight.

"Commissario," he said, his hands raised in the air, as if to appease the gods, his eyes still glued to Capucine's breasts. "Of course, of course. *Che tragedia! Che orrore!* I'll call the helicopter service immediately, immediately. You must forgive me. This is Porto Cervo. All we have here is movie stars and celebrities. Everything is an emergency. I had no idea you had undergone such an *enorme tragedia.*"

He searched frantically though a dog-

94

eared phone directory on the desk and punched in a number. The ringing at the other end could be heard clearly through the phone's handset. As they waited, an even younger man in a white uniform with entirely unadorned black epaulets rushed into the room and whispered in the ensign's ear in eager sibilants. He was waved away in irritation.

The man cupped his hand over the mouthpiece of the telephone receiver. "He is telling me that your boat is moored at our stairway, which is normally forbidden. But, Commissario, you are welcome to remain there as long as you like."

His sycophantic smile was interrupted by a voice on the telephone. A rapid staccato of Italian ensued. The conversation over, he smiled warmly at Capucine.

"*Va bene.* They are sending a helicopter. I let you know what they find." He spoke only to Capucine. It was as if Serge was not in the room. "You looka tired. Go sleepa. I call you the *minuto* I heara something. I take cara everything."

Back at the boat, Capucine and Serge found no one on deck and only Aude and Régis in the salon. They sat at either end of the settee. Aude, impassive as ever, read from a very thick book. Régis typed energetically on his laptop. At the sight of Capucine, he sprang up.

"Everyone's gone to bed," Régis said. "They were exhausted. We wanted to wait for you two, even though we're punched out, as well."

"Go to sleep. They're sending out a helicopter. They'll let us know if they find anything," Capucine replied.

Punctuating her words, the drumbeat *thumpa-thumpa* of a helicopter flying close overhead reverberated in the salon.

The next morning the members of the group seemed strained and ill at ease with each other. Alexandre realized that a communal breakfast was the last thing anyone wanted. He, Capucine, and Jacques began the long climb up the mossy stone steps, hoping to find a café not too far off. When they were halfway up, Inès called out to them to wait for her.

They sat at a table on the terrace of the small quai-side café and drank *caffelatte,* made with impossibly thick espresso mixed into frothy steamed milk, and nibbled tasteless industrial buns from clear plastic wrappers.

"I trust it hasn't escaped your attention

that the delightfully raunchy Nathalie was wearing Inès's jacket," Jacques said, surveying the colossal yachts with insouciance, ripping the wrapper off a *cornetto,* an industrial glazed croissant.

"That was the first thing I thought of," Capucine said.

"So you don't think it was an accident?" Alexandre asked, unwrapping with grave suspicion a *bombolone,* a brioche-like industrial pastry. He frowned, having found a topic that interested him more than people lost at sea. "It's curious that the Italians, from whom, after all, we have inherited our gastronomic heritage, have utterly surrendered their art of *boulangerie* to industrial processing."

"Of course it wasn't an accident!" Inès said with verve. "Someone on that boat has been after me from the very beginning. First, I was nearly washed overboard by that so-called gust of wind. Then they tried to run me over in Bonifacio. And finally, they threw me overboard. But it was the wrong person!" She laughed victoriously.

She tapped Alexandre energetically on the arm. "That means someone's worried that I'm on their trail, don't you think, Monsieur le Journaliste?"

Alexandre looked at her. He frowned

deeply, pensively chewing an exceptionally dry-looking Mulino Bianco, and said nothing. Capucine was positive he hadn't heard a word she had said.

CHAPTER 11

On their way back to the boat, Capucine stopped off at the port captain's office. At the desk, a white-uniformed ensign informed her that the port captain was indeed present but was winding up a meeting in his office. If Capucine would care to wait for a few minutes at the very most, the ensign was sure the captain would be delighted to see her. She sat for nearly forty-five minutes before the ensign took her to an office at the rear of the open-plan area. The door had been in full view the whole time, and Capucine had seen no one leave.

Inside the office a man in his early forties with two gold stripes on his epaulets, sporting an officer's cap decorated with the badge of a fouled anchor, looked at her guardedly, ignoring her breasts.

Capucine introduced herself.

"Yes, of course," the man said in perfect French. "The night-duty ensign left me a detailed note. I have also received a report from the helicopter service, which saw nothing, even though they patrolled the area for two hours."

He paused, constructing a melancholy look.

"It's a tragedy, of course, but I'm afraid nothing more can be done. These things happen at sea, I'm sad to say. It's fortunate that none of you were close to the young woman." He shrugged, the weight of the world on his shoulders, and raised his hands slightly, palms upward.

"That's it?" Capucine asked, not bothering to hide her irritation. "That's all the Italian authorities are going to do?"

"I regret the loss of your servant," he said, intensifying his melancholy look. "But you have to understand the situation. The fact that your skipper noted the position of the boat only a good while after he was alerted tells us that we have no idea exactly where she went overboard. An extended search over a broad area would take a small fleet of aircraft, and it is almost certain that it would be fruitless. In my experience it is extremely rare that drowned bodies float."

Capucine sat mute, radiating irritation.

"Commissario, naturally I spoke to my superiors about this regrettable incident this morning." The melancholy look had been replaced by a shrewd, knowing one. "They are, naturally, very deferential to your rank." He paused. "They regret the 'loss' of your servant girl." The quotation marks were heavy in the air. "But a factor exacerbating the futility of the search" — he paused again to let Capucine admire his mastery of the French language — "is that, given the ambiguity of the boat's position at the time of the incident, it is quite possible, even likely, that you were in French waters." Delighted with himself, he smiled at Capucine, leaned over the desk, and gave her an earnest, curtain-closing look.

Capucine sat back in her chair. The penny dropped. The superiors, whoever they might be, wanted no risk of international complications, particularly if it involved a ranking French police officer. Nathalie, even dead, was an embarrassment.

"Commissario, I'm afraid the case is closed." He smiled again, the smile of someone of who had tied up all the necessary loose ends. "Of course, you're more than welcome to remain in Porto Cervo. But I would appreciate it if you could vacate my mooring. My launch is normally tied up there. One of my men can help you find an anchorage, but I'm afraid it may have to be on the other side of the seawall. Marina berths are booked up months in advance, as I'm sure you understand." He favored Capucine with a grandfatherly smile.

"That's very generous of you, Captain. But we won't be staying. We're on our way to Tortoli. We'd planned a dinner there."

"*Va bene.* Have a good sail. And don't forget to check in at the port captain's office when you get to Tortoli."

Despite the glory of the day, the deck of the boat was deserted. Capucine inched down the long flight of algae-slick steps.

Halfway down she stopped. The situation was intolerable. The opera buffa of the Italian authorities would have been charmingly comical if it weren't for the context of the probable death of someone they had shared an existence with, even if only for a few days. This was her world. A world she should be in control of. Of course, she could always make calls to Paris. The most likely call would be to *Contrôleur Général* Tallon, her mentor, now a god in the stratosphere of the Police Judiciaire hierarchy. But she would sound ridiculous. What would she want him to do? Pull strings to the get the Italian authorities to do something? But what, exactly? That was the whole problem;

there was nothing to be done.

She hopped on board. The rest of the party was huddled around the salon table, drinking Prosecco, serving themselves something out of a Plexiglas bowl, looking unhappy.

"We've been kicked out of Porto Cervo," Capucine said.

"Good," Alexandre said.

"Kicked out?" Florence asked.

"Well, not exactly. But we've been occupying the mooring of the port captain's launch. He wants it back. There aren't any berths available in the cove. We were graciously invited to drop our anchor outside the seawall."

"That's safe enough," Florence said. "It's a good, shallow, sandy bottom out there. Fine for one or two nights with the fair weather that's coming up."

"So what do we do now?" Serge asked nervously, poking at the food on his plate.

Capucine squeezed into the banquette. Alexandre handed her a plate scintillating with bright summer colors. He must have found a market and gone foraging. He'd whipped up a salad of Barilla three-cheese tortellini, zucchini, green peppers, cherry tomatoes, and scallions, seasoned it with a delicate lemony vinaigrette, and topped the whole affair off with thinly shaved slices of Parmesan cheese. One of the things Capucine loved most about Alexandre was that, no matter how severe the crisis, his priorities remained inviolate. The salad was delicious.

Capucine refocused on Serge. "Descartes would have been eloquent in explaining we have only two choices, go on or go home."

"Ah, the quaint notion of free will. It's the sort of concept that you could conjure up only if you lived in an oven," Jacques murmured, sipping Prosecco. Capucine half thought Aude smiled at him.

"I don't care what we do as long as we get out of this godforsaken Costa Smeralda," Angélique said. "I'd just as soon move to Hollywood as stay here."

Through the salon ports Capucine could see portly owners of mega yachts on their decks, with bare-breasted trophy spouses being served flutes of vintage champagne by fawning tanned, athletic young things in uniforms of brief shorts and tight T-shirts.

There was a universal murmur of agreement.

"Serge, how far away are we from Tortoli?" Dominique asked. "I know the whole episode has been a shock. But I really don't want to go back to France just yet. I think it would be kind of fun to meet your friend and see the way real people live in Sardinia." Angélique slid her hand into his and smiled lovingly at him. Mentally, Capucine shook her head at Angélique's protean mood shifts toward her husband.

"The timing is bad," Serge said. "It's a ten-hour sail. If we leave now, we won't get there till midnight."

Jacques purred. One of his knacks was attracting the attention of a crowd with a mere murmur. "In that case, my vote would be to stay here and sample the nightlife of this delicious den of iniquity. Nothing is more enticing than the musk of barely teen starlets in rut. Then we can perform our usual trick of stealing off like thieves in the night."

There was a moment of silence as the group chewed over this alternative.

"Could be fun, when you think about it," Angélique said. "I'd like to see the stars at play. Don't you think, darling?" She slid her arm through Dominique's.

"It's what Nathalie would have wanted," Jacques said, cackling his braying laugh. Aude shot him a dirty look, one that Capucine was almost sure she saw.

Half an hour later they were beyond the breakwater. It was hardly the open sea, just a protected cove with no dock. Florence contemplated Serge as he maneuvered the boat, attempting to drop the anchor. He cruised around, found a spot, went too far, turned, came back over it, overshot, went around again. Florence came up beside him at the wheel. She did not even have to ease him aside. He moved away gratefully.

"This is too close to the other boats," Florence said. "We might hit one of them in the night if we drop the hook here. Why don't you go forward and get ready with the anchor while I find us a spot?"

Serge went to the forecastle and opened a little hatch. He extracted a three-foot anchor, a length of chain, and an electronic device that looked exactly like a TV remote control. Régis snapped pictures with the zeal of a paparazzo.

"When are you going to post all these pictures?" Capucine asked.

"Oh, I've already started. Porto Cervo has great free Wi-Fi. I can't wait to post some shots of the anchor dropping into the water. That'll give the blog real local color."

Florence motored the boat over to an area on the other side of the cove, turned it into the wind, held it in position with the motor ticking over, and told Serge to drop the anchor.

He squeezed a button on his TV remote and the anchor chain clanked through the fairlead. After a few seconds the chain turned into ordinary braided rope. Serge leaned far over the bow pulpit, engrossed. "Bottom," he announced to Florence.

Florence put the motor in neutral and let the wind push the boat away from the anchor, drawing out line. After about half a minute, Florence ordered, "Make fast" in a conversational tone. Serge squeezed a button on his remote. Very gently the boat came to a halt.

"It's a good one," Florence said and switched the ignition off.

There was no denying the cove had scenic appeal. They were surrounded by boats their size or a little smaller. The prosperous middle class cut off from the mega rich by the breakwater.

The sun was still high in the sky. The group broke up, some going below to nap, others finding secluded corners of the deck to read or chat. Capucine went up to the bow and let her legs dangle over the side. She was unable to shake her frustration at the administrative indifference to Nathalie's death. No one should be allowed to be erased from the face of the earth so completely, so unnoticed, so unmourned.

"Serge," she called out. "Do you have Nathalie's passport?"

Serge handed it to her. "What are you going to do with it?"

"See if I can find some next of kin to notify."

"Of course. I hadn't thought of that."

Capucine clicked her iPhone on and pressed the speed-dial button for *Brigadier-Chef* Lemercier, the most proficient of her team with the police database.

"*Salut,* Commissaire. Already bored hanging out on a yacht with the idle rich?"

"Salut, Isabelle. Not quite, but getting there. Can you do something for me? We had a tragic accident. One of the crew went overboard. I need you to run her down and see if you can find any next of kin."

"What's the name?"

"Martin, Nathalie," Capucine said and read off the passport number.

"I'll have it for you in a few minutes. Call you back?"

Capucine draped her arms over the top lifeline, holding the iPhone limply, rubbing her big toes together, emptying her mind. The phone vibrated in her hand.

"Commissaire, there's not much. She was born in nineteen seventy-eight in the Bagneux projects. Her mother deceased in two thousand one, and there's no listing for a father. There's a brother, Martin, Emile. He was convicted twice for auto theft but seems to have left the country. Last seen boarding a flight to Melbourne in nineteen ninety-eight. Want me to run him down?"

"No. That one's gone for good. And there's nothing else on Nathalie Martin?"

"Absolutely nothing. No marriages, no leases on apartments, no bank accounts, no credit cards. But I can dig deeper if you want."

"No thanks. She's not a suspect, just a kid who fell off a boat. Thanks, Isabelle. I'll see you in a week."

That was that. Capucine felt depression descend on her like a damp yellow fog. Behind her the group bustled. After a good bit of chatter, soundless in Capucine's brume, the distaff side of the crew moved below to primp for dinner. The males remained in the cockpit, drinking beer, discussing the evening's venues.

Capucine dropped into the cockpit next to Alexandre. He handed her a bottle of Peroni beer, the sweat of condensation running down its sides. She put the bottle to her forehead and let the conversation wash over her, willing her brain to remain empty. There was already a consensus about the nightspots. The Billionaire was to be the first stop. It was world famous for its views from the tops of the cliffs of Porto Cervo and its wall-to-wall crush of stars, starlets, and the superrich. Even the parking lot packed with Ferraris was supposed to be worth the detour. There was some debate about the second stop, but the vox populi settled on the Ritual, housed in an ancient stone building made to look like a Stone Age ruin. The glitterati who weren't at Billionaire were bound to be there.

That was the easy part. Dinner was trickier. One choice was Porto Cervo's most expensive spot, Ristorante Gianni Pedrinelli. Another was Cipriani, the restaurant in Billionaire.

"We'd save on cab fare, and Lord knows that's important in these troubled times," Jacques said.

Alexandre put the kibosh on both by pronouncing that he had it on excellent authority that the food was execrable at both establishments. Even though no one would think of questioning even his most casual statement about a restaurant, Alexandre hammered home his veto by explaining that restaurants that catered to the fast set were invariably indifferent to restaurant critics since their clientele came to be seen, not to eat. He was certain he wouldn't have the clout to obtain a same-day reservation for a ten-top.

As an alternative, Alexandre suggested a restaurant high in the hills just out of town named Tamarind after the owner, an English chef who had left her London starred kitchen to bask in the Costa Smeralda sun. Apparently, the food was "adequate," which in Alexander's lexicon was high praise indeed.

Alexandre made a call to Paris. In a few minutes his cell phone buzzed. He cooed in French gallantly into the device, chortled, rang off.

"That was Tamarind in person. We're on for eight."

Angélique appeared on deck, scowling. "Dominique, I need you to help me pick out my dress for this evening. And I don't want you sloshed on beer, nodding off at the dinner table. Come with me!"

When Dominique rose, Angélique zeroed in on Serge.

"The plan is lovely, but what are we supposed to do? Slip on our little black dresses and our Manolos and glide across the water?"

Serge grinned at her. "There's an inflatable dinghy with a little motor in a cuddy in the transom. I'm going to take you ashore in groups of three. It'll be great fun."

The prospect of an elegant meal was a tonic to the women, who all spent the latter half of the afternoon showering, blow-drying their hair, trying on outfits, and flitting from one cabin to another to borrow and exchange accessories.

At seven, despite the mood of the past few days, the ten passengers gathered on deck, shoes in hand, in wonderful spirits, already in the high of an upcoming adventuresome evening.

The crossing to shore in the dinghy proved to be more challenging than expected. The little rubber Zodiac was no more than seven feet long and looked more like a beach toy than a motorized craft. It was powered by a kitchen appliance–size, two-horsepower outboard fastened to a wooden transom.

Boarding was an adventure. There was a ladder that clipped onto *Diomede*'s stern that was easy enough to descend, but when the last step was reached, the little dinghy had a nasty habit of sliding away, leaving passengers stretched out at a forty-five-degree angle, worthy of a Mack Sennett comedy.

With four passengers the dinghy sank so deeply into the water, it would have been swamped by anything more than a six-inch wave. Serge made five trips with only two passengers for each crossing, and they arrived at the restaurant half an hour late.

They were a little disappointed. The view was as breathtaking as promised, but the décor, with strings of paper lanterns hanging from a rickety wood trellis, evoked a friendly local taverna far more than the sort of place that required an afternoon's primping. Worse even, most of the patrons were youngsters in jeans and fifteen-euro T-shirts. But as the group settled in, they spotted seams of the debonair in Prada and Gianfranco Ferré marbling the dining room like fat running through the choicest sirloin. It was obvious that Tamarind was the venue of preference for the hyper-cool on relaxed evenings.

The food fully lived up to expectations. The special of the day, crispy duck on deep-fried risotto *supplì*, was good enough to brighten Alexandre's eyes with the epiphany Capucine usually saw only in three-star restaurants.

The evening unwound pleasantly. First, the familiar purple pyrotechnics of a Mediterranean sunset, then the faint glow of a string of paper lanterns, and after, the glory of the main course with Tamarind emerging from the kitchen halfway through to greet Alexandre.

"What did you think?" she asked with a disarming smile.

"That London suffered a great loss with your departure and you enjoyed a great gain. I ate twice at the Hornbill and Continent while you were still there. You've become transcendent here. Your happiness radiates in your dishes."

"I think that's one of the nicest compliments I've ever been paid. Are you going to write that?"

"Only if you'd like. I'm just here to eat with my friends."

"Then don't write anything. I have enough golden youths in here already. I like to cook for people who have to work all day and don't give a hoot if they're being seen or not."

Much, much later, after numerous ear-numbing hours in clubs, they returned to the marina. Capucine was relieved that both the dinghy and the motor were still there. She had had misgivings about leaving them without padlocks. The trip back was far rougher than the way in, and they arrived at the boat drenched. A mood of joyous hysteria took over, and they all rushed below, changed into bathing suits, and jumped over the side with loud shrieks and yells. Later, they dried off on deck and sat huddled in thick towels as Serge motored them out of the bay. It was the first evening on the good yacht *Diomede* that was genuinely carefree.

Capucine marveled at the psychology. Did it really take violent death to bring home the sweetness of life?

CHAPTER 12

By one thirty in the morning the club buzz was long gone, replaced by a soggy dampness that even the golden swath from a full moon wouldn't dispel. Serge had the helm. In the distance, the rocky face of an island was outlined in a faint glow.

"We're off the coast of Li Nibani Island," Florence said. "Time to start heading south."

Serge spun the wheel, his eyes locked on the binnacle. Florence winched in the sheets. The boat heeled slightly and picked up speed on a beam reach. The wake gave off faint sparkles in the moonlight.

Capucine sat in the bow pulpit with Alexandre, who puffed the remains of a once substantial cigar. One by one, the passengers drifted below silently. Capucine nuzzled her head against Alexandre's neck. Neither spoke. Capucine noticed that Florence had replaced Serge at the helm and he had apparently gone below. Alexandre tossed the stub into the sea and went below with Capucine. At the foot of the companionway they encountered Serge.

"She insists on staying all alone all night at the helm. I'm letting her do it. I think it takes her back to her racing days. It's a calm night, and if anything happens, I can be on deck in a flash."

Capucine had no doubt that even in a full gale the boat would be safe in Florence's hands, and she wondered if she really wanted to remind herself of her racing days or if she was creating insurance against another incident.

But instead of incidents, the night proved as blissful as only summer nights on calm seas could be. Capucine and Alexandre held each other, giddy in the cocoon-like confines of the bunk. They fell asleep. Capucine turned to face the moon shining through the hazy port, nestling into Alexandre's welcoming, pillow-like embonpoint. Twice during the night Florence made course changes, easing the boat progressively south. At each change the boat came up a few degrees into the wind and its angle of heel increased. The bunk tilted more and more. Capucine snuggled deeper and deeper into Alexandre.

Just before four in the morning they passed Capo Comino, the easternmost tip of Sardinia. Florence altered course to five degrees beyond dead south, the sails close-hauled, as tight into the wind as the boat could go. *Diomede* heeled well over. Alexandre slid across the bunk until he came to rest against the bulkhead. Capucine slid after him and nestled in. When she woke, it was bright daylight, the keel was even, and the motor was throbbing.

She looked at her watch. Eight o'clock. She never got up that late. She slipped on T-shirt and shorts and went up on deck. This must be the port of Arbatax, adjacent to the slightly inland town of Tortoli. It had nothing of a tourist attraction. A long, industrial-looking cement breakwater had been built to create an artificial harbor. At the far end a small yacht marina was only half full.

Florence, even more rested looking than when they had left Porto Cervo, steered the boat into the marina and cruised briskly up and down, looking for a suitable berth. Florence stopped the boat, effortlessly performed her engine-gunning pivoting maneuver, and eased gently into a slip, stern first, tying off the bow line. She jumped onto the dock and made the two stern lines fast.

Rubbing his eyes and stretching, Serge appeared on deck. Two men in the white uniforms of the guardia costiera clattered down the aluminum dock.

"Commissario Le Tellier?" one man asked Florence from under a snappy salute.

"I'm Commissaire Le Tellier," Capucine said from the deck.

"*Bene.* Can you please get your papers and come with us?"

"I should come, too. I'm the skipper."

"*No, no, va bene,* you stay."

Inside the port captain's offices Capucine was shown into a small, dusty room lined with old files in white cardboard boxes. A portly man with a closely trimmed beard stood up to greet her. Capucine divined he was a policeman, not a port official. She wondered how long she could succeed in staving off the plainclothes miasma, if it hadn't stamped her already. She would have to ask Alexandre.

"Commissaire Le Tellier?" the police officer asked in heavily accented French. "Please sit down. May I look at your ID?" For a long moment he held up her ID wallet at eye level, keeping both the card and Capucine's face in his view. He appeared to make up his mind about something. He smiled thinly.

"I'm *Ispettore* Manfredi from the Tortoli Vice Questura There has been a *complicazione* with your case of the missing servant that we must speak about."

"Of course," Capucine said. "But is there any way I could get a coffee? I haven't had my breakfast yet."

"Mi dispiace tanto. Prego, mi scusi. I forget my manners. Of course. These sailors make excellent *caffè."* He opened the door and spoke to a uniformed police officer who stood almost at the threshold. Capucine was surprised to see that a guard had been posted.

As she stirred the half-filled demitasse of coffee, so strong it was almost sludge, Capucine asked, "What sort of complication? We were told yesterday in Porto Cervo that the opinion of the authorities was that Nathalie Martin had gone overboard in French waters and was no concern of the Italian authorities."

"Ah, but something has happened," Manfredi said, wagging his index finger as if about to score a central academic point in a university debate. "You see, what may be a vital piece of evidence has been found."

"What sort of evidence?"

"A sailor's foul-weather jacket." Manfredi raised his eyebrows and leaned back slightly as if he expected Capucine to be stunned by the revelation.

She looked at him, stone-faced.

"You see, Commissaire, there is a hole in the jacket that looks very much like a bullet hole. And what makes it even more interesting is that it was found on a deserted beach on Isola Caprera. In other words, almost at the mouth of the Porto Cervo bay, not far from where you reported Signorina Martin falling overboard. Surely you see the import of the situation."

"I do. Entirely." Had they been in France, she would be slamming the door of a Police Judiciaire van that would be taking the nine crew members to the nearest brigade to be interviewed.

"It is helpful that you understand," Manfredi said with a thin smile. "We are still conducting our investigation. Normally, your boat's crew would be detained for questioning. But since you are a senior police officer of a country with very close ties to Italy, I see no need for sequestration. But I'm afraid I must require you all not to leave Arbatax. And I'm going to ask you to take responsibility personally for the compliance of your companions."

"We had planned on having dinner at a friend's house in Tortoli."

"Yes, *certo.* Arbatax is administratively a part of Tortoli. May I ask who your friend in Tortoli is?"

"Actually, he's the friend of our skipper, a Signore Cardorna. He apparently has a villa in the hills on the outskirts of Tortoli."

The ispettore arched his eyebrows and flattened his lips. "Tommasso Cardorna. Yes, he does possess an imposing villa."

In the middle of the afternoon they arrived in taxis at the sprawling hillside villa of Serge's friend. They had been invited to bring bathing suits and enjoy his three swimming pools, which cascaded one into another down the side of the hill.

In the taxi, Serge had explained to Capucine that Tommasso was one of the investors in his restaurants, and Serge was hoping he would assume some of the financing of a new bar Serge wanted to buy. The visit was more than just a social call.

Tommasso turned out to be a large man made more corpulent by his billowing Hawaiian shirt. He wore the close-cropped full beard so loved by Italian men. As he cheerfully distributed glasses of Prosecco and made small talk, he explained that he was anything but Sardinian. He was proud to be a Sicilian taking a vacation from his homeland "for his health" and had been in Sardinia only for the past three years. Waving his hand at the spectacular view of the bay and the endless emerald sea, which faded into a purple nimbus on the horizon, he conceded that even though nothing could approach the perfection of Sicily, Sardinia was pleasant enough.

A bronzed pool boy in shorts and a T-shirt of brilliant white arrived to take them down the hill to the poolside changing room, while Serge and Tommasso — with faces so serious, they could be on their way to a funeral — disappeared into the house.

As Capucine was about to enter the cabana at the edge of the pool, Jacques hooked his finger into the top of her shorts and held her back. For several long beats his finger explored the cleft between her buttocks. He had something on his mind that had nothing to do with her posterior, but he wasn't sure if he should articulate it. Abandoning the thought, Jacques snatched his finger out of Capucine's shorts.

"I hope our new friend isn't going the make our dear Serge an offer he can't refuse," Jacques said. He barked out his donkey bray loud enough to bring the pool boy at a trot of alarm.

■ ■ ■ ■

At dusk they found themselves sipping Prosecco at the end of a table large enough to seat at least forty people, under an arbor of grapevines, the Tyrian purple sea resplendent in the distance. A servant slowly turned a ten-foot-long spit set into a grill inset into the stone wall.

Tommasso pinched the fingers of both hands together and shook them in front of Alexandre at eye level. Capucine didn't doubt that he had quizzed Serge closely on their biographies during their meeting.

"I'm going to give you something you've never eaten, *Signore Critico del Ristorante*. A real Sicilian barbecue." He pointed at the grill. "Beef, the best sirloin, veal so tender, you can eat it with a spoon even before it's cooked, and wild pigs from the hill above us. 'What's so special about that?' you say. Eh? What's special is the marinade. Onions, basil, sage and wild thyme, oregano, bay leaves, pepper, olive oil, and just enough lemon juice.

"And *still* you say, 'That's not so special. That's the way I marinate my meat for my backyard grill at home in Parigi.' But, you see, my friend, my fire is made with chunks of hundred-year-old olive trees. And there's still another secret. What you don't have in Paris is wine made from the Carricante grape — the base of my marinade — the most beautiful white-wine grape in the world, especially when it grows on the slopes of Mount Etna. My family at home sends them to me."

At the word *family,* Tommasso shot a glance at Capucine out of the corner of his eye. There was no doubt he knew full well that she was a police officer. Capucine wondered if the look probed for schadenfreude or if it was intended to be conspiratorial.

The main course arrived, brought by three servants under the watchful eye of an enormously fat woman, who must have been the cook. The grilled meats were superb, imbued with the marinade but not overpowering.

"But, signore, the best is the last to come. I'm going to give you a wine I'm sure you've never had before, the Alberto Loi Riserva, made from Sardinia's most popular grape, Cannonau."

Alexandre perked up. He was not moved by barbecue in any form, but a varietal he had never tasted was definitely an occasion. A wooden-faced servant poured a glass for

Alexandre and stood at attention behind his chair. Tommasso looked at Alexandre with a rigid grin as he took a sip. Capucine could see that Alexandre hated it, but he smiled bravely and delivered a long encomium on the wine's merits. Tommasso beamed.

Tommasso was obviously in his element. He repeatedly signaled the servants to fill dishes with a second helping, encouraged them to top wineglasses when they were barely half empty, and played the role of commandeering architect of the entire table's conversation. This he achieved with playful asides and friendly kidding drawn from the nuggets of biography he had gleaned from Serge during the afternoon.

Halfway through the dinner he jabbed his finger with mock aggressiveness at Florence.

"I was your biggest fan when you were racing. I went out and got drunk when you won the Route du Rhum the first time."

Florence smiled at him with the barest hint of polite tolerance.

"No, no, I'm serious. Sicily is a seafaring island. I'm from a fishing village near Catania. You could see Mount Etna from my parents' house and drink this beautiful wine every day." He raised his glass, then lowered his eyes for a beat to let his guests share the misery of his exile. "You had a boat with a very strange name. I learned that it was pronounced completely differently from the way it was spelled. What was it? Totoare? Totangee. Something like that."

"Tottingre, spelled Tottinguer?" Inès asked with a strong note of sharpness in her voice.

"Brava! What a memory you have. I had no idea you were an aficionada of sailboat racing."

"It's a bank. A very old one, currently run by a man called André Tottinguer." She looked at Florence with the gimlet eyes of a juge d'instruction questioning a suspect.

"How did you happen to name your boat after a bank?"

Florence laughed. "They paid for it. Ninety-foot, state-of-the-art trimarans cost a great deal of money. In those days I couldn't have afforded even a single sail on that boat. Actually, I probably still couldn't. All big-boat racers have sponsors. That's the way it's done."

There was an awkward silence. No one could think of what to say. With a clubman's horror of conversational awkwardness, Dominique — who had consumed a bottle and a half of the Alberto Loi Riserva — smiled brilliantly at his wife. "*Chérie,* isn't Tottinguer your biggest client?"

Angélique's brows screwed together in

anger, and her mouth tightened into a taut line. "Nothing is more sacred than the confidentiality of an adviser-client relationship." She glared at Dominique. "Even you should know that." Then she glowered back at the table. "I've never heard of this Tottinguer." Her tone was wrathful enough to deal a death blow to the dinner.

CHAPTER 13

The instant they emerged from their taxis at the marina, they saw something was very wrong. Wrong enough to jolt them out of their sleepy, happy mood, where the only thought in their heads was stumbling down the companionway steps and collapsing into their bunks.

Bright lights skewered *Diomede* at her berth. They rushed down the gangway to the boat, their feet ringing out on the aluminum of the floating pier. Two uniformed policemen appeared, blocking their way. The boat had been cordoned off with yellow police tape. Two arc lights on tripods illuminated the scene. All the interior lights of the boat were on. On deck, uniformed police officers shuffled back and forth, scoring the nonslip surface with their boots. Below, more police officers could be seen through the ports, roughly rooting through the contents of the galley. Capucine had the sensation that their homely but honest boat was being raped.

Serge was indignant. "What are you doing! Get off my boat immediately! You have no right. It's a French vessel. You have no authority to be on her." He attempted to shove past the policemen and board the boat. One of the officers put the flat of his hand on Serge's chest and pushed. Serge stumbled backward and nearly fell.

"Capucine," he said, "do something. Make them go away."

"Serge, there's nothing to do. The boat has been impounded. And I wouldn't try to strong-arm a police officer again. That's going to get you a night behind bars, which you definitely wouldn't enjoy."

"So what are we going to do?"

"Hotel," Capucine said.

Serge's face crinkled, as if he was on the edge of tears. "A hotel? How the hell are we going to find a hotel at this hour of the night? Look at this damn place." With a sweep of his arm, he indicated the bleak area behind the marina. The only amenities were a minute convenience store and a grim-looking café, both shuttered. Behind the marina lay a vast deserted industrial area.

"What am I supposed to do? Cruise

around Arbatax in a taxicab in the middle of the night, trying to find hotel rooms for ten people without luggage? That'll be a perfect end to the evening. Merde, merde, merde!" He stamped the metal dock, making it ring.

Serge marched off to the end of the jetty, snapped open his cell phone, punched a speed-dial button, turned his back on the police and the boat crew. In less than thirty seconds he swiveled back, his face alive with a radiant smile.

"Grazie mille, Tommasso. You're a prince among men. See you in a few minutes. *Ciao."*

"Problem solved. Tommasso is going to put us up for the night. He even has a supply of toiletries for his guests. I'm calling us some cabs. I can't get away from these Italian cops fast enough."

Tommasso's joy at their return seemed genuine enough. Capucine was sure that he would dine out for years to come on the tale of the evening he had offered a French police commissaire a room because her boat had been declared a crime scene.

The villa seemed to contain an infinity of suites, made sumptuous by the unsubtle hand of an interior decorator. They were decorated with aggressively endearing peasant furniture and precious scenes of olive trees and fishing boats.

Large survival kits — plastic containers crammed with luxury toiletries, including toothbrushes, shaving equipment, colognes, deodorants, shampoos and conditioners, perfumes — one for men, another for women, had been placed on each pillow. The effect was that of a luxury Relais & Châteaux country inn.

Capucine took a shower, hoping to cleanse herself of the feeling that for the first time in her life she was, somehow, on the wrong side of the law.

She dried herself off and walked through the house, emerging onto the terrace, sure it would be deserted save for Alexandre smoking his final cigar of the day.

She was dismayed to see that Alexandre was locked in an energetic discussion with Tommasso about something they were drinking. Capucine debated turning on her heel and going to bed, but her desire to be with Alexandre won out. She padded out on the terrace in her bare feet.

It was about grappa. Tommasso had placed an array of bottles on the long table and was attempting to persuade Alexandre of the superiority of the Sicilian product over the Sardinian. Capucine knew full well this was the sort of exercise that could amuse Alexandre until the rosy fingers of dawn crept up over the horizon.

"Tommasso, you're right. The Grappa di Malvasia delle Lipari is the clear winner. Bravo, Sicilia!" He downed the last half inch of grappa in his tulip-shaped glass, reached around Capucine's waist, drew her toward him, kissed her temple.

"It comes from a little village a few miles from mine back home. I know the man who makes it very well. He is my godfather. A man of many talents."

Tommasso handed Capucine a glass of grappa made by the many-talented man and refilled Alexandre's. The three exchanged polite banalities. The wind from the hill brought down the odor of wild herbs and ruffled the canopy of grape leaves above them.

Tommasso put his glass down on the table.

"*Mi dispiace molto.* Nothing would give me more pleasure than chatting with the two of you all night long, but I'm afraid I have a very early meeting and must go to bed. But please, stay and enjoy the night."

The night was indeed magical. The moon had finally become entirely full, a perfectly round orb.

"Let's go down and sit by that pool in the rock grotto. It's perfect for an evening like this," Capucine said.

Alexandre led her down three flights of steps cut into the rock to a natural grotto, which had been enlarged by architects and fitted with plumbing to make it appear to be a natural pool.

"A whole night of having you in my arms, far away from any living creature, on a night like this. It's my definition of *heaven,*" Alexandre said. But at the grotto Alexandre deflated when he saw Jacques sitting at the edge of the pool, facing the sea, his legs dangling over a twenty-foot drop.

With some trepidation they inched out over the rocks to Jacques's side and sat down, Capucine between her cousin and her husband. Alexandre passed one of the glasses to Jacques and shared his with Capucine. Alexandre lit a cigar.

They said nothing, staring into a moon so incandescent, it cauterized the shock of the police defilement of the boat.

Jacques's loud voice shattered the calm.

"*Petite cousine,* for once, I'm going to extract you from the bouillabaisse before you even know you're in it. Aren't you impressed?" He extended his empty glass to Alexandre for a refill.

Capucine sat up straight. "Jacques, not now. It's been a very long day. Let's just go to bed."

"Petite cousine, all this sea air is making you dull. As I'm sure you've told your corpulent consort many a time, the best things in life come in small packages. And I have one for you right here in my hand."

He held out his closed fist, fingers down, to Capucine. Despite her pique at being teased, she opened her palm under his. He stretched his fingers open.

It was difficult to see what it was in the dark. Alexandre lit his lighter.

"A shell casing," Capucine said.

"Look a little closer."

It was a nine-millimeter shell casing marked SPEER around the bottom edge. It was from one of the so-called safety-tipped American rounds that the French police had started issuing three months before. A shell casing that could only have come recently from a French police weapon.

"Where did you find this?"

"It was wedged into the little recess at the edge of the deck on the forecastle. I noticed it as we were approaching the coast on our way into Porto Cervo after Nathalie went overboard."

There was a long silence, punctuated only

by compact little cumuli of Alexandre's cigar smoke rising into the moonlight.

Capucine reached into her pocket, produced her iPhone, fussed with it.

"Here," she said, handing the phone to Jacques. "Show me exactly where you found it."

The picture on the little screen was a close-up of the foredeck area.

"It's Régis's blog," Capucine said. "I've become an avid reader. He posts endless pictures of our trip. This picture was taken before you found the shell casing."

Jacques put his finger on the screen. "Right here."

Capucine took the smartphone back, zoomed in on the image. Régis's pictures were very high resolution. It was obvious there was no shell casing.

"Is there a chance it rolled there after the picture was taken?" Capucine asked.

"None whatsoever. It was wedged in tightly. So tightly someone must have jammed it in so it wouldn't get lost." Jacques beamed his Cheshire cat grin on Capucine. "Aren't you glad, little cousin, that it was me who found it and not one of those heavy-booted *carabinieri*?"

He held his palm out flat in front of Capucine. Automatically, she placed the shell casing in his hand. In a single fluid motion, Jacques crooked his thumb and projected the shell like a small boy shooting a marble. It rose in the air, the moonlight glinting on its polished brass surface, and fell into the thick undergrowth far below.

"It won't ever be found down there. That's one thing we can count on."

"Jacques! That was evidence."

"That's precisely the point. *Now* we can go to bed."

CHAPTER 14

The next morning, as they were all eating breakfast on the long table on the terrace, a Fiat police squad car tore up the driveway and braked sharply, spraying gravel. Capucine assumed she was being picked up for an "interrogation," one step up from an "interview" in the hierarchy of police investigation. Capucine wondered if she would be taken away in handcuffs.

Two police officers, elegant in red-striped trousers and tunics with polished chrome buttons, emerged from the car and, with great politeness, inquired after Commissario Le Tellier.

As Capucine descended the steps to the driveway, both officers came to attention and saluted smartly. This was certainly not the way suspects were picked up in France. One of them apologized for the intrusion and said that the *vice questore* had requested her presence at the *questura.* "But at your entire convenience, Signora Commissario." The officer smiled conspiratorially. "Please, finish your breakfast. We will be happy to wait." Definitely not the way people were picked up in France.

At the questura, she was taken to the vice questore's office, a room imposing enough for a junior minister. The vice questore looked like anything but a police officer — aristocratic aquiline nose, silver hair brushed back from his forehead, well-tailored brown summer suit. With smiling lips and frowning eyes, he rose from behind an antique desk, circled to her side, and motioned her into a wooden armchair cushioned in red silk embroidered with gold thread. Without saying a word, he sat facing her in a matching chair. Two men eased into the room. One was Ispettore Manfredi; the other, a few years older and considerably more muscular, looked like an old-school hard-nosed cop. They took seats in opposite corners of the large room.

So, this was to be an interrogation, after all, but there was definitely something odd going on. The tension in the room was palpable. Capucine admired the vice questore's interviewing technique. After a good many long beats, the vice questore introduced himself. "Vice Questore Piras. And, of course, you've met Ispettore Manfredi. And this is *Commissario Capo* Deiana."

A senior commissaire. There was a lot of brass in the room. Too much brass for an interrogation.

Languidly, the vice questore crossed one long leg over another, taking great care not to flatten the knife-sharp crease of his trouser leg.

"We are faced with an exceedingly delicate situation, Commissario," the vice questore said. "I understand the ispettore explained to you yesterday that evidence has been discovered that strongly indicates the disappearance of your employee was the result of foul play."

"Yes. Apparently, a sea jacket with a suspicious hole in it."

"Precisely. The forensics unit has completed its analysis. The hole was unquestionably made by a nine-millimeter bullet."

"Were there any traces of blood?"

"No. But the forensics experts say all traces of fresh blood could have been washed off by the salt water. But there was evidence of gunpowder singeing around the edge of the hole, indicating that the shot was fired at close range."

He gave Capucine one of his expressionless looks, inviting her to comment. She said nothing.

"The interesting thing, however, is that there is a name printed in indelible laundry ink on the jacket's white manufacturer's label. The name is not Martin, the victim's, but Maistre. I understand you have a Signorina Inès Maistre on board. What can you tell me about that?"

"When Mademoiselle Martin fell — went — overboard, she, Mademoiselle Maistre, and I were keeping watch on deck. There had been lightning in the distance, so all three of us had brought foul-weather gear up on deck. It was far too warm to wear the jackets, so we bundled them up on the cockpit sole, under our feet. Mademoiselle Martin got up to go forward and relieve herself. Apparently, she was experiencing some form of gastric distress. Just as she stood up, the storm broke. She grabbed a jacket and rushed to the bow. She must have picked up Mademoiselle Maistre's by mistake."

The vice questore nodded repeatedly, looking a little like a Chinese porcelain sage with its head set on a spring. After a long pause — his interview technique really was very good — he went back and sat behind his desk, opened the center drawer and, with two long, almost skeletal fingers, extracted a plastic evidence bag as if it took a great effort to even touch something so filthy. He placed the bag on the desk. A Beretta Px4 Storm Type F Sub-Compact. The gun was smudged with white aluminum fingerprint powder.

"The pistol is stamped to indicate that it is the property of the French government. The only French agency, military or civilian, that is issued the model Px4 is the Police Judiciaire. Would this pistol happen to be yours, Commissario?"

"It could well be. It's the standard Police Judiciaire off-duty sidearm."

"It was found in a drawer in your cabin." He held the bag out imperially in the direction of Ispettore Manfredi, who approached the desk briskly. Manfredi removed the gun from its plastic envelope, pushed the button releasing the clip, caught it, and held it out to Capucine.

"It would seem that there are only twelve cartridges in the clip. One is missing," the vice questore said.

Capucine said nothing. She knew she had a very bad, even dangerous, habit. Common sense and police regulations dictated that the chambers of automatic pistols be left empty. If a cartridge were left in the chamber, there was a risk that the gun could go off if dropped or if it was on the belt of an officer who was knocked down. Still, Capucine always left a cartridge in the chamber. A gun that required both hands to be armed struck her as imprudent no matter what the risk. She burned with desire to ask if there had been a cartridge in the chamber, meaning that two shots had been fired, but knew that silence was the order of the day.

The vice questore said, "It's very suggestive that a cartridge is missing." He let one of his long silences do some more heavy lifting.

At length, the vice questore opened the center drawer of his desk once again and extracted another, smaller, evidence bag. He zipped it open and let a small brass cartridge case, dusty with fingerprint powder, fall on the mahogany inlay of the desk. He slipped a wooden pencil in the shell and held it up for Capucine to see.

Capucine was stunned. There had been a second shot. It took an effort to maintain her wooden face.

"This was found on the bow of your boat. It is made for the French police by a company called Speer. They are not available to the public. The forensics experts will determine if the markings are from the firing pin of your gun, but I think we can assume they will be."

Very slowly, the vice questore tipped the shell casing back into its bag, opened the center drawer of the desk, swept the evidence bags into it with his arm, closed the drawer with an audible *thwunk*. There was a sense of finality to the gesture.

He smiled conspiratorially at Capucine. "Commissario, as a police officer, I'm sure you will agree with me that — pending the results of the investigation, of course — you are the principal suspect. You were on deck in the middle of the night with the victim, and there is evidence that she was shot on deck, and that she was shot with your gun." He shrugged his shoulders, raised his eyebrows, and frowned, as if to ask, "What more could you want?"

Capucine had been over the facts many times in her head, but she was surprised and dismayed at how compelling the case against her was when it came out of the mouth of someone else.

"Yes, Vice Questore, I agree there is some circumstantial evidence, but what possible motive could I have for murdering someone I had met for the first time only a few days before?"

The vice questore snorted in laughter and

turned to share the joke with his two officers, who chortled back politely.

"Commissario, every police department on the entire coast of Sardinia deals with incidents on the yachts of the rich all summer long. Almost all of them involve young boat hands. They are invariably hippie types with very loose morals. The sea is nature's most powerful aphrodisiac.

"It could easily be argued that you discovered your husband with the girl. Later, in the middle of the night, you shot her under the cover of the storm. No jury in the world would refuse that as a motive." Elbows on the desk, he spread his hands palms upward in a papal gesture, underscoring the strength of the argument.

There was another long moment of silence. Capucine was certain that in the next few minutes she would find herself in a detention cell.

"That is why my men and I have spent a good part of the night working together and conferring with our superiors to find a solution. Happily, I have just received confirmation from my superiors that we have succeeded.

"Part of our inquiry involved consulting the marine-current expert of the guardia costiera. He produced some extremely good news. It seems that the currents that flow through the Strait of Bonifacio, the body of water separating Corsica and Sardinia, are extremely complex." This said in an almost jovial, dinner party tone. "There is some sort of compression phenomenon due to the funnel made by the two landmasses. There are vortices and whorls and all sorts of complicated little tricks created by all the little islands." He paused dramatically, setting up his punch line.

"The expert concluded, without the slightest possible shadow of a doubt, that your boat was in French waters when the tragic incident occurred. I had a lengthy meeting with the magistrate this morning, and he agrees with me that you are free to leave, at your entire convenience, of course."

"So you're dropping the case?"

"Hardly. We're merely referring it to the proper authorities. Rendering to Caesar what is Caesar's, as it were. The evidence" — he rapped the desk with his knuckles — "will be sent to France. It is up to the French to decide what to do with it."

Capucine had always heard that *vice questori* were more politicians than policemen. Now she understood why.

"And so the French are to investigate the case?"

"Ah, Commissario, how can I possibly tell *you,* of all people, anything about the workings of the French police?" He made a curious wringing motion with his hands, which, Capucine guessed, was a subconscious expression of his washing his hands of the whole business.

"But I will offer you a personal consideration, an observation from one colleague to another. Your boat is no longer sequestered. It would be in your interest to depart quickly. You know the vagaries of politics. Who knows when someone may change his mind? I have been ordered to release you with the presumed assumption that you will return to France to assist with the investigation. But, of course, I have no means to determine your final destination. I understand Brazil is a charming country with no extradition treaties of any kind. And the yacht club in Rio is said to be one of the most beautiful in the world."

He stood up and, with fluid courtesy, escorted Capucine to the front door of the questura.

Capucine was returned to the villa by the same squad car. She found everyone at lunch on the terrace. Capucine slid into a chair that had been left vacant for her next to Alexandre.

"Well, what did the police sa—" Serge started to ask eagerly but was cut off by Alexandre's raised hand.

"*Ma chérie,* do you have any appetite at all?"

Capucine kissed his cheek. Bless his sense of priorities.

"No. I couldn't eat a thing. Maybe a glass of wine, though. We're free to go. In fact, we're encouraged to go quickly. Their marine-current expert has decided that poor Nathalie went overboard in French waters, and they're sticking with their original decision to wash their hands of the whole business."

"Fabulous," Serge replied, jumping up. "Best news I've ever heard. I need to get back to my boat and see if those awful policemen have drilled holes in the hull or something. We can provision up and get the hell out of here in an hour."

"But where will we go?" Aude asked, her glacial eyes deeper and more impenetrable than ever.

Serge sat back down in his chair with a thump.

It took less than a minute to resolve the question. Enough was enough. Saint-Tropez was fifteen hours away under sail. Back in

France they could finish their vacations on their own, happy on dry land. There was not a single demurring murmur. Taxis were called. A rapid note was written by Serge to Tommasso. They all scribbled their initials on the bottom.

In the confusion they had called too many cabs. Alexandre and Régis commandeered one and made off for downtown Tortoli to buy provisions. Capucine and Inès found themselves in another. The others took the third.

"So what did the vice questore really say?" Inès asked Capucine.

Capucine gave Inès a summary, not omitting the comment about Brazil.

"They'll send the evidence on the diplomatic pouch," Inès said. "Your vice questore is convinced you'll be arrested the minute you set foot on French soil. But he's wrong. Even if the evidence and the vice questore's explanatory memorandum arrive tomorrow morning, it will still take the magistrates a week, or even more, to sort out the jurisdictional issues. But sooner or later, the case will be handed over to the police. There's no doubt about that."

Capucine said nothing for the rest of the ride down to the marina. There was a flaw in Inès's logic. The police couldn't be suspected. It wasn't that they were above suspicion. It was that they weren't in the game. You could hardly give a referee a red card, now could you? Those were only for the players.

Once again, Serge fretted on deck waiting for Alexandre and Régis to arrive with groceries. Once again, a good hour and a half late, they appeared, struggling with an overladen shopping cart, both of them serene despite Serge's choler.

"Are you two crazy? We're not sailing to Latin America. We'll be home tomorrow," Serge said.

Inès shot him a sharp look.

But Serge's rage hit its acme when he noticed that — in addition to a full larder of vegetables, Italian charcuterie, cheeses, meats in brown wrapping, dairy products, and an abundance of eggs — they had acquired a family-size pasta-making machine.

"Do you think you're going to open a restaurant on my boat?"

"Hardly," Alexandre said. "But we're not going to leave Italy without eating some proper pasta, and Régis and I are going to make it. *Voilà, c'est comme ça.*"

Getting out of Arbatax was the work of

ten minutes. Docile under Florence's hand, *Diomede* set off on a northerly course toward the Strait of Bonifacio. The afternoon wore on as peacefully as on the most halcyon of sea cruises. Alexandre and Régis joyfully stretched long ribbons of pasta across the salon, some read, and Jacques and Aude communed silently, their legs over the boat's side. The mood had crossed back over its watershed.

Alexandre, in honor of the traditions of final-night dinners laid down by prewar luxury liners, prepared his most sumptuous meal of the trip. Given the fineness of the evening, they ate in the cockpit. He announced the meal would his version of *cuisine sarde* — Sardinian cooking. The meal started out simply enough with an antipasto dish of thin slices of melon topped with slices of Parma ham. The melon's flesh was so pale, it was almost blue, and as sweet as if sugar had been added. The Sardinian note appeared in the pasta dish, *ceci e fregola* — a stew made with chickpeas and semolina pasta balls, unique to Sardinia. The pasta balls and the chickpeas were exactly the same size. Alexandre had decorated the dish with pecorino wafers made by grating a slice of the cheese from the huge wedge he had brought on board onto a baking sheet and grilling it in the oven until the pieces fused.

The *primo piatto* — the first course — was *cefalo arrostito* — grilled fillets of Sardinian gray mullet. Régis ceremoniously brought the platter up through the hatch, placed it on the cockpit table, then served it on the boat's plastic dishes. Only four people sat round the table. The others had spread out around the deck. The mullets were light, flaky, delicately seasoned with a hint of garlic and caraway thyme, a variety that grew wild only in Corsica and Sardinia.

Next came Alexandre's pièce de résistance, the *secondo piatto* — the second course Régis brought up a large casserole and placed it gingerly on the table.

"This is a great Sardinian classic, *coniglio alla sarda,*" Alexandre announced. "A stew made of the cousin of the hare and local vegetables, seasoned mainly with tamarind."

There was happy chuckling at the name of the dish.

Inès, who was sitting with Capucine just above the hatch opening, said, "What do you mean 'cousin of the hare'? Is that a ra—"

Capucine put her hand over Inès's mouth.

She shook it off, furious. "What are you doing!" Her anger increased as the laughter rose to a peak.

"There's a certain animal that can never be named on ships or boats. It's believed it will bring catastrophic luck. Of course, Alexandre's provoked the ire of the gods by actually bringing the animal on board, but there's no point in adding insult to injury," Serge said, shooting Alexandre a poisonous look.

"What animal? What are you talking about?" Inès asked. "A rab—"

Capucine clapped her hand back on Inès's mouth before the word escaped. There were roars of laughter.

Despite the risk of bad luck, everyone had seconds of the stew and ate so much that Alexandre's platter of Sardinian cheeses was deferred to snacks for the watches during the night and people only pecked at dessert, which was *pardulas,* pastry tarts filled with soft cheese and sprinkled with powdered sugar.

Grappa and coffee were served below. The bittersweet parting mood became so pronounced, Jacques broke into a satirical chorus of "Auld Lang Syne." The group laughed uproariously, but the sadness remained.

Much, much later, as most of the group staggered off to their cabins, Jacques, Capucine, and Alexandre made for the bow pulpit for more grappa, with a final cigar for Jacques and Alexandre.

"You need another lifeline out of the bouillabaisse, don't you, petite cousine?" Jacques asked.

Capucine smiled a long-suffering smile at him. "I probably do, but you can't work your celestial Rolodex in the middle of the Tyrrhenian Sea, can you?"

"You're just miffed I didn't throw your little popgun into the sea when I had the chance. But that's my profound sense of allegiance to *la patrie.* Government property is sacred."

"Actually," Alexandre said, "I think she's disappointed you didn't intercept the second shell casing."

"Oh, don't worry about that. She'll figure out that part of it in the end. You have to be patient with the poor dear. She's not as quick as the rest of us, but she's much better looking."

"Inès seems to want me to believe I'll get arrested the second I set foot in Port Grimaud. That's ridiculous. I'm a commissaire in the Police Judiciaire, after all." She was crestfallen when the comment didn't draw a corroborating snigger.

"Cousine, I'm afraid you're going to have to accept that that's a fairly accurate assessment of the situation," Jacques said.

Capucine pouted. "I can hardly jump overboard and swim to the isle of Elba, now can I?" she asked.

"Even if you could, it would be subpar as an idea. I understand Napoleon didn't have all that much to say for the place."

"So I'm *foutu,*" Capucine said, accepting another shot glass of grappa from the bottle Alexandre had brought on deck.

"Cannes, little cousine. Think Cannes. The film festival is over. It's possible once again to get into restaurants, and the beaches will be free of those dreary paparazzi."

"Jacques, don't joke. How would we get to Cannes? I can hardly suggest to seven people, one of whom is a juge d'instruction, to make a detour to Cannes and keep it a secret."

Jacques smiled at her with his all-knowing Cheshire cat smile.

"Well, there's always the dinghy."

"You're joking!"

"Not at all. Bligh covered thousands of nautical miles in a leaky rowboat. And you have a high-tech craft with a state-of-the-art internal combustion engine at your disposal. All you have to do is pitch it into the sea, hop in, and putt-putt your way into Cannes.

What could be more simple?"

Capucine furrowed her brow.

"It'll be as easy as taking a *sucette* from a toddler in a stroller. And I'll create a smoke screen so dense, no one will notice that you two weren't there for the arrival in Port Grimaud."

Lightning flickered soundlessly in the distance, lighting up a small segment of the horizon. Sensing her concern, Alexandre shook his head. "Probably just a local storm. Nothing to worry about. Let's go to bed. I'm thinking we're not going to get much sleep tonight."

An hour later Capucine was jolted awake by a clap of thunder. Eyes open, she lay in the bunk, Alexandre's arm across her torso and the slight roundness of his stomach pressed into her back. Like a child at camp, she counted the seconds between the cracks of thunder and the flashes. Three miles away. Despite the fact that Florence was at the helm, Capucine fidgeted, on edge, a poker player about to slap her last card on the table, a card she didn't like very much when you got right down to it.

Taking to the open sea in the tiny dinghy with a storm coming on was lunacy. But there was no alternative. It was the damned rabbits. What *had* Alexandre been thinking?

She sank into an uneasy doze with a vision of a sinister rabbit twitching his nose at her, laughing maliciously.

CHAPTER 15

Despite Jacques's assurances, when they got down to it, it turned out to be a very far cry from snatching a lollipop out of a baby's hand.

At four thirty in the morning Capucine and Alexandre came on deck, miming a couple seeking a snap of cool air to bring on sleep. Serge, at the helm, had switched on the autopilot and sat on the stern rail, struggling to stay awake.

Serge was delighted at their arrival. "Can you two look after the boat? I'm going below to make something to eat. I need something to get revved up."

"There's some excellent *prosciutto di Parma* in the fridge, and the eggs are farm fresh from the outdoor market," Alexandre said. "Put some butter in a skillet to fry the eggs, and when they're nearly done, put the ham in for a few seconds, until it just begins to stiffen and turn brown."

"Sounds fabulous. I won't be more than ten minutes."

As Serge started to go below, he brushed up against Jacques, who was coming up the companionway, yawning and stretching.

"Couldn't sleep. Our cabin is like an oven. I need a good jolt of the briny."

"We all do. I've had my fill of standing watch, and I'm going below to stuff my face. The worst part is I've got another two hours before we make port." He shook his head to demonstrate the full extent of his heroic suffering.

The instant they heard Serge rattling pans, Jacques got to work soundlessly. He tripped a release catch just above the transom, popping open the long, thin cover with a muffled clunk. All three froze, praying for Serge not to come back up. Capucine thrummed. Jacques pulled her over to him.

"Your course is dead north. I just checked our position on the GPS. We're twelve nautical miles south of the coast. When the dinghy goes in the water, you need to get right on board. I'll hold on to the painter, but at the speed the yacht is making, the dinghy will surf with its nose out of the water. Capucine, you'll go first and kneel in the bow to keep it down. Then you switch places with Alexandre and move to the stern. Tubby Hubby's avoirdupois is just what we need to keep the dinghy level. I'll cast you off, and you sit quiet as ship rats for at least fifteen minutes before starting the engine. That's all there is to it. Even you two can pull it off with your fingers in your nose. Okay, off you go, now."

Jacques jerked the dinghy out of its niche and in the same motion knotted the painter around the stern rail.

The tiny dinghy, barely long enough to lie down in, rose half out of the water, weaving a crazed, erratic wake.

The idea of leaving the yacht seemed beyond suicidal.

"Get your ass in gear, cousine," Jacques said with steely eyes. Capucine could easily imagine him shooting a recalcitrant agent slowing up a field mission.

Holding on to the rail, she lowered herself into the bucking dinghy. Alexandre followed immediately. For a split second they hung on the line running around the gunwales of the careening dinghy. Jacques cast off. The dinghy stopped as short as if it had hit a wall. *Diomede* receded into the night.

Capucine and Alexandre sat on folded Indian legs on the wood slats of the dinghy's sole and watched Jacques disappear, happily waving a vaudevillian good-bye.

For the first time in her life, Capucine came close to a genuine panic attack. All she wanted was the normal context of her life restored. Instead, the only thing they could have called home was already almost over the horizon. What had she gotten them into?

Conversely, Alexandre sighed contentedly. "How satisfying to leave behind all the silly squabbles of that plastic boat. Let's have breakfast. I'm starved."

"And I suppose if we ring, a steward will appear?"

Rather than reply, Alexandre produced several film-wrapped packages from the pockets of his Windbreaker. "Prosciutto and mortadella *panini*. I made them while you were getting ready." He produced a large bottle, which he opened with a resounding pop. "This is that excellent Prosecco we bought at the market yesterday. I know it's a bit early in the day, but a little bubbly *does* make for a perfect breakfast."

Capucine's world came partially back into focus. Bless Alexandre's priorities.

The first rays of the sun winked over the horizon just as they finished breakfast, and they attacked the diminutive outboard lashed to one of the dinghy's gunwales. Clamping it on the wooden transom and hooking up its tiny gas tank was easy enough, but getting it started was a whole other matter.

Both Capucine and Alexandre yanked the starter cord to no avail. Despite the early morning chill, they both began to sweat.

Capucine stopped to rest. She noticed that there was a rubber bulb in the middle of the fuel line. She remembered her early teen years in La Baule, in Brittany. There had been plenty of outboards in those days. Of course, they had been the boys' purview, but she had been an attentive observer.

"I wonder if you need to pump it up to get it going?" Capucine asked.

"All the girls ask that."

Capucine shot Alexandre a mock scowl and gave the bulb three vigorous squeezes.

The engine caught at the first pull of the cord with the purr of an oversize cat. The dinghy advanced, bouncing cheerfully over the miniscule waves of the lake-flat sea.

Capucine turned on her iPhone and frowned. It was dead.

"Don't worry about it, about not having the GPS. France is a big country. If we keep the sun on our right hand, we're bound to run into it sooner or later."

It all seemed simple enough. Capucine almost began to enjoy herself as the morning wore on tranquilly with the bubbling burp of the outboard.

Without warning the outboard gave a moribund cough and fell terminally silent. Capucine lifted the gas container and shook it. Dead empty. The dinghy turned until it steadied, facing the rising sun.

"We seem to be heading toward Pisa. Not an unpleasant place, of course, but at this rate we won't get there till la Toussaint," Alexandre said.

"There must be oars on this thing."

There were. Two toylike objects that required assembly like the shafts of beach umbrellas.

Alexandre began to row. It was obviously hard going. The broad-beamed rubber boat seemed immovable. After twenty minutes he looked at the palms of his hands and frowned.

"Think of that wonderful scene in *A Farewell to Arms* when Frederic and Catherine row all the way across Lake Maggiore to escape to Switzerland," Capucine said.

Alexandre frowned again. "As I recall, that particular boat trip ended a bit tragically."

In another ten minutes, Alexandre sagged and let go of the oars. The dinghy immediately resumed its easterly direction.

Capucine grabbed Alexandre's hands by

the wrists and twisted his palms toward her. Blood oozed down his wrists.

"Change places with me. I need some exercise," Capucine said.

It took some discussion, but Capucine finally gained control of the diminutive oars. She was astounded how difficult it was to get even the slightest motion out of the little boat.

"How far from the coast would you guess we are?" she asked.

"Jacques said we were twelve nautical miles off when we started. With any luck we're halfway there, maybe less."

Capucine deflated. Square one. They might just as well be in the middle of the Atlantic.

In the stern, Alexandre contracted his brow, deep in thought. He inserted his index finger in his mouth and then held it up in the air, nodded, and checked the position of the sun. He broke into a broad smile and sang two bars of cracked Verdi "We're going to be all right," he said. "We're being pushed along by a wind from the south."

"The sirocco?"

"No, its friendly little cousin, the Ostro, mild and humid, not harsh and dry with desert air."

Over the next half hour they became

skilled jury-rig sailors. First, they discovered that if they kneeled upright side by side, the little boat would actually move in the right direction, even though it was impossible to steer. Then it dawned on them that they could make a perfectly serviceable sail by threading an oar through the sleeves of their Windbreakers and zipping them shut. Steering with their hands in the water, they managed to produce a bow wave almost as satisfactory as with the outboard.

Within an hour Capucine smelled land. She didn't actually smell it, but she knew without a shadow of a doubt it was close to hand. Seagulls appeared. Half an hour later they were lifted by a compact breaker and gently deposited on a gritty beach. The grotesque cruise was at long last over. They were ashore, on a rational, ordered, and — above all — normal shore. Capucine's heart soared.

They sat on the sand, basking, catching their emotional breath, rejoicing that they had survived an adventure that, in retrospect, had been conceived in folly and could have ended tragically. But it had worked. Here they were, back in France. Mere steps away from the chic of the Midi, well stocked with haute couture and gastronomic delights.

Sighing in well-being, Alexandre dug through the pockets of his Windbreaker, extracted an aluminum cigar tube, and removed a cigar, which he rolled lovingly in his hands. Capucine shared vicariously in his return to rational order. Alexandre bit off the end of the cigar and patted his pockets for matches. As he prepared to light up, an ancient man, in clothes so old they were almost rags, a heavy burlap bag slung over his shoulder, shuffled over to them double time. Both Capucine and Alexandre smiled at him. Alexandre lit the cigar.

The man broke into a run. *"Non, non, non!"* he shouted. "No smoking. It is forbidden!" He snatched up the cigar — a prized Hoyo de Monterrey Double Corona — flung it down on the beach with a grunt of disgust, ground it into flakes with his heel, and continued his amble down the beach, growling in irritation.

Chapter 16

As the prized cigar was reduced to shreds of tobacco, Capucine's euphoria popped like a soap bubble, filling her eyes with tears. This was even worse than being back at square one, drifting pointlessly on that bathtub-size rubber dinghy. She looked up at Alexandre, expecting to find him sharing her despondency. But, on the contrary, he seemed in his element, delighted with life.

"This is perfect! I have a feeling I'm about to realize one of my life ambitions."

Capucine's jaw muscle relaxed, separating her lips.

"You know what's going on?" she asked.

"I'm pretty sure we're on the Île Saint-Honorat, a tiny island a mile off Cannes that has been a Cistercian monastery since the fifth century. About thirty monks live here and make wine and a bit of lavender honey."

"And just how has all this information

popped full blown into your head?"

"Well, a while back the paper asked me to write a piece on the gastronomic divinities monks are held to produce. You know, all those fudge truffle cakes, flavored beers, that sort of thing. I was supposed to tour all the monasteries in Provence and get the lowdown."

"You must have had fun."

"Au contraire. It was a total bust. First off, they would let me in, and the only good stuff they actually made was produced by commercial firms and labeled by them. The Abbaye de Lérins was the worst of the bunch. They rule with an iron hand. Uninterrupted introversion at all cost. Total silence. No laughing, ah, no radios, no fires — much less any thought of smoking. Just peace and prayer. They threw me out on my ear."

"And what makes you think they're going to be so welcoming this time around?"

"Ah, things are different now. St. Benedict, the granddaddy of all monasteriers, was famous for his desire to provide succor to needy pilgrims. And if we don't qualify, I can't for the life of me imagine who would."

"I'm not too sure about the shipwrecked part, but I'm definitely in need of sustenance. A nice country breakfast with gobs of locally made jam would definitely hit the spot."

The island was so tiny, it took less than ten minutes to locate the monastery. As they threaded their way through a labyrinth of outbuildings toward the main portal, a barely perceptible undertone became increasingly pronounced.

"Sext," Alexandre announced.

"Come again?"

"Don't be vulgar. We're in a monastery, after all. Sext is the noon hour of the liturgy. When it's over, they spend the afternoon deep in prayer until dinner. Our timing is perfect."

Alexandre had thumped the portal with the hefty wrought-iron knocker. As he spoke, the door rasped open, revealing a man in a milky, ankle-length alb, over which he wore an ebony scapular. His frigid glare put small talk at the bottom of the list of priorities.

"I am allowed to speak if necessary. Do you require assistance?"

"We're shipwrecked. We were on our way to Cannes when our boat sank. We just barely made it to your island on the life raft. We haven't eaten for days."

The monk appraised the cut of Alexandre's and Capucine's yachting clothes and seemed to stumble with the reconciliation of the chic of their turnout and the tall tale of their putative circumstances.

Alexandre attempted to lubricate the potential gaffe by introducing himself and Capucine with a clubman's conventional cheer.

"You're not by any chance the same Huguelet who writes the food reviews for *Le Monde*?"

"None other. But this is the last place on earth I'd expect my columns to be read."

This was greeted by a supercilious smirk. "The Lord acts in truly unfathomable ways. We here at the monastery were all once men of the world. The fact that we have chosen a different life by no means implies we resigned from beauty. Appetite is one of the Lord's greatest gifts. I myself was the *saucier* at Chez Le Bec Fin before I found my calling." Alexandre's eyebrows rose in amazement.

He went on. "Our cooking system is simple. Each night one of us prepares the evening meal, whether that person has any skill or not. We eat what we are given, and thank the Lord profoundly, even if it's not the best thing we've ever eaten. Tonight it was Father Simon's turn. But he is at the bottom of his bed in the infirmary. Another of the Lord's little blessings," he said with a wry smile.

"We were going to have to make do with the breakfast leftovers, hard cheese and dried bread. But you are here, and with a little nudge of my tutelage, I do believe we'll be able to prepare a respectable squash, leek, and chickpea stew." The monk crossed himself and glanced heavenward with gratitude before leading them to the kitchen.

The monk's lips pursed in thought. "I'll need you to get going right away with soaking the chickpeas. When they're soft enough, I'll give you a hand and we'll get down to work." The man of the cloth was transforming himself into a man of the chef's toque.

He became so engrossed in his recipe, he didn't notice Capucine slip her iPhone out of her shorts and fiddle with the buttons. Alexandre wondered who she was texting. She wore a pleased little secret smile. The monk barely noticed. As he collected kitchen paraphernalia for the stew, he glanced at Capucine and made an apologetic comment that the use of phones wasn't allowed on the island and that they worked only on hilltops, anyway. Capucine smiled sweetly and pocketed her phone.

The dinner was a joy. The monks sat around a large U-shaped table, facing each other, not exchanging a word. But their eyes never left one another's, and despite the silence, they managed an exchange in depth entirely with eyes and facial expressions. A powerful electric intimacy streamed freely across the table. When it was over, Capucine had the feeling that she had had a more significant exchange than at most of the Paris dinner parties she was used to.

After the meal, the monks retired to the chapel for compline, and the tomb-like Great Silence began. Alexandre and Capucine stole off for a quick constitutional before retiring. They climbed a hill high enough for them to see the lights of Cannes wink in the distance.

Capucine produced her phone.

Pic U up @ 8 am 2moro. Dvd, was the text on the screen. A sweet normality expressed in the banal lingua franca of the day. She would sleep well that night.

CHAPTER 17

On the dot of eight the next morning —
sated on toasted dark bread slathered with
salty farm butter and monastic strawberry
jam, the lot washed down with milky coffee
served in bowls — Capucine and Alexandre
arrived at the island's diminutive dock,
uncombed, unmade up, and ungroomed,
despite their best efforts in the abbey
bathroom. A dilapidated commercial fishing
boat, broad streaks of rust blood disfiguring
its hull, was tied up to one of the cement
breakwaters, its idling motor thumping at
half time.

A young man appeared on deck, stylish
enough for the pages of *Vogue Hommes,*
smiling so broadly his face risked splitting
open. David Martineau, formerly *Brigadier*
David Martineau of the Police Judiciaire,
had been a key member of Capucine's team
until he resigned from the force to run for
mayor of the village where he'd been con-

ducting an investigation and to reassert his meridional origins. His political career was currently propelling him apace toward a seat in the Chamber of Deputies.

"Welcome aboard," said David, followed by two fishermen wearing ramshackle smocks so typical, they might well have been supplied by central casting. The deck was crusted with decades of seagull droppings and was fetid with fish stench. David stepped forward, at a loss on how to greet his former boss, whom he hadn't seen for two years. Alexandre rescued the moment by clasping David's hand in two of his.

"*Ravi de te voir, Monsieur le Maire!* Delighted to see you, Mr. Mayor." The combination of the familiar *tu* and the mayoral title amply did the trick. To complete the tableau, Capucine presented her cheek for an air kiss.

But despite the warmth of the moment, there was still a hint of awkwardness.

"Do we cast off, Monsieur le Maire?" one of the fishermen asked.

"*Oui, Jean.* Let's get going. I need to be back before lunchtime. I have a meeting I can't miss."

They puttered away from the breakwater, heading west along the coast. David produced a thermos of strong, sweet coffee. He filled enameled tin cups, then served everyone, including the two fishermen.

"David," Alexandre said, "I definitely prefer your yacht to that extortionate plastic contraption we've been cooped up on for the past week."

David laughed. "I got the gist of it from the commissaire's cousin. Jacques and I had a long chat on the phone last night. By the way, this is Jean's boat." David indicated the elder of the two fishermen with his head. "He's a good buddy. He fishes out of Bandol and was generous enough to give up half a day's work to help us out."

"Anytime, Monsieur le Maire. You know I'm always at your service." Jean flashed a broken-toothed smile accompanied by a respectful head bob, which David accepted as his due as a celebrity. He had clinched his new career by writing a runaway best seller about a murder, including a racy account of the victim, a rock-star chef originally from the village.

As David sat on the gunwale, chatting with Jean, Capucine watched him ceaselessly preen his locks with his fingers. His love of clothes and his vanity about his hair were still very much there, but he had changed. He had added the mantle of power. He wore it casually, but it was still manifest.

In Bandol, the fishing boat motored past the gleaming white sailboats and tied up at the plebeian rusty end of the marina. Walking through town, David came close to being mobbed. Everyone seemed to want a word in his ear. At one point David disappeared into a branch of the Crédit Agricole and returned in a few minutes with a thick envelope.

"You both need to get kitted out. This should do for a reasonable spree."

Capucine peeked into the envelope. The sum surprised her.

"David, I'm embarrassed. I'll pay you back the second this is all over."

David flapped his hand in dismissal. He looked at his watch.

"*Oh là là.* I'm late already. You two go shopping and meet me at a restaurant called Les Pieds dans L'Eau in an hour. It's right over there," he said, pointing down the quai. "If I'm a few minutes late, don't worry. These meetings with constituents tend to run over, but missing lunch is inconceivable in the Midi."

An hour and a half later Capucine and Alexandre were seated, one row in, on the terrace of the restaurant, contentedly sipping rosé in the sunshine. Capucine wore a short, bouffant, frilly skirt with a pink stripe and a loose white cotton shirt with a low neckline. She finally felt comfortable in her skin. A leather-trimmed teal-green canvas bag sat by her feet, holding the rest of her acquisitions.

David burst onto the terrace, beaming a public smile.

"*Désolé.* I'm sorry I'm late. It was impossible to extricate myself."

"Your timing is perfect. We're in heaven here," Alexandre said. "They have Ott's Rosé Cœur de Grain, which is by far my preferred rosé. It's the only rosé that has such a prolonged note of honey. It —"

Capucine cut him off. Even in difficult moments Alexandre could monologue about wine for hours if unchecked. She grinned internally. She was definitely back in her world.

"How was your meeting?" Capucine asked.

"Very positive." David sat down. "I don't know if anyone told you, but I'm exploring the possibility of running for *député du Var.* The election is in the spring. I was elected mayor of my village only a little more than a year ago, so it's very quick, but my supporters have almost convinced me I'm a viable candidate."

The waiter arrived. David stood up and gripped his hand tightly. They exchanged a few words about the waiter's children. Sotto voce David said something that had the tone of a promise. It wasn't difficult to see why David's supporters were so enthusiastic.

When David leaned over to fill his glass, he said in a murmur, "Discretion is the order of the day. When you're in office, everyone knows who you are and risks cricking their neck to pick up even the tiniest crumb of gossip." And then, in a much louder voice, he added, "You'll love this restaurant. The owner used to be a fisherman. He has a beautiful eye for seafood. No point in even looking at the menu. The *patron* will decide for us."

The owner turned out to be another character who easily could have been served up by central casting, a short man of nearly spherical rotundity, radiating bonhomie. He bustled up, complimenting them on the serendipity of having picked that particular day to eat at his restaurant. It just so happened that he had *rouget,* red snapper, of a perfection never before equaled in Cannes. And not only that, but he had exactly three of them, each more beautiful than the next.

"And I'm going to start you out with *an-*

chois, baby anchovies, dusted with a hint of flour mixed with *piment d'espelette* and *fleur de sel* and then deep-fried. I want you to trust me. When we get to the snappers, don't forget they were alive barely two hours ago, and I'll be serving them the way God intended, grilled very lightly, not cleaned out, and not scaled. As the great novelist said, 'A rouget without its liver is a Paganini without his violin.' "

The rouget were even better than vaunted, as round-bellied as the patron, moist and light, brimming with the sea and the inimitable flavor of red snapper. There was a great deal to be said for fish that had traveled a mere fifteen feet from boat to table.

After lunch, they rattled off into the hills in David's ramshackle little Peugeot.

"I live in a *mas.* That's what they call farmhouses around here. I bought it with the money I got for the book's movie rights. I want you to think of it as entirely yours while you're here." He smiled and squeezed Capucine's arm. "We're going to need to buff up your cover story. I let it drop in the village that my Parisian uncle was coming on vacation with his beautiful young wife."

"*Tonton* Alexandre!" Capucine said. "It suits you."

"Provençal villagers will never breathe a

word about anything to an outsider, and outsiders include even the people from the next village. But they don't like not knowing every last thing that goes on in their own village. Trust me, they'll quiz you both to death. We need a killer story and certainly new names. *Tonton* Edouard suits Alexandre perfectly."

"So, I think we should give La Cadière-d'Azura a miss tonight, until we get everything sorted out. I have Magali, an old widow who 'does' for me, as they say down here, and she cooks well, or at least I've gotten used to her cooking. Tonton, do think you can rough it for one night?"

"Don't get fresh with your uncle, *fiston*," Alexandre said with a broad smile.

"Also," David continued, "I've confiscated five or six cell phones from some teens. Don't look at me like that. They all owe me a favor or two for getting them off the hook for little run-ins with the gendarmes." He nudged Capucine's arm, then pulled back, thinking he had gone too far.

"Cap . . . Commissaire, you can't imagine what a kick I get when those local gendarmes come to attention and salute me."

"David, if you don't start calling me by my name, I'll have to start calling you Monsieur le Maire, and I don't think that's going to help our cover story."

"These cell phones are the pay-as-you-go kind, so they're impossible to trace. Just what a perp on the run or the head of the local police force needs, right?"

The mas might have started life out as a simple farmhouse, but it had come a long way. It sprawled out in all directions and embraced two large pools. Capucine flapped a hand in semi-mock admiration.

"What kind of farmer lived here when you bought it?"

"The kind that makes a lot of money on Wall Street and then gets hit hard by the recession. I'm afraid I had him over a barrel and was not quite as gentle as I could have been. Wait till you see the bathrooms. I still can't get used to brushing my teeth out of gold faucets."

Capucine spent the better part of the afternoon sitting somewhere deep in the fragrant hills, brooding, trying to make sense of her situation. How could she possibly cope without the authority of her badge, the use of her brigade of police officers? She brooded on. It was even worse than that. She was manacled by her exile. She couldn't call her friends, her family, not even her mother. She was naked in a wilderness. A wilderness with gold faucets, yes, but a wilderness, nonetheless.

She rubbed the tears out of the corners of her eyes and dragged her heels back to the mas. She found David and Alexandre on the long trellised patio, sipping pastis and smoking cigars. Alexandre had found a store in Bandol that sold authentic Havanas and had spent more on Vuelta Abajo leaf than she had on clothes. Here she was, deep in mourning over her lost identity, and Alexandre was as serene as ever. For him it was just another cheerful adventure, one that he was already polishing to regale his cronies with.

Capucine sat with them and was given a milky white glass of pastis. The two men fenced with quoted lines from the Provençal poet Frédéric Mistral. The sensual aroma of Havana leaf mingled with the heady aroma of wild thyme, blending with the unaccustomed licorice taste of the pastis. The sun dappled through the overhead canopy of vine leaves.

Maybe it was just the odors, but a sense of peace descended over Capucine. She had found sanctuary. Her problems were probably as irresolvable as ever, but hopelessness wasn't possible under that marquee of vines. She reached out and took David's hand. Alexandre smiled at her.

"*Chaque année, le rossignol revêt des plumes neuves, mais il garde sa chanson.* Every year the nightingale dons new plumage but retains his old song," Alexandre quoted.

What would she do without Alexandre? He was perfectly right. The trappings were the least of things. Gradually, the sun sank in the sky, and the rhythmic violin screeching of the cicadas fell silent.

"Shall we have dinner out here?" David asked. "It's a *poulpe en daube* — local octopus stewed in a wine-based marinade. My guardian angel, Magali, does it very well. She has a little trick we won't tell Alexandre about." He bent over in Capucine's direction and spoke in mock confidentiality. "She freezes the octopus for a night before putting it in its marinade. She claims that makes it much more tender. Excuse me for a moment. I'll go heat it up and come back and set the table."

"You'll do no such thing," Capucine said. "We're in the Midi here, where no self-respecting woman will let a man do a woman's work." She had an irresistible itch for action. She jerked herself out of her chair. Alexandre protested. "No, no. Let me do it."

With an elegant wave of two fingers, David quieted him.

In the kitchen Capucine found a long table covered in antique Provençal tiles, much larger than, but not dissimilar to, the one in her own kitchen in Paris. She wondered when she would ever see that again.

The *daube* was still warm in a stoneware cocotte. She bustled around the kitchen, looking for plates, glasses, knives, forks, then took it all out to the patio with two bottles of a red Mourvèdre from Bandol.

The daube lived up to David's promise, not the slightest bit chewy, rich with the flavors of the wine marinade, olive oil, and a good number of local wild spices.

After the daube came the cheeses — Annot, a strong goat cheese shaped like a doughnut; Banon, wrapped in chestnut leaves and tied with raffia and dotted with specks of blue mold; and Brousse, a goat cheese so mild, it came to life only when sprinkled with local wild thyme.

"I can't tell you how happy I am that you're here, Com . . . Capucine," David said. "How long do you think you'll be staying?" He caught himself. "I certainly wasn't suggesting you leave. To make me perfectly happy, you and Alexandre would stay all summer."

"David, it may well come to that."

"Look, Commissaire —" David flicked his hand in front of his mouth in irritation. "Look, Capucine, I used to be halfway okay as a brigadier, right? Well, I have a lot of free time right now, and, well, if you want, you can use me as if I were on your team. Give me orders. Send me places. All that stuff. Truth be told, I miss it. Actually, I miss the rest of the team more than I ever admit to myself."

Capucine was grateful for David's enthusiasm, but it unsettled her.

"The way your cousin described the situation, the intended victim had to be the juge d'instruction, Madame Maistre, right?"

Capucine said nothing.

"And the perp, or at least the man running the perp, was pretty obviously that investment banker guy. Are we going to be investigating him?"

"Him and others. Yes."

David beamed. Capucine knew why. Despite herself, she had spoken in her commissaire's voice, even though it was unlikely she'd play the role of commissaire for quite a while yet.

CHAPTER 18

Only half paying attention to what she was doing, Inès erected a protective rampart from the thick pile of clothbound legal files, which populated the desk of nearly every lawyer in Paris. She had placed an oversize business card upside down in the exact center of her blotter and tapped an irritated tattoo on it with her fingernail. Finally, with an exasperated snort, she flipped the card over. Beneath the raised engraving were two lines of fastidious handwriting in emerald ink. She pushed her reading glasses firmly up the bridge of her nose and read.

Madame le Juge,
    Apologies for the inexcusable tardiness of this invitation, but it would give me the greatest pleasure to invite you to lunch at the Cercle Interallié tomorrow. Can we say 1:00?

The card was from Etienne-Louis Lévêque, senior partner of Lévêque, Fourcade, and Levy, by far the largest and most prestigious law firm in France, with offices in twenty-five countries and several hundred lawyers on its payroll.

She'd never met Lévêque, but she'd seen him speak a number of times. What lawyer hadn't? He was at the epicenter of the legal power structure, an intoxicating speaker, a big man with a shock of silver hair and a gravelly voice that rolled like thunder. He was supposed to be over eighty but looked forceful enough to be in the prime of his life.

The invitation was enigmatic. Inès guessed it was a tickle at a job offer. Having a former juge d'instruction as a criminal litigator would be a feather in the cap of Lévêque, Fourcade, and Levy. Of course, it was well known that she was as faithful to the *magistrature* as a nun to her convent, but still, the rumors were abounding that the function of juge d'instruction would be discontinued in the near future. These were hardly the times to turn one's nose up at anything. Still, places like the Interallié gave her hives. She certainly wasn't going to join the ranks of those who took three hours for lunch and returned to the office tipsy. No, she wasn't going to show up.

The problem was, she'd let the card sit on her desk since the day before. It was too late to beg out, and simply not showing up was clearly not an option. When you got down to it, she really had no choice but to go.

In the oak-paneled foyer of the Interallié, a liveried servant informed Inès she was expected in the garden. She walked through the painted, gilded, mirrored rooms of the rambling *hôtel particulier* and emerged into the brilliant summer sunshine. Blinking, she took a moment to become oriented. She had eaten there a few times. The over-manicured eighteenth-century garden abutted an area graveled in white marble chips, filled with white-painted metal tables capped with oversize parasols. Hermès ties and the latest in summer frocks were the order of the day.

In a far corner, *Maître* Lévêque waited for her, standing, magnificent as a statue in a light beige suit, his nimbus of white hair glowing preternaturally in the sun.

When Inès reached his table, Lévêque smiled at her in greeting, bent at the waist to kiss her hand in a *baisemain,* remembered just in time she was not married, transformed the gesture into a two-handed clasp. Despite the silliness of his antediluvian manners, Inès was struck by his majesty of power.

"Madame le Juge, please accept my apology for the abruptness of this invitation, but I have been wanting to meet you for quite some time, and I thought with the suddenness of your return from vacation — you weren't expected back for another week — your calendar might not be overcharged."

Inès wondered how — and more importantly, why — he was so well informed.

It was deliciously cool under the tentlike parasol. Beyond its rim, the sun beat down ruthlessly.

"Maître," Inès said, "I'm amazed you're out and about in this impossible heat."

"You're absolutely right. Paris is no place to be in August. I'll be off in a few days. I have a little house on the beach in Loctudy, in Brittany. The weather there is glorious. Even at this time of year one has to wear a sweater in the evening."

Flutes of champagne appeared. Inès felt that she was at the rim of the vortex of the world she abominated. Lévêque prattled soothing banalities. Food arrived, followed by even more food. The service was as impeccable as the cuisine was mediocre:

savorless smoked salmon, pallid chicken paillard salad. It went on and on. Over-dressed people sauntered by to nod obsequiously at Lévêque. Inès didn't have a clue what she was doing there.

Over the *fraises des bois* sorbet, the penny finally dropped. It had to do with a European consortium created to house several major French and German airplane and missile manufacturers. A Frenchman was at the head of the consortium, which had recently missed the due date of a large order of jumbo passenger planes to an American airline. A few weeks before the announcement of the delay, the French chairman had exercised his options and sold them hours before the stock plummeted. The shares had been "portaged" by Tottinguer & Cie to safeguard the anonymity of the transaction.

It took Inès a while to decode her role. At first Inès thought she was being offered the smaller fish, the son André, on a platter if she would keep her hands off the biggest fish — his grandfather, the chairman.

But as the sorbet transformed itself into *coupes* of champagne, the scenario became murkier and the meaning clearer. Underneath the multiple layers of circumlocutions, she was being offered the grand prize: all the top brass at Tottinguer — as long as she forswore investigating the conglomerate itself.

Various governments and senior politicians had to be immersed up to their eyebrows. The object of the exercise was to limit the list of "blamables" to salaried executives and to avoid interfering with political careers and the eternal European diplomatic ballet.

Reflexively Inès bridled. She gathered her legs under her chair to rise and stalk out. But as her toes took her weight, she had second thoughts. This vastly exceeded anything she had ever imagined. She had had no idea Lévêque operated at this level. This could easily prove to be the watershed of her career. Despite her self-control, her cheeks flushed in excitement.

A large, well-larded, toad-like man appeared at the table and extended his stubby-fingered hand to Lévêque. Inès had seen his picture often in the papers, Charles Bufo, cabinet chief for the minister of the Interior. Lévêque invited him to sit. Champagne was brought. Was he part of the package?

No. The half-spoken proposition was snatched from the table like a bad egg. Tone and substance became banal. In a cocktail party voice Lévêque went on about a new committee Bufo had just been placed in charge of to centralize the intelligence and police departments. He had just finished merging the DST — the internal espionage agency — and the RG, the agency in charge of the investigation of individuals on French territory. Next were the Police Judiciaire and the juges d'instruction. But all this was at such a high level that any change would be imperceptible at Inès's level.

Lévêque smiled at Bufo. "You really need to consult with Madame Maistre. She will have some very valuable insights into the definition of the juge d'instruction's role."

"Oh, I will, most definitely." The tone was clearly one of dismissal.

"Oh là là," she said, looking at her watch. "I'm already fifteen minutes late for a meeting." She rose. Her hand was shaken.

"I'd like to finish our chat. Very soon," Lévêque said, rising. There was a strong sense that too much had been said.

Inès wound her way through the tables. She almost ran into an elderly waiter lurching under an enormous tray. She stopped and moved aside to let him pass. Her heart went out to him. He smiled at her.

Behind her she heard Lévêque scold Bufo. "You really need to learn to become more closemouthed. You made a complete balls-up of the situation in the Tyrrhenian

Sea. And if I weren't here to stop you, you'd do it all over again. Sooner or later, you're going to have to learn how to clean up your own messes."

CHAPTER 19

At two o'clock in the morning Capucine woke with a start, convinced she was still on the boat and something was wrong. It took the odor of wild thyme carried by a warm breeze to bring home the fact that she was at the mas. The sense of worry volatilized but returned with redoubled force. Then it hit her.

She might not be on the boat, but she was confined to the mas and she had a crime to solve, and fast. She burrowed into Alexandre's stomach, but sleep would not come. As the black of the night began to pale, she got out of bed, snipped the price tags off a new pair of shorts and a T-shirt, and went down the hall to the kitchen.

A crone of a woman with two teeth missing was fussing in the kitchen.

"Magali?"

"*Oui, M'dame* Capucine. *M'sieu* David told me you'd be up with the sun, so I've got your coffee all ready."

The promised coffee was poured into a white porcelain bowl, then placed in front of her, along with a jug of warm milk and a tin of sugar cubes. While Capucine sipped, Magali boiled eggs, toasted bread in the oven, and cut thick slices from a whole ham kept on the counter, under a linen towel. David walked in, leaned over to kiss Capucine on the cheek, this time without hesitation. Capucine squeezed his hand. David turned to Magali and chattered away in a language that sounded almost like French but of which she could understand only one word in ten.

"You speak Provençal?" Capucine asked.

"Of course I do. Don't forget I grew up in a small village in the hills just behind Cannes." He laughed. "We were forbidden to speak Provençal at school. There was a big sign in the courtyard that said, 'Be Clean. Speak French!' But we all spoke Provençal to each other when the teachers weren't around."

Magali put the eggs, toast, and ham on the table.

"Here almost all my older villagers still speak Provençal at home. The irony of the situation is that now that the language is tolerated, even encouraged, it's dying out.

Our *école primaire* actually has a class in it. But they teach it as a foreign language."

Magali said something incomprehensible. David laughed and patted her arm paternalistically.

"So, Capucine, what are your plans for the day?"

"I'm going to try to get to work on the case. I'm going to start with the telephone."

"Good. I've moved a desk into a room in the corner of the mas and left you all five of those confiscated telephones, along with the chargers. I also put a box of office supplies in there, pads, Bics, stuff like that. There's also my spare laptop." He put down his bowl of coffee and gave her a severe look. "Jacques warned me to not let you use it to send e-mail. He said it would be easily traceable back to here. He said the plan would be to have you type up your e-mail messages on word-processed documents and then to copy them onto a new e-mail account from an Internet café. I put a flash-drive stick next to the computer and can take it into Bandol this afternoon if you want."

"I know the technique. It's too cumbersome for me. I'll just use your cell phones." She broke the top of one of the soft-boiled eggs with the back of her spoon. "And what are you going to be doing today?"

"What I do every day. Go down to the village, sign papers in my office, walk around, sit in the café, hear endless requests, keep the village heading roughly west."

"Holding court?"

"That's the very last term I'd use, but it amounts to that. You can come look. Last night I convinced Alexandre to spend the morning with me and then have lunch at the village café. It would be wonderful if you could walk down the hill and join us. I just sent Magali to your room to make as much noise as possible cleaning up. That should get Alexandre out of the rack."

In a few minutes Alexandre appeared at the breakfast table, visibly put out at having been turned out of bed before his accustomed hour of ten o'clock. In less than thirty minutes Alexandre and David went off, rattling down the hill in the ancient Peugeot. Capucine explored the mas, looking for her new office. Inside, the house was far larger than it looked from the outside. The rooms seemed endless. Only a few of them had been furnished. It was like wandering through an empty hotel that was in the process of being decorated.

She finally found the office in the farthest corner of the building. It was empty except for a large, ancient, heavily distressed oak kitchen table, which must have been scrounged from the detritus of one of the mas's numerous outbuildings. Many of Capucine's Paris friends would kill to have it in their Sixteenth Arrondissement kitchens. The phones had been dumped unceremoniously in a cardboard box, all of them fully charged and fully functional.

She started with Inès.

"Capucine, ma chérie. How *are* you? What a harrowing experience you're having. Are you comfortable where you are, at least?"

"Oh yes, very. We're staying at a sumptuous mas in the Midi that belongs to a good friend of mine. I feel quite secure here."

"Perfect. But don't get too comfortable. I need you to get to work. Tottinguer has become even more of a priority. Why don't you start by mapping out a plan of attack?"

"But what about the Nathalie case? Don't forget, I'm the prime suspect."

"Oh, that. The Italian box of evidence doesn't seem to have arrived yet. And when it does, it will still take forever for the police to inform the magistrates and for the magistrates to get going with a case. We have plenty of time on that one."

"The last time we spoke, you led me to

believe my arrest was imminent."

"That was then. This is now. Let's focus on Tottinguer."

There was a long, leaden silence on the line.

"Capucine, listen to me. You're overreacting. The Nathalie thing will go away. I don't even know if the magistrates will decide it's a French case. We have bigger fish to catch. Map out your plan and call me back this afternoon."

Capucine squeezed the OFF button on the phone and tossed it into the box. She extracted another cell phone and called Isabelle Lemercier, David's former partner at the Police Judiciare. The call lasted so long, the phone beeped to warn that the battery was about to die. The timing was perfect. Isabelle's assignment was fully mapped out. She would be very busy for the next few days.

Eleven thirty. Time to find her way down the hill to lunch.

Capucine changed out of her shorts into a skirt and blouse, which she knew would be more acceptable in the village, and walked down the hill. The scrub grass was hard and dry, the few trees were gnarled and scrawny, and the sawing of the cicadas was almost deafening. It was a world apart from Paris.

Capucine wondered how David had lasted so long in the City of Light before returning to his homeland.

La Cadière was built around a dusty earth square with a fountain in the middle. Even though the green-painted, wrought-iron fountain tilted far more than the Leaning Tower of Pisa and hadn't spouted water for well over half a century, it was a source of pride for the villagers. When Capucine arrived, six men played *boules* — or *pétanque,* as Capucine knew they called it locally — in the dust with all the solemnity and concentration the game required. At the far end of the square was a café with a half dozen deserted green metal tables baking in the sun. Capucine ducked under the awning and walked inside. The ageless ceramic-tiled floor, flyblown mirrors, and zinc bar could easily have been a set for a 1930s Pagnol movie. Alexandre and David sat at a table with an old man. Each had a thick, V-shaped glass of pastis in front of him.

Alexandre motioned for Capucine to come to the table. It was clear from the discreetness of his gesture that they were at a delicate moment in the discussion. The instant she sat, a man, clearly the proprietor of the café, arrived and, without a word, pointed at one of the glasses to inquire if she wanted a pastis. In a whisper, Capucine asked for a Lillet Blanc.

In a Midi accent so thick it could have been eaten with a spoon, every third word in Provençal, the man told his story. His livelihood was his olive grove. It was known to one and all he produced the finest olive oil in the region. David himself used it with great joy, as did the café, as did the villagers of discernment. And just imagine! His next-door neighbor, that dried-out, withered twig of a man, had done research in the village cadastre and had discovered that a tiny corner of the grove was on his land. The neighbor had stretched a rope, cordoning off the part he thought was his, and had told him he would shoot if the line was breached.

How was he going to get to his most precious olive trees to harvest the olives? Could Monsieur le Maire send the gendarmes to allow him access?

David explained that no, Monsieur le Maire could not, because he had verified the cadastre himself and had been out to examine the property, and it was true that that tiny section of the grove was, as claimed, on the neighbor's land.

But, the man explained, it made no difference who owned the land. They were his trees, not the neighbor's. He had cared for them and nurtured them ever since he had been a boy. They existed because his sweat had dripped into their roots. The man was close to tears.

The noon Angelus sounded. Everyone in the café looked up and finished their apéro quickly. Capucine suspected that lateness at family lunches was not tolerable.

The man looked at David with pleading eyes. What was he going to do?

"Leave it to me," David told him with a soothing look. Capucine had seen him use it to great effect with battered wives when he was still with the police. The man was to come back to the café on Friday for some *pastaga,* and he would see that everything had been restored to order. The man, only partially mollified, shuffled out on legs bowed with age.

Before the old man was out the door, the owner of the café appeared with a serving bowl, three dishes, and a large carafe of rosé. He clunked them on the table and disappeared through a door behind the bar.

Alexandre poured wine for the three of them and tasted. "The *cépage* is Mour-vèdre, of course," he said, identifying the varietal most common to the area, "but that's as far as I go."

202

"It's from a tiny vineyard in the Plan du Castellet. Inexpensive, but a village staple," David said. He ladled out the stew. "And this is a daube made from beef cheeks marinated in red Bandol. The owner's wife made it for lunch. Like everyone else in the village, Casimir goes home to eat with his family. But he got in the habit of feeding me at noon when I was staying upstairs" — David pointed with his thumb — "when you sent me down here two years ago. Over the years the habit became permanent, and I eat lunch here every day, even though the café is closed."

"What are you going to do about that poor man?" Alexandre asked. "His case seemed impossible."

"*Pas du tout.* That's one of the easy ones. It's already settled."

"But if the land really is the neighbor's?"

"You have to understand the brain of the Provençal *paysan.* It has only four things in it. Pétanque, pastis, probity, and *patrimoine* — land. This whole story has an underlying narrative, what my editor would call a subtext. What the neighbor really wants is to buy a plot of land in the hills behind his mas. He wants it so his goats can graze there. But it's owned by an old man in his late eighties who has no use for it but won't sell it to him. It has to do with a quarrel so ancient, no one remembers what it's about. The game the neighbor is playing is aimed at getting me to intervene with the old man. If he can buy his hillside plot, he'll be happy enough to sell the tiny hunk of olive grove — which contains only three trees, by the way — to his neighbor. I saw all this coming two weeks ago and have already spoken to the old man."

David laughed and took a bite of his daube. "Of course, I'm going to make damn sure that the neighbor pays a stiff price for the plot on the hill and sells back the three trees for next to nothing."

"Are all politics in La Cadière like this?" Capucine asked.

"Most of it. The mayor acts as a kind of buffer. But he also has to implement his vision for the village."

"And yours is?" Alexandre asked.

"Quite simple. We remain in the sweetness of the era of Pagnol, but everyone will have an iPhone and cable Internet."

"Implementing an oxymoron seems like quite a challenge," Capucine said.

"Not as challenging as a Police Judiciaire case. I have to admit I miss those." He paused for a few seconds, tracing an imaginary pattern on the surface of the table.

"And, of course, as I told you last night, I miss my partners, Isabelle and Momo."

"I just spent an hour and a half on the phone with Isabelle. I set her to work on the case."

"You know, Capucine, I wasn't kidding when I suggested you use me as a brigadier. I have plenty of free time right now, and I really do miss police work."

"Careful what you wish for. I might just take you up on that," Capucine said.

CHAPTER 20

After lunch, Capucine and Alexandre left David, who went off to a meeting of his *conseil municipal* — his town council. They walked up the narrow lanes through the hills to the mas. The heat was intense, shimmering up from the baked earth and radiating down from the sky. The only sound was the raucous sawing of the cicadas. The hills seemed deserted. Alexandre pointed at large rusty patches in the scrub.

"Know what that is?"

Capucine shook her head. Alexandre led her out on the grass, holding her hand. Close up, the rusty patches were made up of squat little plants with tiny purple flowers. Alexandre reached down, yanked out a handful, crushed it in his fist, opened his hand under Capucine's nose.

"*Serpolet* — sweet wild thyme — the backbone of one of France's most imaginative inventions, herbes de Provence."

"Invention?"

"Of course. It's like the fiction of the *Gaulois* resisting the Romans from their tiny fishing villages. The real paysans down here have a very delicate hand with their wild herbs. They pride themselves on dosing them one by one for each dish. They're hardly going to let a big bag of premixed stuff sit in the back of their cupboards so long, it turns into sawdust."

Alexandre was as enraptured by wild herbs as he was by the mushrooms of the damp autumn forests of the Île-de-France. He foraged and presented Capucine with the spiky stems and bulbous violet and purple flowers of wild rosemary, white-flowered savory, yellow-flowered fennel, and a big bunch of lavender, which Capucine wadded, sniffed, and stuffed in the pocket of her frock.

They reached the crest of a hill that overlooked the mas. The hills seemed to roll on eternally. There was not another house in sight. They sat down and held hands like little children, fingers intertwined.

"Are you feeling a little better about things now that we're home?" Alexandre asked.

"We're not home. We're abusing the generosity of one of my former flics while I sit flopping on the ground with my wings clipped."

"You're overreacting."

"Oh, am I? Well, let me tell you, then. From what I've seen, I'd guess David has more than a fair chance of getting elected to the Assemblée Nationale. He has the potential for an important career in politics."

"Of course he does."

"But what I think you've forgotten is that every mayor in France is also a representative of the state and, technically, an officer of the Police Judiciaire, in addition to head of the local police force, if there is one. That means that if a warrant for my arrest is issued, David would be obliged to arrest me. If he continues to hide me, he could easily be removed from office and sanctioned. That would be the end of his political career."

"Should we move to a hotel?" Alexandre asked.

"I've thought about it. Not just yet. But maybe soon. Just as soon as I figure out a way to break out of house arrest."

They didn't arrive back at the mas until six. David was waiting for them with his brow slightly furrowed.

"Bad news?" Capucine asked.

"Not at all. Isabelle e-mailed back. She came up with only slim pickings. I printed out two copies so we could go through it together. I'm assuming I'm working with you on this. Right?"

"Of course it is. Let's see what Isabelle came up with."

The printouts were barely a page long.

from: femmelib17@wanado.fr
to: dmartineau348@hypermail.com
subject: Stuff for the Commissaire

Hey, numnuts!
Still enjoying your endless vacation while us poor working stiffs sweat it out in the city heat?
Pass this on to the Commissaire.

Bisou,
Isa

1 attachments: Commissaire_Le_Tellier-_Informtion.doc

Capucine's mood brightened. This was like the old days, when she'd put her feet up on her desk during a meeting and Isabelle would admire her legs and David her shoes. Capucine put her feet up on the chair next to her.

"Oh, my God, Capucine! Where did you

get those horrid sandals?"

"In Bandol. You don't like them?"

"*Loathe* would be the appropriate word. Those ribbons going up your leg destroy the line of your calf. No more shoe shopping in Bandol without me. If you know where to go, there are actually one or two little shops that have some very cute things."

David snapped his page and read. So did Capucine.

NOTE ON NATHALIE MARTIN

Commissaire, there's not much in our database on Martin. I made a couple of phone calls before I ran out of time, since you wanted stuff back today. We need to talk about next steps.

Martin is one of these people who manage to live under the radar. There was a brother — Martin, Emile — who emigrated to Australia and left no trace. I'm guessing he must have died about three years ago, but the Australians can't produce a death certificate. Other than him, there's no record of any kin.

She did the usual schooling, all in Paris. She stayed at a lycée in Paris until the age of sixteen and never graduated. I got the class list, but no one really seems to remember her. After that there's no trace. No residences listed, no tax returns, only a postal bank account with a handful of euros in it. She always listed the boat she was working on as her residence. There's one fourteen-month absence from the territoire, but the records don't show where she went. That probably was an around-the-world cruise of some sort.

She's your classic boat bum. The boating ports are full of them. The fact that she's not leaving a paper trail doesn't mean there isn't a slime trail a mile wide. It's even possible she's had a handful of runs-in with the local flics, but they probably wouldn't even show up in the local databases.

For my euro, you need to get someone down to the main pleasure ports and dig around for her story. Once we get the names of the people she worked for, her pals and stuff, then stuff will start popping up. This is a hands-on job, not a screen one. No doubt about that.

Sorry there's not more.

Isa

David dropped his printout on the table. "I'll go check her out? Nothing could be easier. These boat girls are all pretty much the same. They love the life of the sea but lack the skills and the muscles to get work on big-time ocean racers. So they hook up with skippers of crewed charter boats and pretend they're cooks, even though all they really do is clean out the heads. But it gets them rides and good times. They're on boats, get fed, laid, and hang out with the boating set. What could be better when you're a teenager?"

"How do you know so much about this?"

"I used to sail a lot. I even spent a few summers working at a yacht charter operation in Villefranche. I still have some pals in the charter business. I think I can get a good rundown on your victim. There aren't many points of departure in southern France. Saint-Tropez, the Îles d'Hyères, Antibes, and Villefranche should do it. I'll Photoshop a few snaps from La Rochelle's blog and have those ports covered in two or three days."

"And you'd do it anonymously, without using your mayor's card?"

"Of course. Mind you, I used to be well known in those ports and still have a lot of pals down there, but the risk of anyone making the connection is slim."

Capucine's brows wrinkled.

"Look, Capucine. It's not like I'm some amateur. I used to do this for a living, remember? It's the middle of August. I'm entitled to some vacation. What's more natural than a guy like me sipping pastis with my old pals on the Riviera?"

CHAPTER 21

The next morning Capucine found David in the kitchen, squabbling in Provençal with Magali. Despite the fact that Capucine could pick up only a word here and there, it was clear the tiff revolved around David's attire. David's fashion-plate outfit had been replaced by a greasy, moth-holed T-shirt sporting the faded logo of an ancient boat race, high-tech shorts with an unwarrantable number of zippers, and — the pièce de résistance — a pair of decrepit boat shoes as flecked with dots of paint as a Jackson Pollock painting, with one sole separated enough from the upper to provide an unobscured view of David's right big toe.

"Going in for disguise, are we?"

"Of course. That business of *l'habit fait le moine* — the habit making the monk — is pure dead on. No habit, no monk. That's all there is to it. This is all stuff I've kept from my sailing days. It's going to be just perfect."

He performed a little pirouette. "I'm off. I'll keep in touch through your collection of cell phones. And I'm leaving you the Peugeot. I have a plain-vanilla rental car. Much more anonymous."

Capucine opened her mouth to speak. David bridged her lips with a finger reaching from the point of her chin to the tip of her nose. "Don't worry. I'm just a happy-go-lucky guy looking for a ride on some boat in the Porquerolles race and hoping maybe to run into that hottie I met last summer. What was her name again? Oh, right, Nathalie. It really would be a shame to lose that one from sight."

When David left, Capucine was surprised to find herself mildly disoriented. She felt awkward going to La Cadière without him and decided instead on an expedition with Alexandre to the open market in Bandol.

The market was laid out under the stare of the Cyclops's eye of the town church, the stands protected from the sun by flaxen parasols casting a golden light over the produce. Alexandre was overjoyed.

"I'm going to make you stuffed artichokes, the excellence of which you've never even dreamt. Now, what we need is a proper market basket. We can't wander around like Parisians. They'll try to palm off on us the rubbish they were about to throw out. Look at those baskets over there. One of them would be perfect for us back in Paris."

At the mention of Paris, Capucine felt an unpleasant chill ripple up her back. How long would it be before that happened?

At the stand, Alexandre investigated the baskets with care. "There's an optimal size to these things. Too small and they're useless. Too big and they're too heavy to carry."

As Alexandre rooted through the bags, Capucine amused herself by trying on floppy straw hats. Abruptly, she snatched one off the rack and clapped it on Alexandre's head.

"Hide your face. It's the Le Galls, complete with all three of their impossible children."

Alexandre admired himself in the mirror the stall provided, chuckling. "Ah, the secret snobbism of my flic wife, whose only true aspiration is to burrow into the grit of the mean streets. Just because Bandol has a reputation as the poor man's Saint-Tropez doesn't mean we aren't going to run into anyone we know here."

"You're right. It was a stupid idea. Let's go back."

"No. We can do better than that. I really want to buy some of those artichokes and those unbelievable mackerel. The mackerel will be perfect as *maquereaux grillés à la moutarde* for dinner. But before we go back, I'm going to take you to a little restaurant on a back street. A hangout for locals. Guaranteed to be completely free of Paris vacationers."

Lunch was as delicious as it was simple: sea bass on a bed of layered fennel, wild thyme, preserved lemons, carrots, zucchini, yellow onions, cooked in pastis. As promised, there were no tourists. In fact, there was even a healthy smattering of Provençal in the buzz of conversation.

Lunch over, Capucine didn't dare go back to the town and scurried straight to the Peugeot, the brim of her new hat pulled well down over her face.

They spent the rest of the afternoon wandering through the hills behind the mas. Capucine was dismayed. In her mind's eye she had had a clear swath of safe country all the way from the mas through La Cadière down to Bandol, an hour away by car. Now Bandol and her access to the sea had been cut off. Her *espace vital* had been reduced drastically to the mas, the village, and the corridor in between. Capucine was well aware her paranoia was blossoming but was unable to keep it in check.

■ ■ ■ ■

The next morning, when Capucine took her second bowl of coffee into her "office," the cardboard box of phones buzzed and rattled, as if filled with insects. One of the phones was ringing.

"Good morning," Inès said. "There's news."

Capucine sat heavily.

"The evidence from Italy has arrived. It seems it took so long because they really did send it through their post office, if you can believe that. The Police Judiciaire have put the case in the hands of a Commissaire Garbe from La Crim'. Do you know this Garbe?"

"I've met him a few times. Never worked with him. Lean, tall man, late fifties, cheerful as an undertaker."

"That's the one."

"So you've seen him."

"Yes, he came to my office to 'consult' with me, but, in fact, it was nothing more than a standard interview. The useful part was that he went over the basic facts the Italians have.

"There are three main pieces of evidence. The shell casing, my jacket, and your gun.

On top of that, there are all their notes and photographs of the boat. The evidence went straight to forensics, even before Garbe was appointed. They confirmed that that hole in the jacket was, in fact, from a nine-millimeter bullet and that there were traces of gunpowder on the entry hole, but no blood. They determined from the firing-pin marks that it was your gun that had fired the shell."

"Nothing new there," Capucine said.

"No. Garbe was put out that Jacques and I were the only two passengers on the boat he was able to contact. From his comments Jacques must have given him a very hard time, indeed."

Capucine smiled, imagining Jacques being interviewed by a police officer.

"The key point for Garbe was that you did not return immediately to Paris and report the incident to Police Judiciaire headquarters, particularly since, to use his words, you are far more than 'a simple observer' in the case. He also found it curious that your cell phone is apparently switched off.

"I played the *naïve* and said that you and Alexandre had decided to continue your vacation and that you probably thought there was no point in reporting an incident that would remain hearsay until the evidence arrived in Paris. I also said I had a notion that you had gone to Corsica and might be in the hills, where there was no cell phone coverage, so it probably wasn't that your phone was off, just that there was no signal."

"It sounds plausible enough when you say it."

"Not to Garbe. He made a report to PJ headquarters, and they involved the Inspection Générale de la Police Nationale — the police of the police — who have assigned a lieutenant to liaise directly with Garbe. The idea is that there is to be an investigation of your conduct regardless of the outcome of the case."

Capucine frowned. "How did you find that out?"

"The juge d'instruction assigned to the case, an old friend, Joseph Léonville, invited me to lunch. It was awkward, to say the least."

Capucine said nothing.

"Capucine, this is not going the right way at all. These two bovines are perfectly capable of destroying my case against Tottinguer once they figure out the link. I can't allow that to happen. I need to get going right away."

There was a long, awkward pause.

"Look, Capucine, you understand the urgency. Do you know anyone in the fiscal brigade who could take over? Just for the time being, naturally, until you are back in circulation. No one has anything even close to your talent."

CHAPTER 22

That night, Inès left her office punctually at seven thirty, as she always did. She had finally caught up with the pile of work that had accumulated while she was away, and was looking forward to getting home to her little apartment, having a cup of green tea from Mariage Frères, her sole extravagance, and spending time mapping out a plan to get the Tottinguer case moving with Capucine in hiding. She told herself for the thousandth time that going on that boat trip had been lunacy.

Before the trip everything had been perfect. She had had just enough evidence to open a criminal *instruction* on Tottinguer. She had lined up the ideal Police Judiciaire detective to handle the investigation. Not only was she almost without peer at criminal investigation, but she also had considerable financial expertise. And it had all come unglued because of a brass shell case.

Ruminating over the wisdom of replacing Capucine with another detective, she walked slowly down the cement staircase of the underground parking lot where she kept her little Citroën during the day. Deep in thought, she sauntered the narrow tunnel, only wide enough for a single row of cars on either side. The place always made her think of an endless mine shaft.

By the time she reached her car, she had almost, but not quite, concluded that replacing Capucine with another officer was the right thing to do. Even if Nathalie's murderer were found, it was possible the IGPN investigation of Capucine would result in her dismissal from the force or reassignment to an administrative function. In any case, she really couldn't wait any longer, now could she? The tricky part was going to be finding another officer even half as good as Capucine.

There it was, her little Citroën. It was so old, it was getting unreliable. She really should replace it. But buying a car was such a hassle.

She squeezed into the tight space between her car and the one next to it. As she leaned forward to slide the key into the lock, she was struck by a violent blow in the middle of her back. She found herself on her hands and knees, her head spinning, with no memory of falling. She shook her head to clear it. She was dealt an even more violent kick to her buttocks, slamming her face down on the cement floor. The world began to ease away from her. She felt squeezed into a closet-size room with walls of grainy cement flecked with red. Her nose was plugged shut, and she couldn't suck enough air through her mouth to fill her lungs. She heaved and gasped, the loudness of the tortured sound scaring her.

Strong hands jerked her up onto her knees. While she was still being held from behind, a man loomed up in front. Her head sagged. The one behind her reached deep into her hair, scratching her scalp, and snapped her head up.

The one in front was just a slip of a boy in his teens, at the edge of emaciation. Jeans designed skintight dangled around his skinny legs; a long, thick chain hung from belt loop to pocket; his eyebrows were decorated with an almost comical number of piercings; a large ebony disk distended one earlobe.

The boy slapped her. She saw his arm move and she heard the report, but she felt nothing. It was as if she was observing the scene from inside her little room.

"Bitch. I'm going to teach you to keep your place and not stick your ugly face where it doesn't belong."

She heard another report and felt a jolt like an electric shot. The pain shocked her. Her lungs froze. She was drowning. Her body willed her to convulse forward, but her hair was still held tight. After an eternity the pain subsided enough for her to take shallow puppy breaths, which brought no relief and instead intensified her agonized want of air.

Through a dun mist she saw the boy's hand unzip his jeans and extract a member so long and skinny, it could have belonged to some barn rodent. She wanted to look up at his face, but her eyeballs refused to obey.

"Open up, bitch!"

The command made no sense to her.

Another violent slap. The ebbing tide of her consciousness slipped away. The boys began punching her face rhythmically, as if performing a gym exercise. Again, she could see the fists arriving and could hear the blows resonating in her cranium, but could not feel them. She noticed his member had become flaccid and he needed to hold it up with the hand he was not using to slap her. Everything went chalkboard black-gray. She had no idea exactly at which point she lost consciousness. Later, she was aware of rising up on her knees, her forehead still resting on the ground. She was alone. She could breathe through her mouth. Not well, filling her lungs. She remained immobile on her knees for an eternity.

The world sharpened into focus. The pain had become a whole separate, not entirely unwelcome, presence. She was elated. She had a profound sense of achievement.

Her handbag, implausibly, was right next to her. She extracted her BlackBerry and touched the speed dial for her secretary.

"Oui, madame."

"Marie, listen to me very carefully. I need you to call both *Le Figaro* and TF1 and tell them that I've been assaulted in the parking garage next to the office. Tell them they both will get an exclusive to the TV and print story, which is breaking right now. When you've done that, wait for exactly half an hour — you're going to need to give them time to get here — and then call emergency and have the SAMU come and pick me up. I want the SAMU fully covered on TV. Do you understand?"

"Of course, Madame. You want a close-up of you being loaded into the ambulance."

"You've got it! You're a treasure."

Inès remained on her knees. Her elation evolved into an even deeper sense of contentment. Far sooner than she expected, she saw the flashing yellow light of the first news truck reflected on the far wall. She started to smile. But it hurt her mouth terribly and wouldn't look right on TV, anyway.

CHAPTER 23

Alexandre had become a devotee of the village. Every morning after breakfast he would amble down the hill to buy newspapers, kibitz the pétanque game, and drink an apéro at the café. Then, at the first note of the Angelus, he would wander back to the mas to lift the lid of Magali's cocotte and let the aromas of her lunch stir his appetite.

Capucine used this interlude to shower and administer all the *petits soins* so dear to Frenchwomen. That morning, when she switched off her hair dryer, Capucine heard the shrill vibration of one of the confiscated cell phones in the cardboard box on her desk. She bounded down the hallway, trying for the phone before the caller hung up.

It was Inès.

"I'm glad you called," Capucine said. "I was going to try to catch you before lunch. I've had some ideas for the case."

As she spoke, Capucine caught sight of the *Midi Libre,* one of the local newspapers, propped up on a stack of books in the center of the desk, undoubtedly left by Alexandre.

PARIS JUGE D'INSTRUCTION ASSAULTED IN PARKING GARAGE.

Beneath the headline was a sooty picture of someone being loaded from a gurney into a SAMU paramedic van. An official photo of Inès was inset in a corner.

Crusading Juge d'Instruction Inès Maistre was found assaulted and severely beaten in a parking garage in Paris's Eighth Arrondissement last night at eight o'clock. She was taken to the Hôpital Beaujon, where her condition is listed as stable. It is not known when she will be released from the hospital. The police have issued a statement that "satisfactory progress" is being made in the apprehension of her assailants.

"Inès, this is absolutely horrible. What happened? Are you okay?"

"Of course I'm okay. I was beaten up, but it's nothing that won't heal in a few days. The worst of the injuries is two cracked ribs. The good news is that today the bruises are gruesomely photogenic. I'm even scared to look at myself in the mirror. There's going to be a small press conference in my hospital room, which will be glorious for our case."

"Glorious?"

"Don't you see? It means that the Tottinguers are panicking. But they've blundered. Not only am I not in the slightest bit intimidated, but they've also transformed me into a latter-day Joan of Arc."

"Inès, you're sounding very stressed, almost a little irrational. This is no time to be thinking about work."

"Capucine, listen." Inès grunted from the pain of sitting up. "There's been a development I haven't had the chance to tell you about yet. Last week Maître Lévêque invited me to lunch. He proposed a deal, not too thinly veiled. If I agreed not to investigate EADS." The international consortium that now owned most of the European defense and aeronautic industry had become one of the most powerful indistrio-political institutions in Europe.

"Lévêque, would make sure I was leaked enough evidence to prosecute not only the son, André, but the entire management board of the banque Tottinguer, as well."

Capucine said nothing. There was an awkward silence. Inès's breathing rasped painfully. The rasping had a decidedly artificial quality to it.

"Did you accept his offer?"

"Of course not. The Tottinguers are whitebait. Lévêque made it clear there are salmon in the river. I'm going after them."

There was another long pause with more labored breathing.

"But I intend to eat the whitebait as an appetizer before I get to my main course of salmon, and you're going to help me net them. The first step is to get young André behind bars, in *garde à vue.* That has to happen this week. I need you to get the evidence. Once you get that done, you and I will begin to put pressure on the wife. She's sure to cave in. She's the biggest chink in their armor.

"And once I've relished my whitebait, I'm going to put together a large squad from the fiscal brigade and carefully take EADS apart brick by brick. Of course, you'll be a key member of the team. You're going to be amazed at how large our salmon will be. I think we'll be setting some world records."

"The last time we spoke, you were talking about finding someone else to work on the Tottinguer case."

Inès made a guttural noise, which Capucine at first thought was pain but then realized was irritation.

"That was before they blundered and attacked me. Now timing has become all important. I can't afford to wait for the PJ headquarters to assign me someone and then bring him up to speed. And, anyway, no one's going to be as good as you are. I want you to come to Paris immediately."

"Inès, aren't you forgetting that I'm virtually a fugitive? How can I traipse around Paris, interviewing people and making arrests?"

"You're not even close to being a fugitive. So you've been a bit sloppy, not calling PJ headquarters and reporting the Nathalie case, but so what? They'll get over it. All you need to do is get a few brigadiers who are loyal to you to do the legwork and make the arrests, and when you start working on the Tottinguer wife, wear a wig or something and have one of your brigadiers sign the procès-verbal. The only downside will be that a brigadier will get all the credit."

"Aren't you forgetting about the internal police?"

"Capucine, be reasonable. Your brigadiers can keep their mouths shut, can't they?"

Capucine opened her mouth to remonstrate. The situation was absurd. Inès had definitely become irrational. It must be the painkillers.

Capucine heard the voices of several people on the terrace. Could Alexandre have been irresponsible enough to invite some of the villagers to lunch? It was exactly the sort of thing he would do.

"Inès, there are people outside," Capucine said in a whisper. "I'm going to have to get off the phone."

She slipped into a pair of jeans and a T-shirt and walked out to the front of the house, her hair still damp. She was nonplussed. David, Isabelle, and Momo were standing on the terrace, talking and joking, while Alexandre passed around glasses of pastis.

When they caught sight of Capucine, Isabelle's and Momo's eyes softened with affection, then tightened in concern. Isabelle stepped forward to kiss her boss's cheek but instead hugged her awkwardly. Momo emerged from behind Isabelle and enfolded Capucine's hand in his hamsize paws.

"You look like you've been under a lot of strain, Commissaire," Isabelle said.

"Not at all. That's just because my hair's wet. I'm fine."

Isabelle made a moue of doubt.

"What prompted you two to come down

233

here?" Capucine asked.

Isabelle gave Capucine a blank look of incomprehension.

"We've both been following up on the stuff you gave us to research, right?" Isabelle asked. "And we found a bunch of things that might be useful. I was going to write it all up and e-mail it to you, but David suggested we leave work early, hop on the TGV, come down for the weekend, and report in person. He picked us up at the station in Marseilles."

"David?"

"Yeah. I've been talking to him a couple of times a day about the case."

Capucine guessed that David had fallen back on his PJ habit of making a daily report to Isabelle, his former direct superior. The two might find it impossible to make small talk without bickering but formed a tight-knit team when it came to police work.

Alexandre emerged from the house, holding a massive stoneware cocotte.

"*Allez, les enfants.* Lunch. Magali and I have been working on this dish, which comes straight from heaven, for the past two days. As the *Guide Michelin* says, this alone is worth the trip. David, I left two open bottles of Domaine de La Laidière on the counter. Can the rest of you go get what we

234

need to set the table?"

When everyone was seated, Alexandre removed the cover of the cocotte with a flourish.

"*Nougat de bœuf.* Six different meats — beef rump, beef shank, salt pork, fresh pork rind, calf's foot, and oxtail — are marinated for a day and then cooked for five hours with garlic, tomatoes, orange zest, capers, onions, carrots, leeks, anchovy fillets, a bottle of red wine, and a four healthy shots of cognac."

"No nougat?" Capucine asked.

"Of course not." Alexandre frowned histrionically at his wife. "The nubby nature of the thing is supposed to make you think of nougat candy with fruits on it. Or at least the Niçois did when they came up with the dish."

There was a long silence as the dish was savored and the Bandol sipped.

At first, the conversation was as congenial as any first meal of a weekend house party. But gradually, a note of strain arose between David and Isabelle. Capucine expected it. Isabelle was always hostile to authority, and now her former subordinate was a mayor, and was rich and on the road to a position of power in the Assemblée Nationale.

"Quite some shack you've got here, Monsieur le Maire," Isabelle said.

David looked sheepish. "Yeah, well, my book sold very well, and I got a very nice advance for the next one. I didn't really know how to invest the money. As it happened, the American banker who lived here lost a lot of money in the U.S. recession. He came to see me at the *mairie* to see if I could help him sell. It had been on the market for months, and he had no takers. He was ready to let it go for far less than market value. So I snapped it up, even though I don't really know what to do with so much space. Maybe I can turn it into a school."

Isabelle snorted. "A school for hairdressers or a school for fops?"

Delighted, David grinned broadly. They were back to their sibling banter. This was as good as old times.

Just as Momo began to serve himself a second helping of the nougat, Capucine asked Alexandre to clear the table.

"I'm sorry, dear, but we really need to get to work."

Everyone stood up. With visible reluctance, Momo put the serving spoon back in the cocotte. Alexandre, who had an oil-and-vinegar complicity with Momo, filled his plate to overflowing and poured him another glass of wine.

"Les enfants, don't forget to do the dishes. I'm going to stay out here with Momo, catch up, and not let this most excellent La Laidière go to waste."

It took Capucine a good half hour to herd her team back to the terrace table. Alexandre smiled at them, lit a cigar, and wandered off into the aromatic hills.

"Let's start with you, David," Capucine said. "How far did you get with Nathalie?"

"How far did I get? How far didn't I get? Remember, my cover was that I was a guy who had had a fling with her and was looking to hook up again. I hit the yacht clubs and sailing bars in Îles d'Hyères, Antibes, Villefranche, and Saint-Tropez and added Porquerolles. It was a rich lode. I ran into nine guys who had been over the course a few times and were more than happy to compare notes on the roughs and greens in great detail."

This was said purely to goad Isabelle, who cocked her arm to deliver a punch to his upper arm, thought better of it, contented herself with a deep growl. Momo barked a seal-like laugh. Capucine smiled.

"No one knew the slightest thing about her past. She never talked about her hometown, her family, or anything like that. She'd

237

been a boatie for as long as anyone could remember. Mostly, she did pickup jobs on crewed charter boats, but she also made it on a few ocean races. She'd sign on as cook and stand her watches on deck with no set job. In other words, she was galley slave and rail meat."

Isabelle stood up in a fury.

"Isabelle, it has nothing to do with sex," David said. "Get your head out of the gutter. On a racing boat anyone who isn't doing anything sits on the windward rail, dangling their legs, using their weight to help the boat heel a little less. They're called rail meat."

Isabelle ground her teeth.

"But she didn't get many ocean-racing rides. Her normal MO was to hook up with some skipper and sign on crewed charters with him. Charter companies like that. They want the skipper and the cook to be an item so chartering hubby doesn't get carried away. Anyway, word has it that she was kicked off a lot of boats because charter hubbies *did* get carried away. The last time that happened, her skipper hookup didn't want to have anything more to do with her. He knew he'd never find gigs with her in his baggage.

"So she hung around Mediterranean

Anchorage Yachts, sucking up to yacht charterers, hoping she could find a berth as a boat girl. The guys I had a drink with in Port Grimaud said her marketing technique was something to behold."

"Good work, David," Capucine said. "What about you, Isabelle? Tell us what you found out."

Isabelle drew herself up. Skilled as she was at her job, she was always nervous when put on the spot.

"Since Monsieur High-And-Mighty Mayor is so keen on boats, let's start with those. I told Momo to check out Florence Henriot at the Agence France-Presse. Tell her what you found, Momo."

"Well," Momo said. "I spent a couple of days over there, in what they call the morgue. It's only half computerized. They have computers where you look stuff up, and it directs you to a box in this big warehouse. Then you have to look it up in the publication it appeared in. If you want copies, you scan them on the computer. They had a ton of crap on Henriot. Most of it was pictures of her showing up, winning some race, looking all beat to shit but still kind of pretty in a kick-ass way, if you know what I mean.

"So after a big race, the second Route du

Rhum she won, you start seeing pictures of her in the society magazines, all dolled up, looking like a million euros, wearing fancy clothes, with her hair all up high on the top of her head. You know what I'm talking about, right? These postage stamp–size pictures of the fat cats having a good time at parties, trying to show every last one of their teeth. Well, the funny thing is that in a lot of these pictures she's with this Tottinguer guy." He paused, looking at Capucine to see how this went down.

"That's not all that surprising," Capucine said. "His firm was sponsoring her boats. It's natural enough they'd get the maximum publicity value out of her."

"Yeah, sure. So then I notice that a lot of the listings were in the not so hoity-toity press. A few of them were in these celebrity gossip magazines that are getting sued all the time. In those you see her in places like Ibiza with Tottinguer. But he's not going for publicity. He's usually got his arm around her waist, and her boobies are swinging free. In one or two of them he's giving her a good, deep, wet smooch. The only thing I can add to that is she's got one hell of a rack."

Isabelle emitted her growling grunt.

"Calm down, Isabelle," David said. "It's

another sailing term."

Capucine suppressed a smile. "What else, Isabelle?"

"Momo's not done. He found out some interesting things about your chum Angélique Berthier at Agence France-Presse. Tell her, Momo."

"See, it turns out that their database can run linked names, in addition to single names. So it will list references to two or more people in the same article. Isabelle told me to run Berthier's maiden name, Thévenot, and Tottinguer as a link. It produced eleven references." He paused to make sure everyone understood.

"It takes a while to find the stuff, because the database doesn't give you the page numbers, just the publication and date. It turned out that all eleven of the listings were from the same goddamn society pages with the postage stamp–size pictures. In most of the cases Berthier and Tottinguer were in pictures on the same page, but at different events. But in two pictures they're sitting next to each other, in fancy duds, at charity dinners. They're not smooching or anything, but you kind of get an impression that they're more than just pals, if you know what I mean."

"That *is* curious," Capucine said. For a

few seconds she drew imaginary circles on the table with her finger. "Isabelle, when you looked into her finances before, did you get the impression she was wealthy?"

"No, I told you. She makes a lot of money for someone in her early thirties, but she's definitely not rich. This time I checked it all out. Right down to her brokerage accounts. Solid, but definitely not massive. She does straight buys of good, conservative stocks and hangs on to them. With one exception."

Capucine's eyebrows rose in query.

Isabelle scowled, as if she had been accused of doing something wrong.

"It was only one stock, and the trade wasn't all that big. It was that missile and airplane conglomerate, EADS. You know, the one that defaulted on an airplane contract. She shorted some stock just before the announcement. I wouldn't have thought she'd know how to execute a short trade. Anyway, it was no biggie. She made only a bit over fifty thousand euros on the deal."

Capucine made more circles on the table. "You have the dates of all of this, right, Isabelle?"

"Obviously, Commissaire." Isabelle tapped her notebook, which was lying on the table.

"Did the pictures in society pages continue after her marriage?"

Isabelle flipped through the pages of her notebook. "No, the last one was two years before she got married."

Capucine nodded. "And the EADS trade?"

"A few months after the wedding."

Capucine smiled thinly. "Isabelle, I need you to look into Dominique Berthier. But you have to be very discreet about it. Scour his finances. Check out his family. See if you can figure out a family tree that goes back a couple of generations. You should have no trouble getting that from the birth records."

Isabelle nodded and scribbled in her notebook.

"In fact, it wouldn't be a bad idea to have a very close look at the finances of all of them," Capucine said.

"Sure. What else do you want us to do?" Isabelle asked.

"That's it. You've already done too much. I can't have you putting your careers at risk."

"Look, Commissaire," Isabelle said, "that's why we came down here. We're your team. You're not going to get this solved without us, you know."

"Don't think I don't appreciate it, but that

just can't happen. You both have to be back in the brigade bright and early Monday morning. Think about it. If you start doing legwork, you're going to have to go on the stand at the perp's trial, right?"

Momo nodded.

"That would mean that even with a conviction, you'd still face a serious problem with the IGPN not only for abetting a fugitive, which is what I'm going to be, but also for investigating a case without being ordered to. There's no way they'd let that drop. You'd get kicked off the force and could even face criminal charges."

"I don't give a shit about that," Momo said. "There's more to life than police work." The statement sounded proud but rang hollow.

"Momo's right, Commissaire," Isabelle said. "You can't solve a case sitting in front of a screen in the hills of the Midi. You have to get out on the street."

Capucine did not reply for several beats. Instead, she stared intently at Isabelle and Momo. "You both have done a lot. Way too much. You've already advanced the case a great deal. I'll have it tied up in a few days, and things will get back to normal. Let's all stop worrying the damn thing to death."

There was a belligerent silence. Capucine,

Momo, and Isabelle avoided each other's gaze. The sawing of the cicadas grated.

"In any case, we can't do anything until after tomorrow," David said. "It's the feast of Saint Veluton, the imaginary patron of the village. I get to make one of my beloved motivating speeches, and then the whole village shares a table of potluck dishes. I know for a fact Magali is determined to outdo herself."

The next morning the village square was as packed as the Paris Metro at 6:00 p.m. The instant David's speech was over and loudly cheered and he was absorbed into the melee, a determined phalanx of paysans appeared with trestle tables. They spread them about and covered them with tablecloths and the trappings for dinner. Finally, a platoon of village matrons marched in to place an earthenware cocotte at the center of each table. An expectant hush settled over the crowd.

"Monsieur Alexandre." Magali had sidled up to Alexandre and drew him with some occult magnetic attraction to her table. She edged the lid of her cocotte to one side and inserted a spoon. "You're going to have news for me," she said with a flirtatious

smile that transformed her back into a teenager.

The dish was a Toulouse cassoulet: white
beans — known as *lingots Tarbais,* ingots
from Tarbes — goose confit, salt pork, garlic
sausage, and tiny white Toulouse sausages.
A classic recipe, but to Capucine's nose, in
a class entirely of its own. Surreptitiously,
Magali spooned out samples for Capucine
and Alexandre. Alexandre exuded an orgas-
mic groan.

Capucine dropped to her knees. Alexandre
assumed it was the vulgarity of his eructation.

"I've lost a contact lens!"

"You don't wear contacts."

"Of course not, you idiot. It's happened
again. This time it's the Chambourdons."

"You don't wear contacts."

"We've got to get out of here right now.
The church . . . Hurry up!"

Inside the church Capucine vanished into
one of the tiny transepts. And from there
out a small door in the sacristy leading into
a field at the back of the church. Alexandre
was hard on her heels.

"Curse those Chambourdons," Alexandre
said. "It was a truly heinous crime to
abandon that cassoulet."

"I'm sure Magali will make you another.

We're not going to be leaving the mas for a while."

When they reached the house, Alexandre puffing, they stopped on the terrace. "I need sustenance after all that emotion. Wait out here and I'll get us both some pastis."

"Not out here. Let's drink it in the kitchen."

"The kitchen? There's no light in there. The windows are tiny."

"That's just the point."

To compensate for the gloom, Capucine had a Lillet Blanc and Alexandre a double pure malt Scotch. Gradually, Capucine relaxed. She fluffed up the back of her hair in a feminine gesture.

"Tell me," she asked, "how do you think I'd look as a blonde?"

Chapter 24

For once, Inès was having a good day. Such a good day that she hardly noticed the poisoned seesawing between the unbridled ambition and desire for acceptance that ordained her life.

Years before, while still in law school, she had decided to consult a psychiatrist about it. All her friends had assured her that the process would make her feel far more comfortable in her skin and would heighten her productivity. Instead, the shrink had announced she had a serious case of something he called "dissociative identity disorder." She had looked the term up and discovered it was the latest in cocktail party psychobabble. Her skin fit perfectly. So perfectly it was the font of her success. She had stalked out of the office. Just who the hell did that quack think he was talking to?

The trigger for her good mood was her discussion of a case with a *procureur* at the

Palais de Justice. The prosecutor had been beyond admirative.

"This is beautifully prepared. Absolutely perfect," he had said, tapping the bundle of papers tied up with a cloth tape between traditional red binders. "Even the greenest of procureurs couldn't fail to get a conviction with this one. Your talent exceeds your reputation, and it's quite a reputation. I know you have detractors who claim you're a press hound, even a sensationalist, but that's pure jealousy. You are by far the most talented juge we have."

The meeting over, Inès smiled a tight but pleased smile and started down the marble staircase of the Palais de Justice. Of course, the culprit in the case was only a tiny fish, a mere anchovy, part of the management of a small private bank, specializing in so-called mid-cap deals. He had tried to sweeten his fees on a transaction by getting a cousin to buy a good-size hunk of a company he had been mandated to sell to an international conglomerate. Yes, a very little fish, but it was still a joy to think of him in the van on his way to prison.

At the bottom of the staircase, she could see the *procureur de la République,* an enormous man, made even larger by his long bloodred and black robe trimmed in

faux ermine. He was encircled by a sycophantic entourage, a crimson shark in a
cloud of pilot fish. Since he was titular head
of all the Paris prosecutors, his function was
primarily that of a senior government official rather than that of an actual practicing
prosecuting attorney. Inès had shaken his
hand three or four times at receptions, but
they had never exchanged more than a few
polite banalities.

When they were fifteen feet apart on the
staircase, the procureur de la République
dismissed his retinue with an imperial
gesture and bounded up the steps with
unexpected energy. He stopped on the step
below Inès but still towered over her.

"Madame le Juge, what a happy coincidence. I was just going to call to ask you
to lunch."

"Lunch?" Inès said, unable to mask her
surprise.

"Absolutely. I've been reviewing your
cases. Your approaches are always innova-
tive. I've been remiss in not spending more
time with you." Below them the cortege
hovered; above, a small crowd accumulated,
too deferential to descend.

"Why don't we go to my chambers, have
a little apéro, and see if we can't find a suitable date?"

Inès assumed the chambers would be imposing, but was nonetheless surprised by the opulence. A huge oil of Jean Domat, the father of French jurisprudence, framed in dripping rococo, dominated the room. The piece belonged in the Louvre.

The procureur disappeared into a side chamber to remove his robes and returned in an immaculately cut suit with the red rosette over a silver ribbon of the *grand officier* of the Légion d'honneur conspicuous on its lapel. He produced a chased crystal decanter and two stemmed goblets.

"Pineau des Charentes," the procureur announced. "A good friend of mine sends it to me from the Charente-Maritime."

Inès's seesaw reached its tipping point. Pineau des Charentes, an oversweet fortified wine, was the sort of thing working-class people gave their aged grandmothers, not something you offered a peer. The perceived slight felt like a slap and stung.

The procureur smiled at her over the rim of his glass, relishing its content. "Not only are your cases always brilliantly prepared, but you tie them up in record time. In many ways our work is like that of light cavalry. It's all in the speed. The main thing is to strike before the enemy has time to organize its defense, don't you agree?"

"No, I don't. I prepare cases against guilty people, and I demonstrate their guilt with enough proof to resist even the most carefully structured defense." Inès wondered where this was going. Bizarrely, he really did think the Pineau was something special. Maybe she had misunderstood.

"And your case against Tottinguer? Is that going to resist all defense, as well?"

Inès sat back in her armchair and waited for the rest. There was an eternal five-beat silence.

"The halls of the Palais are alive with rumors that you intend to investigate the son, André."

Another five-beat silence.

"Sooner or later, these rumors will reach the outside world."

Another silence. The procureur drained his glass and raised the decanter in Inès's direction before he realized she hadn't taken a single sip. He filled his glass and set it down on the table with a click.

"If your intentions reach the outside world, your case will be compromised. You may even be sued by the Tottinguers. That would be a good diversionary tactic for them to try, don't you think?"

Another long silence. He had the sense of timing usually found only at the Comédie-

Française. Inès decided she would drop in on one of his court appearances to see how he performed on his feet.

The procureur toyed with his glass, then looked up sharply, his eyes boring into Inès's. She definitely was going to have to go see him in the *parquet.*

"I also understand there is a possibility you might be able to receive enough corroborative evidence from inside the banque Tottinguer to present your case very quickly, which would be key tactically. As our Anglo-Saxon friends like to say, it's time for you to either fish or cut bait, my dear."

Inès stood up, smarting at the slight of being given a specific instruction. It took control not to storm out, slamming the door. But she had to admit he was right. Her timing on the case was off. And he was dead right that timing was all.

"Thank you for the apéro, Monsieur le Procureur de la République. You have a most excellent Pineau."

He smiled at her. She was not sure if in complicity or mockery. As quietly as she could manage, she walked out.

On her way down the stairs she remembered that the question of lunch had not arisen.

Back at her office she told her secretary to

go to the café and bring her back a *sandwich jambon-beurre* — ham in a baguette spread copiously with butter — and an Orangina. When her lunch arrived, she pushed the sandwich to one side of her desk but sucked greedily at the Orangina through a straw. The sweet-sharp taste of the soda erased the taste of the Pineau.

The more she thought about it, the more she realized how completely right he was about the timing. She slurped at her straw, enjoying the loud, vulgar rasp when she reached the bottom. The specter of Lévêque lurked. She hadn't expected his tentacles to be so far-reaching.

She picked up her phone and buzzed her secretary. "Call our HR contact at Police Judiciaire headquarters. Have him prepare a list of suitable commissaires in the financial brigade to take charge of investigating a case. If possible, I'd like to review his suggestions this evening. I want to get going on this first thing tomorrow."

She just had to face up to reality, awkward as it sometimes was. It made no sense at all to wait for Capucine.

Chapter 25

Alexandre and Capucine drove north on the A52 autoroute, cutting a swath dead straight through unending fields of Tyrian-tinted lavender. Capucine was as keyed up as a convict who had just pulled off a jailbreak. It took all her self-discipline to keep from shouting for joy and pumping the accelerator of the borrowed compact Renault to the floor. Her brand-new blond bangs snuck into her field of vision under her oversize sunglasses. She blew the strands away with a jubilant snort.

Alexandre contemplated her from under sleepy lids.

"It's just not you, that hair."

"That's precisely the idea, *mon ami.*" Capucine puffed again.

Capucine and David had spent the better part of the prior day doing her hair. Early in the morning they had donned rubber gloves and attacked it with a thick concoction of L'Oréal powdered bleach and three different kinds of whitener. It had looked exactly like the industrial mayonnaise Alexandre proscribed from their Paris kitchen. When David had bolted off to a town council meeting in the village, Capucine sat in her bathroom, steeping in a chemical miasma despite wide open windows, scrutinizing her creamy mop, occasionally teasing out a lock with the pointed handle of a styling comb to check the color. The process left her simultaneously despondent and jubilant. The beloved auburn hue of her hair was gone, but she was going to be unrecognizable.

Hours later, David had shaped her light golden blond tresses with scissors and rollers. His first attempt evoked Catherine Deneuve's tousled bedroom curls in *Belle de Jour.* Capucine liked the look. It was one she could grow into.

"Non, non, non!" David had said. "Like that, you are too lovely, too noticeable, and too feminine for police work."

He had gone at her hair a second time. She had emerged from the fray with long bangs descending well over her eyebrows, the top teased high and blown full, and the sides cut back to just below the level of her ears. The look was overdone, démodé, even slightly cheap. Capucine hated it.

"Perfect!" David had said. "You look like anyone but you."

"I had no idea hairdressing was one of the skills taught in the Police Judiciaire," Alexandre said.

"He has a real flair for it. Isabelle used to kid him and tell him that he'd missed his true vocation."

"Well, he's certainly found it now." Alexandre crossed his arms over his chest and pouted. Getting up before ten always made him testy.

When the fields of lavender finally morphed into military rows of grapevines, Alexandre perked up.

"You know, we'll be in Nîmes before long. We're in no rush. Why don't we explore the Roman ruins, have an apéro, and then lunch at one of my favorite restaurants? Appropriately enough, it's called Alexandre. Two stars in the *Michelin.* They have some spectacular dishes. One is a fillet of *taureau* — bull — in honor of the bullfighting in the Roman Colosseum."

Alexandre leaned forward with a grunt, patted his pockets, and dug out his phone. "I'm sure they could find us a little nook for lunch."

"Don't even think about making that call.

The last thing we need is you broadcasting our presence to the restaurant world. Even if you buy an even faker beard, the only bull meat you're going to be eating is in the Golden Arches of a service area."

Alexandre crossed his arms and pouted.

"And we *are* in a rush. We're going straight to Perpignan. We can have a sandwich in a café there." Alexandre grimaced. "I've wasted enough time as it is. High time to find Nathalie's murderer and end this nonsense."

As it happened, even though it wasn't in a Michelin-starred restaurant, they unearthed a lunch that Alexandre deemed "perfectly acceptable," high praise in his lexicon. They arrived in Perpignan at twelve thirty and decided on a brief recce of the downtown area to see if they could spot someplace suitable. They wandered into the place de la République, a spacious, traffic-free cobbled square surrounded by inviting *restaurant-cafés* with parasol-covered tables on outdoor terraces. One was conspicuously more crowded than the others. Fifteen minutes later they were eating *carré d'agneau* with a crust of tapenade, washed down with an excellent Languedoc-Roussillon red that the waiter had praised to the skies.

"You're absolutely right, my dear. I've let

myself become enslaved to haute cuisine. This is haute enough for any mortal, and it's a joy to sit outside in this sun, especially with a sexpot blonde like you."

Capucine frowned. Alexandre took her hand.

"So what are we doing in Perpignan? You've been a bit cagey about that."

"I'm here to see Angélique. I need to launch a proper investigation. I'm going to see them all, and I might as well start with her. She's spending the last of her vacation here."

"And how did you discover that?"

"Nothing simpler. I dialed her cell phone. I told her we were driving around the Midi and would love to have a drink with her when we got to Perpignan, which just happened to be today."

"And she didn't think it was odd that we weren't on the boat when they got to Saint-Raphaël?"

"Not at all. They were so anxious to get off the boat, they scampered like rats fleeing a sinking ship the second they touched the dock. She even apologized to me for her rudeness in leaving in such a rush and not saying good-bye."

Alexandre lost interest in the subjects of boats and police work and settled into his mode of luncheon raconteur, waxing on about Languedoc-Roussillon and Perpignan. Capucine had known it was the last town on the coast before you reached Spain, but had had no idea the place was so dear to the hearts of the Catalans.

"Indeed it is," Alexandre said. "Perpignan is the true capital of Catalan culture. So much so that Salvador Dali maintained Perpignan was the center of the world. He even claimed that the exact center was the Perpignan train station and went so far as to paint a picture to that effect. Apparently, every time he sat in the waiting room, he experienced a tempest of creativity and got all his best ideas there."

"I'll have to give that a try," Capucine said.

After lunch, Capucine dropped Alexandre off near the cathedral — he was planning a tour of the shops to sample the local foie gras — and told him she would meet him later at the train station. She wished him a whirlwind of inspiration in the waiting room and drove twenty minutes out of Perpignan to the Château du Riell, a luxury hotel nestled in rocky gorges, where Angélique had been staying since she'd left the boat.

They met on a terrace on one of the château's crenellated ramparts overlooking the dramatic craggy terrain. Angélique shrieked when she saw Capucine's hair.

"You look just fabulous. Fabulous! It's a whole new you. I almost didn't recognize you."

She circled Capucine to admire the hairdo.

"Where did you get this done? Have you been back to Paris? Nobody down here could possibly have that kind of genius."

"It was someone I found near Bandol," Capucine said, settling at a glass table beneath an oversize white parasol.

"You have to give me their number. I might just make a detour on my way back to Paris. I've never seen you look so pretty."

The tea Capucine had been promised materialized as gin and tonics. Angélique snatched hers off the waiter's tray before he had a chance to serve it. Capucine suspected she had had at least two or three already.

Their chat started out pacifically enough, revolving around the last day of the cruise. Capucine was astounded Angélique actually believed both Capucine and Alexandre had been on the boat right until the end, and even recalled a discussion she had had with Capucine after they docked at Port Grimaud.

The minute the waiter hovered into sight,

Angélique made an impatient gesture for another gin and tonic. Flustered, she took a deep draught when the drink arrived.

"Capucine, I'm sure you heard us fighting in our cabin on that last day. Of course you did. Everybody must have. You heard those horrible things he said to me, didn't you?"

"Who? Dominique?"

Angélique nodded, and a tear ran down her cheek, leaving a black slug's trail of mascara. She waved irritably at the waiter for another drink.

"Of course Dominique. I threw him out before we left Port Grimaud. I told him to take the car — my car — and go wherever he wanted. And then I rented another car and drove here. And I'm having a good time. A *very* good time." Angélique paused, downed the remaining half of the gin and tonic and made a tipsy gesture at the waiter for yet another.

"What an odious, loathsome, vile man Dominique is. I can't understand how I could ever have married him. Do you know that while we were having dinner in Bonifacio, in that restaurant with the fabulous view, he was down on the boat, *fucking* — yes, that's the word, *fucking*! — that slovenly boat girl?"

Angélique had screeched loudly enough

to turn heads at surrounding tables. Capucine guessed that she was a single drink away from a loud scene with the waiter when he refused to serve her.

"Are you sure?"

"Sure? Of course I'm sure. That bastard will put his pecker into anything that's warm and damp."

More heads turned. An elderly couple got up and left the terrace, clucking and shaking their heads.

"Thank God, I was spared actually seeing him in the act. But still, I know perfectly well what happened. Right after lunch, when it became obvious Dominique wasn't going to join us, I went looking for him. Naturally, the first place I looked was the boat. No one was in the salon, but I thought I could hear something going on in that awful girl's cabin in the forepeak. So I walked out on deck as quietly as I could, and sure enough, two people were *fucking* in there."

Angélique was puce with rage. She had finally been loud enough to prompt the waiter to action. He appeared, looking simultaneously stern and apologetic.

"Madame, je vous en prie," he said with hands outspread in supplication.

"Okay, okay. I'll be a good, quiet little girl if you bring me another gin and tonic. But if you don't, I'll raise hell," Angélique said, slurring her words. "And make it a double. Hell, a triple!" She giggled.

Angélique leaned over the table and continued her story in a sibilant but carrying stage whisper.

"I couldn't really see who was in the forepeak, and fool that I am, I assumed she was with Serge. You remember how we all thought they had a thing going, right? So I went off to the shops in the lower town to see if I could find Dominique there. And guess who I ran into? Guess!"

The waiter returned with Angélique's gin and tonic. She thanked him in her stage whisper, put her index finger to her pursed lips, making a theatrical shushing noise. The waiter departed without a word.

"I ran into Serge. That was all the proof I needed."

"Couldn't it have been someone other than Dominique?"

"Of course not. I saw the little glances he had been giving her. And that little bitch was a slut, but I don't think she was enough of a slut to haul some guy right off the dock onto her bunk at dinnertime."

Capucine said nothing.

"So I'm divorcing him. That's all there is to it. I've called my lawyer and started the proceedings. I also called my concierge and had the locks on our — *my* — apartment changed. Voilà, it's done."

She slumped in her seat, eyes half closed.

"I'm sorry, Capucine. I wanted our day to be a happy one. But this has been such a trial for me. Dominique has always been despicable with women. And I put up with him because I thought he would get over it. But I learned I was building a castle in the sky. I feel terrible, but I also feel much, much better . . . free at last to be the real me."

She squinted, having trouble focusing.

"I think I need to lie down. I'm sure you understand."

Capucine helped the swaying Angélique into the hotel, put her in the elevator, and drove back to Perpignan. She felt a little numb.

CHAPTER 26

Capucine was dismayed by the vaunted waiting room of the Perpignan train station. In the flesh, it was no different from any other small-town SNCF waiting room: low ceilinged, overbright with flat fluorescent light, the walls relieved only by a row of vending machines dispensing tickets and candy bars. The focal point was a glass window labeled ACCUEIL, allowing potential passengers to yell questions at a sullen clerk through a *Hygiaphone,* a glass labyrinth, which not only protected the clerk from airborne germs but also obliged customers to strain to make themselves heard. The only distinctive note to the room was the ceiling, which had been decorated in amateurish polka dots joined by primary-color whorls, apparently in some sort of oblique homage to Dali.

Capucine made a quick lap of the room, stopping only at the tiny news stall to purchase a postcard reproduction of Dali's painting. The painter, incongruously, arms and legs akimbo, floated into a giant sunburst in the sky, surrounded by figures from Millet's praying peasants. Capucine felt she was missing some sort of joke.

Capucine sat on a hard oak bench and pondered the postcard.

After a few minutes, she put it in the pocket of her jacket. Her plan of action had appeared full blown in her head, mapped out as clearly as if it had been honed in a long series of team meetings with her brigadiers. Maybe Dali was right and the waiting room *was* the creative center of the universe.

She pulled out her iPhone and searched through the directory. Then she extracted one of the borrowed cell phones from another pocket and punched in David's number.

"Salut, David. How are things in La Cadière?"

"Blissful, as they have been since time immemorial."

"Would you have time to do a little police work for me?"

"I'd like nothing better."

"Good. Here's what I need you to do. I want you to go to Bonifacio and find out as much as you can about the movements of certain people on a certain date."

"Hang on Com . . . Capucine. Let me write this down."

When he came back on the line, Capucine gave him the date of the group's lunch in the town and their departure from Bonifacio. "Now, David, I want you to go online and find the blog of someone called Régis de La Rochelle. He's been posting a good number of pictures of our cruise. They are tagged with the names of the people involved. I'd like you to make portraits of the eleven of us and interview anyone permanently involved with the marina — port captain's office, bars, food stores, whatever — about their movements around lunchtime on the two days in question. Pay particular attention to Nathalie Martin."

"The victim?"

"Exactly."

"I'll get the pictures out of the computer right away and then drive down there. There's a car ferry direct from Marseilles to Bonifacio. I'll take the first one out tomorrow morning." He paused. "Can you tell me more about what I'm looking for?"

"Nothing specific. I just want to know who came and went from our boat around lunchtime that day."

268

Capucine slipped the phone back in her pocket and looked around the waiting room. The same four people still sat on different benches, waiting as endlessly if they had been there since the beginning of time. Of course, she undoubtedly gave them the same impression.

With her mind's eye she transported herself to her office. She was sitting behind her desk, leaning back in her chair, feet on the desk, lecturing her three brigadiers in her commissaire's take-charge voice.

We still need to do work on five possibles — Serge, Régis, Aude, Florence, and Dominique. I'm going to start with Florence. There's too much I don't understand about her. I want you to try to figure out where the other four might be. They haven't been answering their cell phones.

Capucine shook herself back to the material world. She had only one brigadier on the case, and he was fully utilized. It was all up to her.

She pulled out her own iPhone, searched for Florence in her directory, then rooted for one of the borrowed phones in her pockets, feeling ridiculous. She dialed Florence's number.

"Oui."

"Salut, Florence. C'est Capucine."

"Allô, Capucine." The voice was surprisingly distant. Nearly outright cold.

"Where are you? What are you doing with the rest of your summer?" Capucine tried hard to project a smile across the ether.

"Nothing exciting. I have an apartment in Carcassonne. I'm here catching up on my reading."

"You are! How wonderful. Alexandre and I are taking a driving tour of the Midi, meandering back to Paris. We're planning on stopping at Carcassonne. We'll be there tomorrow. Why don't we drop by for a drink? You could tell us all the best places to go. Alexandre is always on the lookout for restaurants only the locals know."

There was an awkward pause.

"Tomorrow? Tomorrow might not be ideal. My day is pretty packed."

"I thought you were just catching up on your reading."

"Yes, I am. But I told a friend we'd go clothes shopping tomorrow."

"That's no problem. We won't be arriving until around five. We'll come by then. What's the address?"

Grudgingly, Florence surrendered her address, and Capucine rang off with exaggerated cheer.

Capucine changed phones once again and

rang Inès, who also seemed distant.

"Any news on the case?" Capucine asked.

"News? No. Not really. What about you? Still hiding out at your friend's house?"

"No. I'm on the road, interviewing people. I've decided to let the chips fall where they may and get off my duff and solve this thing."

"Be careful. Have you found out anything?"

"I saw Angélique in Perpignan today. She's decided to divorce Dominique and is drowning her sorrows in gin."

Inès snorted.

"Tomorrow I'm off to Carcassonne to interview Florence."

"Carcassonne?" There was a long pause. Capucine could hear the tapping of keyboard keys. "Carcassonne. Yes, yes, of course. How could I have missed that?"

Capucine waited.

"It's impossible to do proper work without sufficient police support."

"What do you mean?"

"André Tottinguer has disappeared. The day he was released from garde à vue, he vanished. I just remembered he has a house in Carcassonne. I'll bet he's there with Florence. He's bound to have maintained his relationship with her. Capucine, this is a valuable opportunity. I need you to shadow Florence. Find out how involved she is with Tottinguer. Take your time. Plan on spending a week or two. Report back to me tomorrow night and tell me how it's going. Keep me in the loop. This is excellent news. Really excellent news."

Capucine hung up and pursed her lips into a frown that reached up to the bottom of her nose. As she mused, dismayed, she saw a person walking toward her and mistook him for Alexandre. But it wasn't anyone she knew. This person had an enormous ginger mustache cascading down over his upper lip. But he had Alexandre's gait down to a T. It *was* Alexandre! He'd bought himself a disguise. This was too good to be true. Capucine dissolved into paroxysms of giggles. Alexandre stood over her, frowning under his mustache, tapping his foot in indignation. The severity of his expression only intensified her giggles.

Choking, she said, "You look like half of Dupont and Dupond from *Tintin*. You know, in the story where their hair and mustaches keep on growing and changing color."

"My dear, you obviously are a babe in the woods when it comes to disguise. I acquired this at a very upmarket costume shop. It's real human hair. Cost a pretty centime, too.

272

Not only is its verisimilitude beyond reproach, but it also gives me a very distinguished look. I decided we needed to go out for a proper dinner, and since you're in disguise, I shall be in disguise, as well."

Capucine continued giggling.

"Pull yourself together, my dear. I've booked at a one-star restaurant here in Perpignan, La Galinette. The chef is well known for his vegetables. He has his own little farm where he grows the forgotten ones. He does seven varieties of eggplant."

"Wait a minute." Capucine's face went dead sober. "How did you get a reservation in a one-star restaurant for the same day without using your name?"

"How you underestimate me, my child. I called a chef I know in Paris who happens to be a buddy of the chef of this place. The chef in Paris told him we were called Estouffade. That's our new name for tonight. Voilà," Alexandre said, sensuously smoothing his mustache.

"So now this chef in Paris knows where we are."

"Oh, please. The police are hardly likely to interview every last chef in Paris to see if anyone knows where I am. Besides, you know how chefs are. They never tell anyone outside of the business anything."

Capucine was mollified. She was on the road back to her normal persona, and that definitely included eating in starred restaurants.

"I suppose you're right. And we'll be in Carcassonne tomorrow, anyway."

"Even better. There are two restaurants there I'm dying to try out."

They walked out of the train station hand in hand, Alexandre fondling his mustache, his new love.

"And don't you dare even think about growing one of those," Capucine said, butting Alexandre with her hip.

CHAPTER 27

Capucine had never liked Carcassonne. It was, of course, one of the great architectural wonders of France, with not one, but two intact medieval fortified walls still encircling the city. And it was a thrill seeing the fortifications dominate the hilltop when one first drove up. But once inside, the medieval architecture was crabbed and the walls were claustrophobic.

Florence's address was on a narrow cobbled street at the edge of the vertiginously high wall. Capucine tapped the brass knocker on the white-painted wooden door. Nothing happened. After a few seconds, she raised the knocker a second time, but the opening door pulled it out of her hand. It dropped with a clunk. Florence scowled.

"Come in, Capucine. You've done something with your hair. You cut it short, is that it? It was much better before."

Originally home to a tradeperson, the little

house was the typical middle-class vacation residence. An architect had attempted to open up the space by demolishing a few of the interior walls, leaving oversize, bare rooms, monastically furnished with inexpensive antiques from local markets. The look was temporary and unlived in.

The only remotely appealing feature of the house was a closet-size courtyard with a tiny square pool fed by a plastic ignudo urinating angelically. Capucine wondered why Florence had not had it removed when she bought the house.

Dominique, barefoot in white trousers and a white shirt open down his flat stomach, was stretched out in a child-size canvas lounge chair, his feet propped up on the edge of the diminutive fountain.

He stood up and sneered insolently.

"That hair color suits you. The touch of vulgarity conveys a definite sense of piquantness."

The eye of the artist, Capucine told herself. "I'm surprised to see you here," she said.

"Angélique gave me my walking papers, so I thought I'd look up our chum Florence." He shot Capucine a provocative glance. "She gave me a very warm welcome."

"Is that what you call it?" Florence said,

carrying in a tray with glasses, a pitcher of dark liquid, and two bowls of supermarket salted treats. "I made us some Negronis. Régis used to do them very well on that ill-fated cruise."

She handed one to Capucine and walked over to stand behind Dominique, her large hand proprietarily on his shoulder, a masculine gesture expressing pride of ownership far more than affection.

"What brings you to our little love nest?" Dominique asked.

"Alexandre and I are taking a little driving tour of the Midi before going back to Paris. We wouldn't have missed Carcassonne for anything, and I thought it would be fun to drop in on Florence."

"You're so right. Florence *can* be a lot of fun under the right circumstances."

Florence smiled tolerantly.

"Actually, Dominique," Capucine said, "I'm glad I ran into you. I wanted to ask you some questions about the day of Nathalie's death."

"Ask away." He put his hand on Florence's thigh. When she did not respond, he let it drop.

"I had a hunch you might have had a little dalliance with Nathalie before you joined us in the old town."

" 'Dalliance'? Is that what it's called in the police?"

"What would you call it?"

"I fucked her brains out."

Florence snorted.

"In her cabin?"

"In her little box, the ideal place. That little slut had been coming on to me even before we left Port Grimaud. I doubled back to the boat when you all went up the hill, and found her half naked, sweating, swabbing out the heads. She was like an animal. She wanted it everywhere. She couldn't get enough."

Florence didn't look at him, but her parted lips were engorged.

"And after, you weren't too tired to climb up all those steps to the old town?"

"Not me. I didn't want wifey to worry."

"But she was irate."

"She's always irate. That's par for the course." Dominique dropped into the chair. "You don't understand Angélique. Jealousy was her biggest turn-on. It made her like a tiger in heat. That night she wanted to go at it all night long. And the storm intensified it for her. She made so much noise, I had to cover her face with a pillow."

Florence gave him a complicit smile.

Dominique slid his hand under her short skirt.

Repelled, Capucine decided to cut the interview short. She'd found out what she wanted to know. Dominique had an alibi — of sorts. It would have no weight at all in court, but it did have the ring of truth. And it didn't look like Florence had any involvement with Tottinguer. High time to find Alexandre and get something good enough to eat to cover up the rancid taste in her mouth.

She got up and left awkwardly.

As she walked to the car, she slid one of her phones out of her pocket and considered calling Inès but didn't have the patience for another burst of Inès's one-track mind. She dropped the phone back in her jacket and drove off to pick up Alexandre. Rumbling over the tortuous cobblestoned streets, she chided herself on not having taken the time for a complete interview. But to what end? She had no doubt about who the killer was. What she needed was proof enough for a court case, and she wasn't going to get that from either Florence or Dominique.

CHAPTER 28

Alexandre opted for the prelunch apéro in the penthouse bar of a brand-new hotel with a sweeping view over the ramparts and out into the hills. With the last of the morning mist evaporating in the sun, the scenery had an overdone look in keeping with the licked perfection of the penthouse's décor. Capucine found the scene cloying. This was always the hard part of the case, the legwork to assemble enough evidence for a judge to put together a viable case. It was dog work that was supposed to be done by brigadiers. The injustice of having to do it while exiled behind the dark side of the curtain of the law was beyond unfair. She sipped her Lillet Blanc. The limp-wristed drink just wasn't doing the trick. She should have opted for a muscled single malt. The new drink in hand, Capucine still couldn't shake the petulance of blaming the whole mess on the Police Judiciaire. Why weren't they on her side, supporting her? Two more sips into the malt she realized the Police Judiciaire had damn well all to do with her predicament and would probably have rallied if only she had just called someone in time. She felt like kicking the leg of the table.

"I take it your efforts this morning weren't crowned with success?" Alexandre asked, appearing over her shoulder.

"In a bizarre sort of way, they were. But right now, lunch is very much top of mind. Where are you taking me? Some multi-starred place where the food will send me into richly deserved paroxysms of delight?"

"There's only one restaurant in Carcassonne that has a Michelin star, La Barbacane. Unfortunately, I know the chef there too well. He used to work in Paris. So I booked at the Domaine d'Auriac. It's a Relais & Châteaux hotel, and their restaurant is supposed to be adequate."

Fifteen minutes later they were sitting on a second-story balcony overlooking a garden of Prussian rigidity. Alexandre grumbled and snorted at the menu, blowing sharp puffs at his mustache, which had begun to irritate him. Even despite the mustache, it was clear he was enjoying hating the restaurant.

"With one or two exceptions, this is

precisely the same menu Relais & Châteaux would present in Abu Dhabi, or anywhere else, for that matter. It's all here. King crab ravioles, foie gras with an apple-rhubarb compote, cocotte-cooked veal in a secret sauce. Chérie, you order for me in a whisper. The element of surprise will add a nuance of drama. While you're at it, I'm going to take a tramp around the garden and smoke the merest of panatelas."

Capucine felt guilty. She had asked too much of Alexandre. He missed his Paris. He wasn't cut out for life on the run. And on top of it all, she was behaving childishly. The mature thing to do was to call Contrôleur Général Tallon, go to Paris, have a long lunch with him, solicit his advice and patronage. In a word, abdicate and begin acting like the civil servant she was.

She knew exactly what he would tell her to do: report immediately for duty at the head of her brigade, confine her activities to non-newsworthy cases in her brigade's arrondissement, and let the palliative police bureaucracy consign Nathalie's putative murder to the oubliettes of the archives. In a matter of months it would be as if the case had never existed. The unacceptable rub was that somewhere there would be a murderer licking his chops in self-congratulation.

For Alexandre, she ordered an anchovy salad — with extolled anchovies from the famous Maison Roque in Collioure, on the Spanish frontier — followed by a fillet of *rascasse,* a small, red Mediterranean fish, well known as the sine qua non of bouillabaisse, and then a risotto made from *fregola,* the little balls of pasta Alexandre had made for their last dinner on the *Diomede.* For herself she ordered the foie gras, followed by the veal. She had none of Alexandre's desire for surprise.

Halfway through the meal, Alexandre put his hand on top of his wife's. "You order brilliantly. It's a great art, knowing what will be good in any given restaurant. The anchovies were exceptional, and, I blush to confess, these fregola are in a class apart from mine."

"But you miss Paris."

"That I do," he said wistfully.

"Good, because we're going back tomorrow."

Alexandre whooped and smiled broadly. The right-hand half of his mustache came away. Capucine creased her brows and made a little circular gesture with her finger under her nose. Alexandre put both hands to his mouth, pressing the mustache back into place.

"How wonderful. I thought we were on the run," he said between his fingers.

"We are. And I may be kidding myself, but I think our disguises are effective enough. Angélique and Florence almost didn't recognize me. And you look like some sci-fi character with that ectoplasm coming out of your nose." She looked at Alexandre critically. "I'm going to give it a little trim right after lunch. You look like you've been straining your soup through the damn thing."

"Good idea. I plan to get any number of decent meals in Paris and don't want any encumbrances."

"Don't get your hopes too high. We're just going for two or three days. We'll be back down here before the week is out. I still need to interview a few people."

"Anyone I know?"

"Your two buddies, Serge and Régis, are at the top of my list. Serge is behaving oddly. His cell phone is eternally off, and the phone in his office announces the business is closed until the *rentrée* in September."

Alexandre continued taking small bites of his rascasse, concentrating on the flavor. He had stopped listening to Capucine.

"This is quite a challenge. Only two or three days, eh? Two dinners and three lunches. That's going to take a bit of planning."

It was supposed to be a nine-hour drive, but Capucine was positive she could shave off two good hours. They were going to leave at eight in the morning, stop in Limoges for lunch at a place Alexandre promised would be delightful, and make it to Paris in time for the apéro before dinner.

Capucine loved to drive, and gallantly, Alexandre was happy to surrender the wheel. Capucine had a *pied de plomb* — a lead foot. The speed limit on French autoroutes was eighty miles an hour, but Capucine felt ninety-five was more than reasonable enough for a police officer. Once or twice over the years she had been stopped, but her police card had produced a smart salute and a friendly chat about the doings in the local gendarmerie.

The route to Paris was almost entirely over expressways. Capucine pressed the accelerator of the Renault hard to the floor. The speedometer gradually crept up to ninety and kept on going until it waved just south of a hundred.

Forty-five minutes away from Limoges,

Capucine saw a blue pulsing light in her rearview mirror.

"*Ah, là là!* What fun. We're being pulled over. Now, not a peep out of you. Let me handle everything."

Like a model bourgeois, Capucine pulled over into the narrow breakdown lane on the right, hands in clear view at the top of the wheel. In the rearview mirror she could see two gendarmes in khaki military uniforms, one talking into the radio, calling in the license plate, the other looking down at his lap, filling out a form.

Despite her delight with the unexpected break, Capucine experienced a slight frisson of fight-or-flight anxiety. So this was what it was like on the reverse of the medal. In real life, stopped at that speed, a normal citizen would find herself on the backseat of the gendarmerie squad car, on her way to a nightmare. And when you got right down to it, she herself might already be on some list that would put her in the same spot.

"*Papiers,*" barked the uniformed gendarme at her window, without the courtesy of a "s'il vous plaît."

Capucine leaned over Alexandre's leg and foraged in the glove compartment, producing a plastic wallet with the car's registration and insurance policy, both in the name of Siméon Flaissières, from Marseilles, the owner of the car David had borrowed.

The gendarme examined the papers with unnecessary attention and ordered, "*Permis de conduire.* Driver's license."

Capucine rooted through her bag and turned to Alexandre. "*Chéri,* have you seen my wallet? It's not in my bag. Do you think I could have lost it again?"

"Not again! That will make it twice this month."

"*Bon, bon,*" the gendarme said. "Where are you going? I'll send the report there, and you can present your license at the gendarmerie."

"We're going to Paris," Capucine said sweetly.

"Paris, Madame Flaissières? In the middle of August?"

"*Bien sûr.* We're having a little vacation in Paris. All by ourselves."

The gendarme gave her a knowing look, then focused on Alexandre. "Monsieur, are you Monsieur Flaissières?"

Alexandre was perfect. He managed to look disconcerted for almost an entire second, then turned haughtily to the gendarme. "What business is it of yours? I'm not at the wheel. I'm just a passenger enjoying the view. I see no reason to give you my name."

The gendarme looked from Alexandre to Capucine and back to Alexandre again, comparing the age difference and noting Capucine's curves and provocative hairdo. "I see," he said with a smirk. "Enjoy your 'vacation.'" He handed the car's papers back to Capucine. "And I understand your rush, madame, but do try to make at least some effort to respect the speed limits."

Capucine pulled out of the breakdown lane, with the gendarme behind her. After a few hundred yards he passed Capucine's car, turned his head, gave her a broad smile, and accelerated on. Capucine and Alexandre burst into laughter.

"You were fantastic," Capucine said. "Have you ever considered a career on the stage?"

"I certainly wasn't acting. I was thinking, Madame Flaissières, about our *cinq-à-sept* — our five to seven — this afternoon. I know just where we will go. L'Hôtel, in the rue des Beaux-Arts."

"That overdecorated place where Oscar Wilde died?"

"The very same. The rooms are redolent with the musk of illicit passion. And the restaurant!" Capucine turned her head toward Alexandre. He touched all five fingers to his lips and cast them heavenward. "A méli-mélo of silk settees in a delightful Belle Epoque jumble, where you eat cuisine that fully merits its Michelin star."

"It sounds as if you know the place inside out."

"A restaurant critic has to be au fait, my dear. But remember, even if many may own my stomach, only you own my heart."

CHAPTER 29

They arrived at L'Hôtel a few minutes before six. Alexandre had spent much of the ride to Paris on one of Capucine's cell phones, calling cronies, using his pull to secure them a small suite at L'Hôtel under the name Estouffade.

Alexandre checked in with ebullient good spirits, providing a cash deposit instead of a credit card number, just like a prosperous provincial farmer showing off. As he signed the register, he repeatedly blew puffs at the mustache to keep stray hairs from tickling his lip. The pretty woman in a dark suit behind the desk assumed the deadpan face of a novice poker player with an exceptional hand and took frequent peeks at Capucine out of the corner of her eye. It was clear she was having a hard time suppressing her giggles.

Capucine had not set foot in L'Hôtel in years. The atrium, narrow and deep as a well, brought back memories not only of her youth but also of *Paris Match* photos of famous rock groups leaning over the balustrades of the top floors, making funny faces. Capucine and Alexandre's room was decorated with cubist furniture made entirely of mirrors. It had a thirties charm, Capucine told herself, she would find amusing for exactly one night.

The restaurant was exactly as she remembered, a heavy rococo caricature, dripping with brocade drapes and hooded lamps, awash in a sea of red velvet and striped silk. They sat facing each other on wide green silk-covered settees, nestled into throw pillows, separated by a diminutive round table inlaid in veneer. The fare was classic one-star haute cuisine. Alexandre chose veal sweetbreads in a dried chanterelle herb broth, and Capucine the wild pigeon in a *sauce diable.* The plating of both dishes was melodramatic, amorphous foams providing the ubiquitous molecular cuisine touch.

Alexandre was back in his element. Capucine could see him framing a review and lamented that it would go unpublished for quite some time. "This is an institution that has been able to hang on to its niche for a good many decades," Alexandre said, punctuating the utterance with a puff at his mustache.

They both looked around the room. There were a handful of Parisians in exorbitant casual attire and a greater number of English people, the men in brocaded waistcoats and luxuriously flowing locks and the women in designer harem pants under silken blouses open to their navels. They all smacked of the world of music or fashion.

"How glorious to be home again," Alexandre said, cheerfully blowing at his mustache.

The next day, Capucine abandoned Alexandre to his mustache and wandered around Serge's part of the Marais, visiting his restaurants to see if she could come up with any news of his whereabouts. She was tranquil that her new hairdo would safeguard her anonymity.

Her first stop was a restaurant-café on the rue Vieille-du-Temple in the Marais, not far from her apartment. It was a bijou place that had been in business for over a hundred and fifty years. The tiny bar was U-shaped, corralling two bartenders, who supplied drinks and snacks to the artsy crowd until the small hours of the morning. At night the bar was invariably packed tight as the rush-hour Metro.

She arrived at the restaurant-café at eleven and sat outside, at one of the four round marble-topped tables on the sidewalk. She was the only customer on the terrace. The waitress, a pretty young girl with long pale chestnut hair, so clean-looking and light it bounced when she walked, came out to take her order. Capucine had never seen her before; she'd never been there during daylight hours before.

When the waitress returned with Capucine's express, Capucine smiled at her in thanks and asked, "Has Serge Monnot been in yet today? I was hoping to see him."

"The owner? I've been working here for a year, and the only time I've seen him was when he interviewed me. I think he comes in only at night. Anyway, someone told me he's on vacation and he won't be back until September. And why should he?"

She looked in at the bar. Capucine followed her gaze. It was completely deserted.

"This place is a wasteland in August. I don't know why Monsieur Monnot bothers to keep it open. He should close down for August like everyone else."

Capucine crossed the street to another *restaurant-café* owned by Serge. This one was essentially a bookstore with a long mahogany bar. Capucine sat on a stool and ordered another coffee. While it was being prepared, she wandered around the long room, examining the titles. The selection leaned heavily to avant-garde poetry and aggressive post-modern literature. Capucine picked up a slim book of poems and returned to the bar. She had also come here frequently with Alexandre for nightcaps. Patrons with books in their hands were a common enough sight, but she had never seen anyone actually buy one.

The bar girl was even more attractive than the waitress across the street. She wore her dark blond hair crinkled in waves cut so it formed an equilateral triangle with a flat base. The hair provided a dramatic frame for her face.

"Vénus Khoury-Ghata," the bar girl said, nodding at the book in Capucine's hands. "A genius. She won the Goncourt for poetry last year. One of the great visionaries of our century."

Capucine had scanned two or three of the poems. She was unable to concentrate enough to get into the verse. She slapped the book down on the table. The bar girl looked up in alarm.

"You don't really want to buy it, do you?"

Capucine smiled at her and shook her head. The bar girl seemed relieved.

"Actually, I was hoping to run into Serge Monnot."

"He's on vacation. He won't be back until September."

Her penetrating amber eyes told a story involving hurt. Capucine guessed that this one had seen Serge a good bit after the initial interview.

She had a similar result at her third stop, a restaurant a hundred yards up the rue Vieille-du-Temple, which was just setting up for lunch. The restaurant, usually packed with upwardly mobile under-thirties, was deserted. It specialized in what Alexandre called Italian light: salads with pine nuts and crumbled mozzarella, white pizzas, anything perceived to be nonfattening. As she walked in, Capucine noticed that the pizza oven had not even been turned on. It really was a mystery why Serge kept his restaurants open in August.

Her interlocutor this time around was a male, with long, lightly gelled black hair, swept away from his face to end in little swirls at the nape of his neck.

"Nah, we never see Serge in the summer. My guess is that he just keeps these places open in July and August so they don't get broken into. We do a little dinner business, but the guys who work in the two bars down the street are bored out of their minds."

Capucine had one last idea. She walked down the rue Sainte-Croix de la Brétonnerie to the corner of rue des Archives. This was the heart of the gay quartier of the Marais. She ducked into a huge magazine shop that prided itself on its range of international publications. She pulled a copy of *Vogue Italia* out of a rack and thumbed through it while peering out the picture window at a large restaurant-café on the opposite corner. The terrace tables were packed with muscular men in skimpy wifebeater tank tops, their multihued tattoos undulating over rippling muscles.

Serge was sitting at a table on the corner with two other men. All three of them wore light linen summer jackets, setting them apart from the more roughly dressed patrons at surrounding tables. One of Serge's companions was slightly effeminate; the other looked like he divided his spare time between the gym and running marathons.

Capucine had heard Serge mention this café several times during the trip and had divined that it was his next target for acquisition. If it was, it was hardly surprising he was having difficulty getting the Mafia as a co-investor, if that was really what he was up to.

Capucine flipped through fashion magazines in foreign languages while peeping
over their tops at Serge. The threesome
consumed two more coffees and went
through a range of facial expressions and
body language: conciliation, new differ-
ences, masked animosity, and finally, grudg-
ing agreement. After half an hour, hands
were shaken and backs thumped. Serge
stood up, expressionless, and began to cross
the street in Capucine's direction. Halfway
across the street — invisible to his companions — he broke into a broad smile. Capucine put her last magazine back in its rack
and went to the glass door of the shop. With
perfect timing she rushed out and collided
with Serge.

There was a scene of irritation instantly
replaced by recognition, happy greetings,
and "What have you done with your hair?"
questions.

"Buy me lunch," Capucine offered.

"With pleasure," Serge said. "But not
around here. I know just the place."

He took her to a restaurant in an enormous room with a high dome, not unlike a
church. The height of the dome and surrounding ceiling created a cool, half-lit, very
welcome break from the August midday
heat.

"This used to be a 'Chez Ma Tante,' you know, a nine-teenth-century pawn shop. I love the term. You took your brooch or whatever to 'your aunt's.' "

When the food came — *salades composées* and a carafe of white wine — Serge said, "How amazing we ran into each other like this. I'm in Paris incognito. I've been negotiating my next restaurant, and I don't want any distractions."

"And, of course, you're going to keep your target a secret," Capucine said with her best smile.

Serge shot her a shrewd look. "Just this morning I reached a handshake agreement with the current owner, but it's nothing to gloat about. There's many a slip twixt cup and lip in this sort of thing. Particularly in this deal. The establishment in question is almost the high temple of a cause, and there's potentially a good deal of unhappiness if it falls into the hands of a nonmember of that cause." He smiled sweetly at Capucine. "I hope that's ambiguous enough to make everything perfectly clear."

"It is," Capucine said with a laugh.

"Actually, I was going to call you," Serge said. "What happened to the investigation of the death of that poor girl, Nathalie? Did the French police decide to investigate the case, or will the French and Italians bounce it back and forth until everyone just forgets about it?"

"As far as I know, the French police have yet to receive a communiqué from the Italians," Capucine fibbed.

"Typical. It's always the same. Do you think we'll ever find out what happened to her?"

"My guess is that the investigation will be dropped." Capucine paused. Serge avoided her gaze, over-scrutinizing the restaurant. "Actually," Capucine said, "if the French police ever get around to an investigation, you'll be the first to know."

"Why me? I hardly knew Nathalie."

"You knew her before the rest of us did. You hired her. You're the first person any flic would interview."

Serge intensified his examination of the restaurant. "Some guy in the yacht charter office recommended her. A paid hand is always a godsend on these charters. I met her on the dock — it wasn't even an interview, just a quick chat — and I hired her. I don't think that really counts as 'knowing her.' "

"And you were with her in Bonifacio when we all went up the hill to dinner."

"That's true enough. I gave her a list of

things to buy for the boat and then headed up the stairs to meet you all in the upper village."

"It must have been a long list. You almost missed lunch altogether."

Serge laughed. "That was because I ran into the port *capitaine* as he was coming out of the capitainerie. I've know the guy for years. He took me for an apéro at the B' Fifty-Two. I'm afraid our apéro turned into drinks with lots of canapés on the side. I only went up the hill not to be rude."

Capucine said nothing. The food arrived. They talked about other things. Toward the end of the meal, Capucine said, "I've always wondered what happened while we were at lunch. Nathalie seemed very relaxed, almost happy, when we were on watch that night."

Serge shrugged, indifferent.

"We'll see what the police make of it, if it ever becomes an official case," Capucine said. "Thank God I won't be investigating. It's the sort of case that is impossible to solve. The investigating officers always look bad."

CHAPTER 30

Inès glowered at the young man sitting across her desk. Proletarian as she liked to believe herself, it took an effort not to curl her lip. He wore an oddly colored, ill-fitting summer suit with a lustrous polyester sheen. Her eyes traveled down his unpressed leg. He was wearing white socks over scuffed black shoes. White socks like a schoolboy! Inès was the last person on earth to believe that civil servants should be subjected to a dress code, but standing out in a crowd was inconsistent with police work.

The man selected one of his four thick notebooks, flipped through to the right page, put it on his lap, and looked at Inès with the eagerness of a dog about to receive a treat. Inès's frown deepened.

She had made a mistake. This was the wrong man to have picked. Probably any officer from the fiscal brigade would have been a mistake, but this one took the cake.

DGPJ, Police Judiciaire headquarters, had first offered her a commissaire from La Crim'. He had come across as an unshaven bully, the last person sensitive enough to win over Madame Tottinguer and coax a story out of her. Lieutenant Lambert had been their next proposal. She had worked with him a few times. He knew finance for sure, but she had had no idea he was so inept with people.

"How did you make out with Madame Tottinguer?" Inès asked.

"Quite well. It was a very positive interview. She was very frank and open."

Inès nodded. "So she confirmed her decision to bring charges against her husband?"

"Not at all. She's decided to drop the case."

"What?" Inès sat up straight.

"Yes. Her husband's been sending her flowers every day with notes apologizing for his conduct. He claims he panicked when she pointed the shotgun at him, and didn't know what he was doing."

"What about the concierge? Did you see her? What did she have to say?"

"Apparently, the Tottinguers are model residents of the building. Not the slightest peep comes out of their apartment. This was the first incident, and it wasn't even really an incident. The man on the second floor who called the police overreacted."

Inès's frown deepened.

"Did you see this man?"

"Oui, Madame le Juge. He's a geriatric. In his eighties, at the least. He doesn't remember a thing. His wife thinks he must have heard their cat push a sugar canister off a shelf onto the floor. I saw the cat. A little trickster, that one. My cat does the same sort of thing. In the middle of the night, for no reason at all, she'll just push something off a table. It's cute, but some-times it can be a bit ir—"

"So you have nothing?"

"Au contraire, Madame le Juge, I've put together a team, and we're compiling a list of all the short sells of EADS stock since the creation of the company. It's early days, of course." Lieutenant Lambert smiled in self-satisfaction. "But even at this prelimi-nary stage, the banque Tottinguer is close to the head of the list. I have high hopes we will get very useful results from this investi-gation." He looked at Inès, expecting praise.

Inès scowled.

"Listen to me very carefully, Lieutenant. Tomorrow morning, early, Lieutenant," Inès said, "I want Madame Tottinguer here, in this office, sitting right where you are sitting now. If she refuses to come, you will send a squad car and have her picked up. Is that perfectly clear?"

As far as Inès could tell, Madame Tottinguer was the standard-issue Auteuil-Neuilly-Passy mindless rich bitch who cared only about her clothes and her dinner parties. Well scrubbed, with too many teeth in her mouth, she hid her nervousness at being in the office of a juge d'instruction well. There was no sign of a tight throat or a dry mouth, which was the reaction Inès was used to from the majority of people she interviewed.

Madame Tottinguer made a show of having fully regained her composure and crossed her long legs at the ankles. Inès noticed she was wearing stockings. In the middle of August. That must be a sign of something, but Inès had no idea what.

"I'm investigating a series of transactions conducted by your husband's bank, which appear to have been based on insider information. As I'm sure you know, that's a very serious crime."

Madame Tottinguer did not react in the slightest. Inès wondered if she had understood.

"Some of these transactions were conducted by a small holding company in the

Channel Island of Jersey of which you are listed as a director. I'd like to talk to you about that."

"The Channel Islands? Are you sure? That can't be right. I've never been there."

Inès opened a thin file and extracted an official-looking piece of paper, which she put on the desk in front of her. She tapped it twice with her fingernail.

"Yes, it was opened four years ago."

Bored, Alexandra Tottinguer shrugged her shoulders. "Does this have something to do with taxes? If it does, you'll have to ask my husband. I know nothing about our money matters."

"Your husband . . ." Inès let the words trail off. The effect went unnoticed.

Inès pulled another sheet from the file, placed it on top of the first one, and gave it a similar tap. Again, the gesture failed to produce a result.

"Your husband was detained last week for attempting to kill you with a shotgun. Would you like to tell me about that?"

Madame Tottinguer laughed. While not entirely joyous, it was carefree enough for any social occasion.

"Our concierge's husband is very fond of his Calvados. Actually, occasionally, it can be a bit of a problem. He's been known to

305

roam in the middle of the night, ranting. One or two people in the building would like to get rid of them, but I don't agree. That would be wrong." She was earnest. "The concierge is very devoted to the building, and she would have a very hard time finding another job." She looked disappointed when Inès did not nod her agreement.

"You see, what must have happened is that the concierge's husband heard my husband come home late from a business dinner, probably making a bit of noise, misunderstood, and called the police." Madame Tottinguer smiled to ensure Inès's empathy.

"But there were reports that a gun had been fired."

"Really? I had no idea."

"And also that you fled your apartment to seek refuge at your sister's."

Madame Tottinguer chortled. "Refuge for sure, but hardly for me. Both of Marie-Chantal's — my sister — children were sick with a summer flu. The kind that makes them retch all night long. Marie-Chantal was at her wits' end. She hadn't slept a wink in three days. She called me for help. She was silly to have waited so long."

"There's also a woman on the third floor who heard the shots fired and heard your husband shouting at you in the stairwell."

"Is this Madame Durand-Lafriche, who lives on the second floor?"

Inès nodded.

"She's eighty-five and completely gaga. Just like her husband. If you asked either one of them if they'd seen Moses himself coming down the stairs with his stone tablets, they'd tell you they had." She smiled at Inès, as relaxed as if at one of her dinner parties. "You must think we live in an insane asylum. Actually, sometime I do, too. But you know, many of these old buildings in the Sixteenth are like that. There are many elderly people who live in apartments they inherited from their parents. They've lost their sense of proportion. Sometimes it can be a bit taxing, but it does give one a satisfying sense of continuity."

"A sense of continuity, I would think," Inès said faintly. This was a disaster. The woman would reveal nothing. Inès had made a tactical error by letting that imbecile Lambert interview her first. He had probably harped on financial matters and convinced Madame Tottinguer he was some sort of a tax inspector from the fisc. All the people of her class were brought up from childhood to believe the fisc were agents of Satan himself who were to be avoided at all costs. Why hadn't she waited for Capucine? *Damn. Damn. Damn.*

"Anyway, if this is about taxes, you really should speak to my husband. I've never filled out a tax form in my life. It's my husband who knows all about that. He's very busy. The poor dear works *so* hard. Right now he's off on a business trip. But when he's back, I'm sure he'll make the time to see you."

CHAPTER 31

She had no idea why, but Capucine assumed that Régis was a late riser like Alexandre and put off her call to him until ten in the morning. Instead of the sleepy male voice she expected, the phone was answered by a harried young woman. There were several other voices in the background, the most strident of which was that of Régis, who was giving directions. She was interrupting a shoot.

"Who is it?" Régis called out.

"Someone called Capucine. She wants to see you," said the harried woman.

"Great. Have her come here for lunch at one, if she's free. We'll eat the subjects." There was a ripple of dutiful laughter.

Capucine arrived at Régis's street, the rue Legouvé — a block away from the now ultrachic Canal Saint-Martin — at 12:40 p.m. and drove around looking for a legal parking spot. If it had been her own car, she would have been happy enough to leave it at a bus stop, but the last thing she wanted to do was impose a mountain of parking tickets on the person who had so kindly lent the car to David. Finding a legal parking spot, something she'd never attempted even in her student days, turned out to be far more difficult than she imagined.

She went around the block twice, found nothing, went farther afield. At 1:10 p.m., she finally saw a man pulling out of a legal spot in the rue des Récollets and shoe-horned the Renault into the space. She was five long streets away from Régis's studio. Rounding a corner, she saw a teenager snatch the handbag of an elderly woman and sprint in her direction. Capucine ducked back around the corner. As the young man passed her, she stepped out, hooked his raised leg with her foot, and lifted just as he was about to put his weight on his leg. The effect was gratifying. He rose in the air and dropped flat on his face, deeply skinning an arm.

Capucine twisted his uninjured arm in a policeman's lock and prodded him to his feet. The boy, fifteen at the most, limp and soft, sneered at Capucine, saliva leaking out of one side of his mouth.

"*Salope. Vieille conne.* Bitch. Old asshole.

What did you have to do that for? What did
I ever do to you?"

Police phrases, subduing and authorita-
tive, formed themselves automatically.
"Take it easy, son. We're going somewhere
to talk this over quietly." The moment of an
arrest was always electric for Capucine.
Beneath the endorphin rush lay a seabed of
moral vindication. There was no joy sweeter
than that of the altruistic avenger.

Reality kicked open the door to the scene.
She had nowhere to take this perp. If she
turned him over to the local Police Judiciaire brigade, she would be required to
produce ID. When her name was run
through the computer, she would be of far
more interest to the officers than a juvenile
purse snatcher.

She heard the *pan-pon-pan-pon* of a distant police car. She released the boy's arm
and gave him a little push.

"*Tire-toi.* Get the hell out of here."

He reached down to grab the purse.
Capucine kicked his hand away. He looked
at her, his pink gums exposed in a sneer.

"*Connasse. Va te faire foutre.* Bitch. Go
fuck yourself."

He skipped down the street, waving both
arms, giving her the finger. The police siren
got louder. Capucine wondered if someone

311

had seen the incident and called them.

Capucine ran off in the same direction as the juvenile. Thank God she was wearing ballet flats. In less than a minute she was at the door to Régis's building. She realized she still had the woman's bag in her hand. She couldn't think what to do with it. She walked a few doors down the street and looped it over a doorknob. There wasn't the remotest chance the woman would be reunited with her bag, but what else was there to do?

Régis's building had been built as a small factory — there was still a railroad track running down the cobbled entranceway — but had been converted to artists' lofts. Régis's unit was at the back of the building. The door was ajar. She wandered down a long hallway until she reached a vast studio. In the very center, a large table was surrounded by a battery of lights and silk reflectors. In the middle of the forest of equipment sat a large, black, battered video camera, only a few inches above the level of the tabletop. The camera was unattended.

Régis sat at a small table a few feet away, a laptop computer open in front of him. Three women hovered nervously. A third sat in a kitchen area in one corner of the room, sipping coffee from a demitasse.

Régis tapped a button on the laptop. The lights came on with an audible pop. Capucine was impressed that he seemed to be able to run everything from his keyboard.

"All right, children. Seventh take. Here we go," Régis said.

Three oval plates, rimmed with the words CHAROLAIS ALLÔ, were lined up at one end of the table. Each contained a different form of steak with a different side order.

"Giselle, we're looking a little dry here."

A young woman darted over to the steaks and sprayed them with something from a plastic squeegee bottle.

"Perfect," Régis said. He touched a button on the keyboard. "I'm rolling. Action!"

Giselle took up the handle of what looked like a miniature shuffleboard paddle running through a wooden frame. Slowly, she pushed the first steak out into the middle of the table, then the second, stopping a few inches behind the first, then the third, a few inches behind the last. As the steaks were pushed out, slight traces of vapor could be seen rising.

"Cut." Régis touched a key. "Let's see what we've got."

A large, flat computer screen on the far end of the table lit up. A close-up of the steaks appeared. It looked like they were being pushed out on the table by unseen human hands. The vapor, looking like wisps of steam, was more apparent on the screen. The meat was astonishingly inviting, hot, moist, cooked to perfection, more luscious than any steak Capucine had ever eaten.

"It's a good one," Régis said. "Let's do the béarnaise shot, and then we can break for lunch. Antoinette, I need new steak. This stuff is already drying out and beginning to look tough."

Antoinette went to the kitchen area, took a raw steak out of a waist-high refrigerator, held it with a pair of pincers, lit an industrial blowtorch, and charred the steak. In less than a minute it looked like it had been cooked on an outdoor grill. She placed it on one of the Charolais Allô dishes and spooned some fries next to it. The fries tinkled as they landed on the plate, as if they were made of some brittle material. She took the plate to the studio table, plumped the steak up with her fingers and then meticulously arranged the fries in a loose pyramid. She sprayed the plate with her squeegee and gave Régis a thumbs-up.

"Here we go. Action!" Régis said.

The plate began to rotate slowly. Capucine hadn't realized the center section of the table was a lazy Susan.

From his computer terminal, Régis muttered, "Good, good." He looked up. "All right, Véronique, cue the béarnaise."

A woman arrived with an antique English sauceboat. A homely woman in a pink halter, cutoff jeans, hair pulled back in a tight ponytail. She wore no makeup. The lazy Susan stopped. The woman extended her sauceboat in the direction of the plate. The hand that held the sauceboat was a study in perfection, not only as graceful as the hand of a Botticelli Madonna but exquisitely manicured. The nails as pure and luminous as mother of pearl, the skin was ivory white and completely blemish free.

The woman tilted the sauceboat. For a long moment nothing happened. Finally, a large excremental blob of chrome-yellow sauce plopped onto the plate.

"Antoinette!" Régis yelled just as Antoinette was already rushing up to collect the sauceboat and the plate.

There was a moment of calm as Antoinette went to work in the kitchen. Régis caught sight of Capucine.

"Capucine, you're here. How wonderful." He did a double take. "You got adventuresome with your hair."

Capucine could see he was searching in vain for something flattering to say about the new hairdo.

"Don't worry. I'm going back to my usual style. Alexandre hates it."

"Let me introduce the team. This is Giselle. She's the prop girl. And the young one is Daphne, the intern who does all the heavy lifting. And the body and brains behind the exquisite hand is Véronique. She's a full-time hand model and not on our payroll, but I use her all the time. I rarely have faces in my ads, but I almost always include hands."

Antoinette returned with a fresh plate, which she placed on the lazy Susan.

"And this is Antoinette. She's in charge of food prep. She's a genius, by the way. I'd be lost without her."

The scene was repeated. The dish rotated; Véronique arrived with the sauceboat of béarnaise. This time it flowed unctuously. Régis had left the monitor on. The béarnaise was creamy, flecked with dark green speckles, presumably tarragon. Capucine could see herself dipping the perfect fries into the perfect béarnaise. It would be superb. She was half tempted to twist Alexandre's arm into giving Charolais Allô a try.

"Okay, children. Got it on the first take. Brilliant. We're done for the morning. We'll finish the shoot after lunch."

The lights died. Antoinette cleared the stage.

"Where is your old devil of a husband? I'd thought you'd be bringing him."

"He wanted to come but had to go to a restaurant he wants to review."

"In August?" Régis raised his eyebrows in a pantomime of incredulity.

"Was that really béarnaise?" Capucine asked. It looked absolutely delicious. There was a titter of laughter from the women in the room.

"My dear, if you put a real béarnaise under those lights, it would separate in less than fifteen seconds. That's one of Antoinette's secret recipes. Guaranteed not to contain a single edible ingredient."

"Isn't that illegal?"

"Of course not." Régis was slightly offended. "The law is quite clear. A restaurant can't show portions larger than what they serve, but they have every right to make their food look as appetizing as they can. I apply makeup to my actors exactly the same way feature-length movie directors make up their actors. Well, it's true the béarnaise is a bit artificial, but think of it as the stuntman standing in for the real béarnaise." He laughed happily.

The women left, and Antoinette led Capucine and Régis to the kitchen area.

"I'm trying out something new on you. I've figured out a way to make those steaks we shoot edible," Antoinette said.

Capucine sat in front of places that had been laid at the kitchen table. Antoinette produced a platter with two tournedos that looked even more delicious than the ones that had been photographed.

"These are some of the understudies I blowtorched for this morning's shoot. These haven't been sprayed with glycerin, so they're perfectly edible. You know, I freeze the steaks before I run the blowtorch over them, so they stay raw inside. They look more appetizing that way. I take the steaks out of the refrigerator and pop them in a two-hundred-degree oven for forty-five minutes. That's all there is to it. Tell me what you think."

Capucine cut a piece out of her steak. It looked like no steak she'd ever had before. Beneath the crisp, charred exterior left by the blowtorch, the meat was a uniform pink monochrome from top to bottom, with not the slightest variation in hue. It was so tender, Capucine was sure it would melt in her mouth if she sucked on it. Still, delicious as it was, its unnaturalness was slightly unsettling.

Antoinette put another platter on the table.

"Nothing magic about this. I can't serve you the fries. They've been coated with silicone. These are some of the potatoes they sent us. I sliced them up and fried them in duck fat for half an hour with a little diced garlic and chopped parsley. Good old *pommes de terre sarladaises.* Nothing better."

She clunked a bottle of Côtes du Rhône on the table and made for the door.

"I'm glad you dropped by," Régis said, pouring the wine. "I'd been meaning to call you and Alexandre. I looked for the two of you on the dock in Port Grimaud, but I guess you'd already left. It really was unconscionable the way everyone disappeared the instant we docked."

"What happened to Aude? Are you still seeing her?"

"Aude." Régis pursed his lips and squinched his eyebrows together. "She vanished in Port Grimaud. She wouldn't even have lunch with me. I suppose she took the first train back to Paris. I haven't seen her since. I've tried calling a couple of times, but her cell phone goes right to voice mail and her landline has been disconnected. My guess is that she's already in the States, looking for a place to live."

He paused, thinking about Aude.

"Nice girl. Beautiful. But very spacey. You never knew what she was thinking. A lot of the time it was as if she was on another planet." He snapped himself out of his reverie. "No point in worrying about her anymore. You can't win them all."

"So what are you and Alexandre doing with the rest of your summer? You're not back at work, are you? Are the police investigating the death of that poor girl, or has it just been filed away as an accident?"

"As far as I know, there's nothing to file away. The report from the Italian police hasn't arrived yet." At the words "as far as I know," Régis looked at her quizzically but said nothing.

"What an awful night that was," Régis said finally.

"I thought you slept through it all and only woke up when Serge started shouting on the radio."

"Not at all. I couldn't sleep a wink. It was Aude who was tucked into her little corner, sleeping like a princess. I was just lying there, watching Alexandre and Jacques play backgammon on the settee on the other side of the salon. They were trying to be quiet, but it was very easy to hear their conversation. Jacques loves to tease Alexandre, doesn't he? He's very funny when he does it."

"And that was it? Nobody came or went?"

"No one. You were the last person to go on deck and the first person to come below two hours later, when you came to get Serge."

"And you're sure you didn't nod off?"

"Positive. I'm a very light sleeper even in my own bed, much less on a sofa in a public area."

Later, as Capucine left, Régis said, "I'm thinking of throwing a big dinner party next week. You know, a party for *Aoutiens* — those of us who are stuck in Paris for the month of August — particularly my three girls and their husbands and boyfriends, but also my clients who want their ads up on the screen the second everyone gets back from vacation. I'd love it if you and Alexandre could come, and maybe Jacques, too. Are you going to be around next week?"

"Next week? What a shame. Alexandre and I are planning on spending the last week of our vacation in a tiny village near Bandol. We have a friend who has a mas there. It's really too bad. Your dinner party sounds like great fun."

As she was walking to her car, Capucine saw a woman on the opposite sidewalk whom she had met at a cocktail party several months before. The woman looked at her, her lips parted for a greeting. She hesitated, then decided she might not know Capucine, after all. The shock was as if Capucine had been hurled into the Canal Saint-Martin. The new hairdo was nowhere near as effective as she had thought. Capucine felt her blouse sticking to her back from sweat. Hugging the wall, she darted to the safety of the car.

CHAPTER 32

Capucine was upset enough to yank Alexandre away from his lunch before he had had a chance to tuck into his dessert and coffee.

"We have to leave right away. Immediately. I seriously underestimated the risk of coming to Paris. Too many people know us here. This is folly. Come on. Hurry up. Settle the check. We're going back to La Cadière right now."

Alexandre well knew when not to oppose his wife. In less than half an hour they had packed their bags, checked out of the hotel, and were on the E60 autoroute heading south.

Capucine kept to the middle lane, scrupulously keeping the car's speed at exactly eighty-two miles an hour, two miles an hour over the speed limit, neither too fast nor too slow to attract the gendarmes.

By seven in the evening, the sun had sunk

low on the horizon. "We're coming up to Beaune," Alexandre said. "I know the perfect little *bistrot* there. We can just hop in and have a little bite *sur le pouce* — "on our thumbs" — and be back on the road in no time at all."

"*Pas question.* But if you're desperately hungry, we can stop at one of those places on the autoroute."

Alexandre was left speechless as a cow dealt a blow to the head with a sledgehammer. Numb, he allowed himself to be led up the steps of a bridge restaurant spanning the autoroute. He remained mute as they were shown to a table by an impassive teenager with bad skin and handed folio-sized menus laminated in thick plastic, lurid with overbright, polychrome photographs. Capucine was delighted. The menu was even more magic realist than Régis's work.

She was less delighted when the food came. Alexandre's overdone entrecôte was shoe-sole thin and filmed over with a slick of garlicky *beurre composé.* Her fried eggs were mucousy, tasteless, evocative of the postage stamp–size confinement of the hen cage, and the geometrically round circle of ham was so fluorescent, it seemed impossible it could once have been the functioning component of a living creature.

They left the restaurant without a word.

Just before eleven they reached the D559 departmental road, which would lead them to La Cadière and then to the mas. Capucine relaxed, slowed down, rolled the window open. The car filled with the humid, tropical air of the Midi and the smell of wild thyme. In fifteen minutes they were at the mas.

At the sound of the car, David emerged onto the terrace, his finger in a slim book. He wore white linen slacks, a long-sleeved broadcloth white shirt open to the middle of his chest, and white espadrilles. When Capucine emerged from the car, he smiled.

"The hurly-burly of the big city was too much for you, eh? I know the feeling."

Capucine sank into his arms and let herself be enveloped in his hug.

"Are you hungry? Magali made a marvelous pissaladière this evening. Most of it is still left. And there's a half bottle of Ott rosé in the fridge. Why don't you just sit out here and let me get it for you?"

In less than a minute, David was back, balancing a tray laden with plates, cutlery, and the dish of pissaladière in one hand and holding a long-necked bottle and three glasses in the other. The pissaladière was an onion tart topped with a crisscrossed latticework of anchovies and olives. Legend had it that it originated in the area around the Italian border in the days of the Roman Empire. The original pissaladière was apparently made with garum, the fermented fish intestines so prized by the Romans. The anchovies were supposed to evoke that taste. Like all of Magali's cooking, this dish was excellent, silky with umami. Capucine rejoiced in Alexandre's pleasure.

"Where did you eat on your way down?" David asked.

"Don't ask," Capucine warned with a coquettish smile. Things were beginning to fall back into focus.

"One of those bridge restaurants they have over the autoroute," Alexandre said.

"Wow. Even in my flic days I wouldn't eat in one of those places," David said.

"Oddly enough, the frites were quite good. I have to write a piece about that. You can knock yourself out at home making frites, but they are never anywhere near as tasty as the ones made by pimply teenagers with two weeks' experience in a fast-food dive. Asian food is just the same —"

Neither Capucine nor David listened to him.

"How did you make out in Bonifacio?" Capucine asked.

"I think I got all there was to get. But this isn't the time to talk about it. You both look punched out. Let's go to bed. We'll deal with it all tomorrow, after breakfast."

By morning the healing of the mas was nearly complete. Capucine slipped on a silk kimono and, barefoot, padded to the kitchen door, where she heard David chattering with Magali in Provençal. The rhythm seemed so otherworldly, her real problems retreated to the threshold of the imaginary.

Capucine waited for a lull in the conversation and walked in. David had the local press open on the table in front of him, and Magali had gutted several small fish, apparently for lunch.

David smiled up at Capucine and tapped the open newspaper with his knuckle.

"If you believe this, I'm the new powerhouse of the Var. I'm beginning to think my candidature for the Assemblée might not be so unrealistic, after all."

Capucine put her hand on his shoulder and scanned the article.

"For years I've known you had gifts as a politician. I think you can make a real contribution to the country. And I'm sure you will. But I still want to know what you found out in Bonifacio."

David laughed and folded his newspaper. Magali shuffled over and served Capucine café au lait and buttered toast made in the oven.

David waited until Capucine had downed half of her coffee before beginning his report.

"Despite all the tourism, Bonifacio is not too different from my village here. It's run by a hard core who look down their nose at everyone else. I drank a few pastagas with some of the key players, the port captain, the owner of a club called the B' Fifty-Two, the man who runs the mini supermarket at the end of the marina, people like that. After a drink or two, they were all very expansive.

"For openers, your Nathalie was no saint. She was well known in the ports. Last summer she had been half of a skipper-cook combo on a crewed charter boat, a very froufrou fifty-foot catamaran. It was a sweet job. The kind of setup where you get a four-figure tip for two weeks' work, in addition to your salary from the charter company. But one afternoon your girl decided to have a go with the charter customer while his wife was out shopping. The wife got wind of it and got so pissed off, she grabbed her husband by the ear and took off in a taxi. There were no tips that trip. Even worse for her, the skipper, with whom she was sharing a cabin, didn't take kindly to her tryst and threw her off the boat. She hung around the clubs for a while but got warned off one by one. Her look was just too scruffy, and she liked to get sozzled and go in for heavy making out at the bar and then ask for 'little loans' from her marks.

"That was the last anyone saw of her until she turned up again on your boat. The port captain noticed that she almost never went on shore. His guess was that was because she had too many enemies on the lookout for her."

"Serge," David continued, "is also known down there. He bought the port captain drinks a couple of times. The port captain said he was a very nervous sailor, very unsure of himself. Probably shouldn't have been skippering a boat the size of yours."

"He might be a weak sailor, but he's not dumb one," Capucine said. "He made a point of bringing along a crew member who had been a champion racer."

"Yeah, I heard about her, too. Seems there was this bizarro love-hate relationship between her and Serge. Much as he needed it, he couldn't stand when she interfered. His hot button was that she would tie the boat too close to the dock for his taste. She didn't want women to have to take a huge step off the stern to go ashore. And Serge was worried that the stern would bang against the dock if the wind picked up. They were always bickering about it on the dock, the stock joke.

"When you guys went up the steps to the old town, Serge invited the port captain for a pastaga. The port captain tried to get out of it, but Serge was insistent. Serge was after him to check their mooring. The port captain couldn't get over it. 'The guy had so little control, he needed the port captain's sign-off for the most trivial stuff,' he said."

"Did the port captain go look at the boat?"

"Of course not. But he said Serge did. After they finished their drinks, he made a big show of checking not only the stern lines but the bow line, as well. The mooring thing seemed to be a very big issue with Serge.

"That's pretty much it. The port captain said that as he was shutting down the capitainerie, he saw one of your crew, Dominique Berthier, rush down the quai in the direction of the boat, patting his pockets as if he'd forgotten something."

"Did they see him again?"

"No. Because they went to a bar that was on a side street just off the quai that didn't have a good view of the marina. The only

other thing he saw was the boat girl struggling with a supermarket cart from the
mini-market at the port."

"When was this?"

"About twenty minutes into their second
drink."

Capucine looked out the window of the
kitchen and into the hills for a few beats.

"When the port captain went back to his
office, was the cart still there?"

"No, he said it wasn't. It was the sort of
thing he'd notice. He's an old lady about
the neatness of the marina. But you can't
conclude it was your boat girl who took it
back. I checked with the mini-market. It
seems that a good number of their customers just leave the carts on the dock, so they
have a boy who, in addition to helping out
in the back of the store, goes up and down
the dock every couple of hours, bringing in
carts."

That evening, around six thirty, at the magic
moment when the cicadas' sawing quieted
and the colors of the hills began to deepen,
David, Capucine, and Alexandre sat on the
terrace, sipping *perroquets* — apéros made
with pastis and mint syrup. A black Merce-
des with darkly tinted windows rolled up
the road at speed and stopped abruptly in a

shower of pebbles.

Capucine felt her stomach twist more tightly than one of Serge's over-convoluted sailor's knots. She half rose, on the way to disappearing into the house.

The door of the car opened.

"What's for dinner? I'm starved," Jacques said.

Capucine collapsed back in her chair with a thud.

"What's this?" Jacques asked as he arrived on the terrace. "I'm used to being greeted with rose-petal confetti and clanging cymbals, and all I see are dropped jaws dribbling drool. Have I come at an inopportune moment? There's not enough dinner to go around? You were planning a quiet three-some?"

"Jacques, how did you find this place?" Capucine asked. "I never told you where we were."

"Little cousin, it may surprise you, but there are actually things I know that you've never told me. Granted, only a few, but there are still some."

"No, seriously. How did you find out where I was?"

"Maybe it was the all-seeing eye of the DGSE's drones in the sky, or maybe I just know how the mind of my little cousin works better than she knows it herself, and have a computer that can look up names and addresses and a GPS in my car that will take me anywhere. Choose whichever solution pleases you best."

Capucine scowled at him. Alexandre beamed.

"We're having a bouillabaisse," Alexandre said. "David has the most extraordinary cook. You've come to the right place for dinner."

"And to stay for a while, I hope," David said with his vote-winner's smile.

"Who could resist the invitation of a future president of the republic?" Jacques said through his Cheshire cat grin.

A glass was produced for Jacques. By the time it was a third empty, the intimate circle had re-formed. Jacques teased Alexandre, finished Capucine's sentences, and poked fun at David's political aspirations. The strain of the circumstances retreated into the hills with the fading light of the day.

The meal over, David and Alexandre cleared the table and could be heard chatting and washing dishes in the kitchen. Jacques and Capucine strolled through the grounds of the mas.

"Lovely place," Jacques said. "Good to see that David finally got over his thing for his boss, Isabelle — isn't that her name? — and struck out on his own. He has far too much talent for the Police Judiciaire."

"His thing for his boss! Are you kidding? She's definitely . . . And I think he may be, too."

"Little cousin. The things you don't understand. So tell me, are you planning on spending the rest of your life here and becoming David's campaign manager? Mind you, you could do worse."

Capucine laughed. "*Quelle idée.* No, I'll be back at work in a week or two at the most. My greatest concern right now is finding enough *pièces à conviction* for a court case against the murderer."

"Whom you've identified, naturally."

"Of course. It wasn't all that difficult." She paused for a few seconds. "Jacques, it might help if you could tell me exactly what you saw the night of the murder."

"Nothing. I'm sure Alexandre has already told you. He and I were on the little settee in the salon, playing backgammon. The poor guy was so besotted, he couldn't bear to think of himself snoring away while his dear wife was braving the elements on deck."

"He doesn't snore," Capucine lied defensively.

"And when you came down," Jacques

continued, as if she had not spoken, "I saw what you saw. You banged on Serge's cabin door, and he emerged, yawning and stretching, wearing his foulie pants and sea boots, the intrepid sailor, ready for the call of duty on deck."

"At the time, I thought his foul-weather pants were dry. Did you get that impression, too?"

"They looked dry enough to me. Do you suspect him of having had wet dreams?" Jacques's piercing bray shattered the calm of the night. "I hope you're really sure you have the killer tagged. There are some nuances to the case that may have escaped you."

Rather than ask the question directly, Capucine queried with raised eyebrows.

"Nothing so complicated it will give you headaches, *ma belle.* If you suspect whom I think you suspect, you're right. But don't ignore the fact that there are any number of eddies and whirlpools in this case. If you're going to get your boat into port, you're going to have to steer carefully around them, or you just might get sucked under. Don't you just love nautical metaphors? They take me back to those delightful days on the briny."

Capucine could think of absolutely nothing to say.

"And if my mentor will permit me the indulgence of giving her a spot of advice, don't spend too much time skulking around this place. It's lovely and all, but like everyone in our family except my father, you need to feel the pulse of urban living to get your cerebral juices flowing. If Paris is too intimidating, go walk around Bandol. You might see things in a different light. Yes, Bandol would do it. Definitely." He smiled his all-knowing Cheshire cat grin.

"And don't waste too much time with me. I know it's almost a lost cause, but you could have a crack at squeezing some juices, cerebral or whatever you can make work, out of Tubby Hubby. Off to bed with you. I have a little errand to accomplish."

Jacques produced a long, thin panatela, the sort of cigar an evil Latin villain smokes in a thriller, and wandered down the hill to his car. In the darkness of the night the pulsing red glow of the cigar looked like a malevolent red firefly as he talked endlessly into his telephone.

CHAPTER 33

In the morning Jacques was gone. His bed had been slept in, he had left a wry thank-you note for David on the kitchen table, but when Capucine rose at seven, his bed was already cold to the touch. Capucine had an intuition, she had no idea why, that he had been out the evening before, returning only early in the morning.

Capucine accepted a bowl of café au lait from Magali and drank it on the steps of the terrace, watching the colors of the hills lighten as the sun rose.

David dashed out of the house wearing a necktie and a well-pressed tan linen suit.

"Town council. You'd think we'd knock off for August, but we don't. I'll be back for lunch."

Before the rattle of his car had faded, the rasping violins of the cicadas had taken over again. Capucine's thoughts wandered. Jacques had been right. He always was. She had grown away from Paris and the Police Judiciaire. She wasn't altogether sure it was such a bad thing.

This was the kind of woolgathering she loathed. The only way forward was to keep working. And she desperately needed to go forward.

Still, what was the point of Jacques's insistence about the urban experience? Had he been telling her to leave the mas and go back to Paris, or did he want her to go to Bandol? Could it have anything to do with where he had gone last night? If, indeed, he had gone anywhere.

Irritated, Capucine stood up. She needed action, motion, anything but sitting, staring at the hills. She went to the bedroom, dressed in white harem pants, a long-sleeved white linen blouse, which she left unbuttoned to just below the level of her breasts, and white espadrilles with long satin ribbons for laces. It was a look she loved. A look she wouldn't be wearing if she were back in Paris.

Within twenty minutes Capucine was striding down the quai des Baux in Bandol, buoyant with the intention of buying the morning papers, sitting on a terrace overlooking the boats, letting a *bain de foule* — a "people bath" — wash over her.

By the time she was halfway down the quai, she had acquired a large plastic bag filled with four newspapers, three newsmagazines, and a softcover edition of the latest Fred Vargas, but she had yet to find a satisfactory café.

She reached the Bar de la Marine, a broad café with a terrace consisting of four rows of tables surrounded by navy blue canvas director's chairs under a broad white- and blue-striped awning. *Perfect.* As she was about to sit down at a table front and center, she noticed Aude sitting one row back at the opposite end. Aude seemed to be looking at her, at least the infinite depth of her butterfly-wing powdery blue eyes were aimed in Capucine's direction. Capucine smiled and thought — or was it her imagination? — that she received a smile in return.

Capucine crossed the distance between them. When she reached the table, Aude's eyes softened in a complicit look. Capucine pulled out one of the director's chairs and unfolded herself into it. A waiter rushed up with zeal uncharacteristic of cafés on touristy quais. Capucine gave her order for an express. Aude shook her head at the invitation to more Perrier.

"Régis told me you'd already left for the States."

"No. I had to finish an assignment for my boss. I'm going tomorrow."

"Your boss at Lévêque, Fourcade, and Levy?"

Aude nodded fractionally. "I work for Maître Lévêque."

Capucine kicked herself internally. How could Isabelle have missed that? It was exasperating to have to conduct a case at a distance.

"I didn't know you worked for him personally."

"There are six lawyers on his team who do the legwork for him." Aude smiled thinly. This time Capucine was almost sure it really was a smile.

"It's a very fulfilling job. And very gratifying, too. My office is two doors down from my mother's."

"Your mother?" Capucine was aware that the repetition made her sound like a halfwit.

"Yes. My mother is Maître Lévêque's personal assistant. Now that the firm has become so big, it's a very grand job. She even has two secretaries of her own." Aude smiled thinly again.

There was an awkward silence. Or, at

340

least, awkward for Capucine. Aude seemed to be serenely biding her time.

"I'll be on leave while I'm at Harvard. Actually, going there was Maître Lévêque's idea. He made sure I got in. My job will be waiting for me when I get back." She paused, her unblinking eyes fixed on Capucine's for several long beats. "But I'm thinking of leaving private practice and becoming a juge d'instruction when I return. I think that's something that suits my talents far better." Her eyes seemed to demand Capucine's opinion.

"Wouldn't it be a different world without having your mother so close at hand?"

"Oh, I'm sure she'll always be close at hand, as will Maître Lévêque. They've both always been the central elements in my life."

"Does that mean you knew Maître Lévêque as a child?"

"Oh, yes. My mother has always worked for him, as far back as I can remember. And he's always been my mentor." There was an odd emphasis on the word *mentor.*

"How do you mean?"

"You see, my mother was a single mother. She never told me who my father was. I sometimes wonder if she even knows. She has always been completely devoted to Maître Lévêque. He was the cornerstone of our lives even when I was a child. Every summer he'd take two months off to go to his house in Brittany and take us with him. He still does. That was where I just completed my recent assignment for him. He never stops working. . . . Those summers were wonderful." For once, Aude's face reflected an emotion, a deep wistfulness.

"He would dictate letters and memos to my mother and make telephone calls from dawn to lunch. Then he would take me sailing all afternoon. He had — he still does — a wonderful old Brittany sloop with brick-red sails. From when I turned ten, he let me skipper it all by myself while he napped in the cabin."

Aude smiled a hint of a smile, parting her lips slightly, revealing a line of flawless teeth. She leaned back in her director's chair, crossed one slim leg over the other, wagged her perfect foot. Capucine's eye was drawn by the motion. The foot was as shapely as a magazine advertisement, with long, finger-like toes, the nails made lustrous with clear matt lacquer. She wore stylish Gucci leather flip-flops with a black enamel *G* at the intersection of the toe and instep straps. She flapped the sandal on the raised foot, making a barely audible slap against her heel. After a few taps the sandal fell off. For a few seconds Aude languidly caressed the alabaster sole of her foot with the strap of the sandal and then picked it up with her prehensile toes and slipped it on. Capucine was mesmerized by the gesture.

"I think that was the best part of my life. Between the ages of twelve — no, thirteen — and seventeen. Yes, I was happiest then."

Capucine understood the allusion as clearly as if it had been expressed in full.

"Did he abuse you?"

"What a term." She placed two long fingers on the back of Capucine's wrist so delicately that Capucine felt only a tingle in the fuzz on her skin. "Police terminology is an open door to a world of vulgarity. There was no abuse of any sort."

Capucine invited the rest with raised eyebrows.

"It began as slowly as the shore grasses swaying in first breaths of the morning sea breeze. We would sail every afternoon and drop anchor in a secluded bay to have what Maître Lévêque called 'our afternoon tea,' a glass of rosé for him and a Coca-Cola and some cookies for me. Of course, when I was older, I was allowed a glass of rosé diluted with water and there were no more cookies. Usually, we were very tired. Those ancient Brittany boats are hard work to sail. Everything is so heavy.

"That particular afternoon . . . the first afternoon . . ." Aude looked deeply into Capucine's eyes to make sure she was understanding. "Is etched in my brain forever."

Her sandal had slipped off again. She stroked it with her long toes. Slipped it on. "The light came off the ripple of the bay like shards of glass. I had a small splinter in my foot from the rough wood of the boat. He wanted to take it out. It was too small to remove with his finger, so he put my foot in his mouth and drew out the splinter with his teeth. He kept my foot in his mouth and very gently sucked my toes. I couldn't help but notice what was happening to him. I was profoundly affected. Remember, I was thirteen and had, quite by accident, enslaved my and my mother's god.

"Without really knowing what I was doing, I responded by touching him with my toes. It was electric. I could feel his soul flow into me." She fell silent and dropped her sandal again, this time with a loud clack.

"And then?"

"Then? Why, nothing. We sailed home, and I helped *Maman* make dinner. We made *sole à la Bretonne,* as I recall. What happened after was what happened after."

Capucine was mystified. She had no idea why Aude had told her the story. Her only conviction was that her session with Aude was anything but an accident. She wondered how much of a hand Jacques had had in it. Could it possibly have been the reason for his trip to the mas?

"I think I would make a very good juge d'instruction, don't you?"

Aude expected an answer, but Capucine could think of nothing to say. The awkward silence lasted for several beats.

"What if I told you, Commissaire, the instructions I would give you if you were investigating this case for me?" The dreamy tone had vanished, replaced by an authoritarian one that did sound very juge-like. There was another long pause. Aude pierced Capucine with her eyes.

"I would tell you to impound the boat we were on and have a first-rate forensics team give it a very thorough going-over. Not just the usual quick look, Commissaire, that forensics teams consider adequate, but the kind of search that involves dismantling decks and looking deep. Very deep. Do you understand, Commissaire?"

"I do." Capucine was tempted to complete her response with a respectful "madame," but bit it back in the nick of time.

A young man, as golden haired and copper skinned as one of Helios's acolytes, appeared at the side of the table, smiled, and moved off to wait courteously for the women to finish their conversation.

"I'm afraid I must leave you." Aude uncoiled from her seat as gracefully as a sea nymph rising from the foam and bent down to kiss Capucine on the cheek. Capucine sensed rather than felt the alabaster flesh against hers, and she heard the merest murmur in her ear.

"Don't get the wrong impression. I am, and intend to remain, intact until the night of my wedding day."

Aude and the golden young man vaporized into the shimmering heat of the quai.

CHAPTER 34

Capucine leaned back in the director's chair and pianoed the black-painted wooden tabletop for nearly a full minute. The waiter appeared and asked what he could bring her.

"A glass of rosé, if you have it by the glass."

"Bien sûr, madame."

Capucine took a sip of the wine and willed the merry-go-round of unanswerable questions to a stop. She drummed the table for a few more seconds, then extracted her iPhone, checked Inès's number, keyed it into one of the confiscated phones. Inès's secretary put her right through.

"I had an insight into the Nathalie case."

"I can only hope it's an insight that will put you back on the active roster of the PJ. I need you right away. I've had a setback. I was thinking you could come to Paris incogn—"

"Inès, listen. This could be important. Can you to get through to the juge d'instruction in charge of the Nathalie case, Liouville — isn't that his name? — and get him to impound the boat and have a first-rate forensics team give it a very thorough shakedown? It might be useful to have Commissaire Garbe, if he's still assigned to the case, present. I have a hunch that might produce enough evidence for a court case."

"I'll have my secretary send an e-mail. But, frankly, Capucine, it's a complete waste of time. The silly girl went overboard. What's to find on the boat? Anyway, it's bound to have been chartered out again and won't be back for weeks. We can't afford to go on a wild-goose chase. No more distractions. I want you back here right away."

Quietly, calmly, Capucine pressed the red END button. Inès had always been obsessive. Now she had escalated to monomaniacal.

As Capucine drove back to the mas, one of her phones rang. She fished it out of her bag and looked at the screen. Inès. She let the phone fall back into her bag.

At the mas she found that David was still in the village and Alexandre and Magali were side by side, engrossed in the making of an *aïoli garni,* a dish of cod and boiled vegetables served with aïoli. Capucine chafed at being ignored.

Capucine sat at the kitchen table and served herself another glass of rosé. While she diced garlic, Magali regaled Alexandre with a long shaggy-dog tale about the wayward daughter of one of her neighbors. The girl was notorious in the village as a *Marie-couche-toi-là* — a strumpet — but her parents refused to admit the fact. The daughter's favorite tactic was to retire after lunch for a nap, close her bedroom door, and slip out the ground-floor window to an assignation with her lover of the week. Even though her escape was in full view of the neighbors, the parents were so solicitous that if anyone stopped by, they were shushed into whispers, lest they wake the poor girl.

Magali delivered the tagline to the story in Provençal. Alexandre laughed uproariously. Capucine didn't understand a word. Her pique rose another notch. She went to the refrigerator for another glass of rosé, vexed that Alexandre hadn't divined her intent and served her before she had risen. She heard one of her cell phones ringing in her bag in the living room and delighted in ignoring it.

Lunch passed uneventfully. David shared village gossip. The aïoli garni was much praised, proclaimed by David to be the only truly authentic version. The dishes cleared, David returned to the village. Alexandre announced his intention of a short nap and looked hopefully at Capucine, who, still irritated at the imagined slight over the glass of rosé, returned a glassy-eyed stare. Crestfallen, Alexandre retreated to their room.

Thoroughly vexed, Capucine walked into the hills, kicking every sizable stone she came across, ruining a brand-new pair of Zanotti flats in the process. She charged up the steep slope of one of the tallest hills in the area. At the top she bent over, clutching her knees, fighting for breath. The effort broke her pique. She sat down in the grass, grabbed a bunch of wild thyme, crushed the spiny leaves, brought her fist to her nose, and told herself how foolish she was being.

Inès was Inès, the eternal aggressor-victim whose life had always existed, and always would, exclusively between the two poles of her beleaguered self and whomever she was currently hunting. But even if Capucine couldn't afford the risk of going to Paris, she could provide Inès with counsel. Behaving like a hormonal teenager wasn't going to help anyone.

She loped down the hillside, bounded back to the mas, snatched up one of her phones, and dialed Inès's number. The secretary stated crisply that Madame le Juge could not be deranged.

Capucine forbade herself to pout. She went to her room, smiled at Alexandre, who was snoring on the bed, then replaced her clothes with a bikini bottom and T-shirt. At the pool, she pulled off the shirt in a cross-armed feminine gesture, then slid into the sun-heated water. After performing a flip, she crossed the pool underwater. As she broke through to the surface, she could hear one of her phones ringing in her bag. She swam back with a strong breaststroke, retrieved the phone with dripping fingers.

"Capucine, you're more difficult to reach than the president of the republic," Inès said. "I spoke to Commissaire Garbe. It took him only a few minutes to find out that the boat has been chartered to someone who is on a cruise to Majorca and will be back in Port Grimaud in two days. He'll have officers at the dock, waiting to impound it.

"Garbe had important news. It seems a body was found on Isola Piana, a deserted, rocky island off the northeast coast of Sardinia, wedged in between the rocks. There are grounds to think it might be Nathalie. The body's been flown to Cagliari for examination. It's in an advanced state of decomposition, but there were no bullet wounds and the preliminary investigation suggests death by drowning."

Inès paused for a reaction. Capucine said nothing, hanging on to the side of the pool with her elbows, forming a small puddle.

"Commissaire Garbe is being sent down to view the body tomorrow, and I want you to go with him. I've already cleared this with the DGPJ, who have agreed to your participation on the Tottinguer case. The DGPJ took it for granted that this discovery exonerates you from the slightest suspicion of wrongdoing, which, they hastened to underscore, they had never suspected you of in the first place." Inès snorted a laugh.

"Capucine, this is excellent news for us. I want you to fly back from Cagliari as soon as you can and get right to work on Tottinguer. We've wasted far too much time."

At the mention of Tottinguer, Capucine bridled. The news had not registered. It was one of those statements that could not be assimilated immediately, like "It turns out it's not cancer, after all." So much so that she did not fully accept that her world had been restored until she was sitting next to Garbe on an Alitalia flight to Rome, which would connect to a Cagliari flight.

Garbe was one of those old-style flics with a salt-and-pepper crew cut and crow's-feet from squinting and looking tough. He was furious he had not been allowed to bring his Manurhin revolver on the plane, and scowled, touching his empty left armpit every few minutes. His face softened slightly when the meal arrived. He tore off the plastic wrapper and prodded the slice of pâté with his plastic knife. He put a small bit in his mouth.

"*Buerk*. This tastes like cat food. Or at least what I imagine cat food tastes like."

Still, he made quick work of the pâté and attacked the main course, a miniscule plastic bowl of what could well have been *bœuf bourguignon* in an airline caterer's imagination.

"And now the dog food," grumbled Garbe. "You know, Le Tellier, it's a goddamn good thing I only have four months, one week, and two days left before they put me out to pasture. The bullshit is getting too much for me." He finished his meal and eyed Capucine's untouched tray.

"Le Tellier, you're really not going to eat that?" he asked, already switching trays.

In Cagliari they were picked up by two uniformed carabinieri. They squeezed into the backseat of a sit-up-and-beg Fiat police car and rocketed through palm-lined streets, the blaring siren importantly proclaiming that two exalted French police officers had come all the way from Paris on an extremely urgent mission.

The Cagliari morgue resembled every other morgue Capucine had seen: air-conditioning blasting lip-blueing cold, floor-to-ceiling rows of three-by-three-foot stainless-steel doors, toxic miasma of disinfectant. A morgue attendant in a white lab coat checked the names on their IDs against a list on a clipboard, then saluted smartly. Capucine felt herself settle a little deeper back into her skin.

After double-checking his clipboard, the technician stepped up to a door at waist level and pulled out a cantilevered rack supporting a corpse. The body, which had spent two weeks alternately washed by waves and baking in the sun, was in such an advanced stage of decomposition, it was unrecognizable. The eye sockets were empty — no doubt plucked clean by birds — and the flesh was so desiccated, the face looked like an African tribal mask.

The body had been slit open with the

standard autopsy Y-shaped incision, and the organs removed. The top of the cranium had been sawed off, presumably to remove the brain, and then replaced. A loose flap of scalp dangled over the partially visible cranium. The hair color seemed to be more or less the russet brown of Nathalie's hair, and although it was difficult to gauge, the length also seemed to be the same.

A second technician, exuding the authority of someone in charge, came in, looked mournfully at the cadaver, consulted a file.

In fluent but heavily accented French he said, "The autopsy revealed death by drowning. All the signs were there. There was even still a good quantity of water in the lungs. We were asked to make sure she had not been shot, and I can say there is absolutely no question of that. There's not much else of interest. She had eaten a full dinner about six or seven hours before death. There was only a minimal quantity of alcohol in the blood. There was a trace of semen in the vagina, indicating she had had sexual intercourse earlier in the day. There were also unhealed minute tears in the external sphincter of the rectum, indicating she had had sex there recently, most probably the same day."

He looked at the body with basset hound eyes.

"I doubt a reliable physical identification is possible given the state of decomposition. I have prepared a tissue sample for you to take back and give your forensics unit. I understand that the woman's clothes and soiled laundry were sent to France, along with all the evidence the Italian police had obtained. Your forensics people should have no trouble making a DNA link if this person is in fact the victim. I also had our dental expert write a description of the teeth, which could be decisive if you are able to find a dentist who treated her."

As he spoke, Capucine flexed her knees and lowered herself until her eyes were at the level of the corpse's hands.

"I'm virtually sure this is the ring she wore."

On the wedding ring finger of the left hand the corpse wore a ring comprised of three interwoven bands. Capucine had noticed it on the boat. The ring was in the style of the popular Cartier wedding band, except that instead of being made of three different colors of gold, this one was made with three different steel alloys. Of course, now the ring looked very different. Two of the bands were oxidized, one bright orange and the other tarnish black. Only the third band, which seemed to be made of stainless steel, had remained unchanged, even though it was duller than Capucine remembered.

"It might be helpful if we could take the ring back to Paris with us," Garbe said. "With your tissue sample we should be able to make a positive identification in a few days. The forensics people already have a DNA profile, which they were able to establish from vaginal discharge in some of her underwear that hadn't been laundered."

The entire session had taken twenty minutes. In the squad car back to the airport, Garbe stared straight ahead, indifferent to the sights.

"You think it's her?" he asked Capucine.

"Virtually certain. The ring, the hair color, the body morphology. Yes, I'm almost positive."

Garbe nodded and said nothing.

That was the last comment he made until the meal arrived on the Alitalia flight to Milan, a soggy-looking veal scaloppine and an unappetizing mass of spaghetti in a chemically crimson marinara sauce.

"These Italians understand airline food. Now, this is what I call cooking."

Capucine could not help thinking that

Nathalie would undoubtedly have liked it, too.

CHAPTER 35

Capucine arrived at her brigade at six thirty the next morning, a good hour before normal. Only the skeleton night shift was on duty. The uniformed officer at the reception desk saluted her without enthusiasm and glanced at his roster sheet.

"You weren't supposed to be back until next Monday, Commissaire. Don't tell me you got bored on holiday?"

The officers at their desks didn't look up as she walked to her office. Her desk was swept clean except for three pink message slips recording personal calls. Her one captain and three lieutenants apparently had had no problem running the brigade in her absence. A sense of alienation rose in Capucine's stomach like bile. She roved around the brigade, chatting with the officers as they arrived for duty. They were happy enough to see her, greeting a colleague or boss who had returned from vacation, but there was no urgency in their greeting. She was disappointed that there didn't seem to be any problem desperately awaiting her return or any sense of a weakly helmed bark awaiting her steady hand. Worse even, they all seemed oblivious to the calvary she had just been through.

When she returned from a particularly long lap, Capucine was delighted to find Isabelle and Momo in her office.

"We heard you were back," Momo said. "Isabelle thought you'd want a report first thing."

Capucine looked at him. She had an odd sensation of the diametric opposite of déjà vu — *jamais vu* — if that was what it was called. It was as if, familiar as all this was, she had never seen it before.

Attempting to punch through the distancing screen, she put her legs on the table, a gesture that had characterized her meetings with her hard-core brigadiers for years. True to form, Isabelle admired her legs, but the effect was spoiled since there was no David to comment on her Stuart Weitzman studded ballet flats.

Capucine tuned in to Isabelle's monotone reading of her report.

"Neighbors and concierge declined to comment on subject. Local merchants know subject well and are forthcoming on subject's personal specifics. . . ."

Isabelle looked up, checking that Capucine had seized the nuance. Caught up in her enthusiasm, Isabelle abandoned her report.

"You know how it works in these fat-cat neighborhoods like the Sixteenth, right? The merchants force the patrons to cultivate them. You're not going to get the choicest cut of beef or the freshest fish if you don't cross their palms with non-tax-reportable silver, right? These guys like to come across as being all feudal and forelock tugging, but they actually have it in for the richies. And they don't miss a trick."

Isabelle paused for effect.

"It seems our Mrs. Rich–Lacy Pants gets beaten up pretty regularly. The butcher I spoke to — who thinks he's one beautiful, macho dude and God's gift to women, by the way — said that at least once a week she shows up with bruises on her cheek that come from slaps. Like, he's a butcher and should know, right? And then sometimes she comes in with enormous sunglasses, and he figures she's had a whaling, you know, closed-fist punching and all."

Isabelle paused, then went on.

"The other *commerçants* told me pretty

much the same thing, except they weren't as expert with . . . with . . ."

"Meat," Momo said.

Isabelle's eyes shot him a flow of daggers.

The report went on and on. Alexandra Tottinguer was unquestionably a seriously battered woman.

Capucine had lunch in a workers' bistro with her senior officers. The nagging feeling of alienation persisted.

After lunch she drove to Inès's office. For the entire trip she toyed with the idea of canceling the meeting but could find no plausible excuse. Maybe Alexandre was right, and she should quit the force and do something more, more . . . more what? That was the crux of the problem.

When Capucine reported on Isabelle's progress, Inès was elated.

"Frequently assaulted?" Inès rubbed her hands in satisfaction. "Excellent. Just excellent. I can't tell you how pleased I am you're back on the job."

Capucine said nothing.

Inès leaned over her desk to lend force to her words. "I'm going to authorize close surveillance. I want you to put a full team on her around the clock. She's bound to seek medical care before long. I want you to know about it and interview her in whatever ER she winds up in. That's when she'll be at her most vulnerable. You have to convince her the only path to personal safety is to co-operate with me. Put your best people on this."

Capucine groaned inwardly. Complete close surveillance required three teams of six officers. The loss of eighteen officers would wreak havoc with her duty roster. By the time she had reached the car, Capucine decided that assigning the three rookie recruits who would arrive at the end of the week was more than sufficient.

That evening Capucine and Alexandre drove deep into the Bois de Boulogne to Le Pré Catelan, the first of the three-star restaurants to open after their summer closures. Alexandre was ebullient. So ebullient, he had even invited Jacques.

"We owe him for the idea of that dinghy ride, which not only got us out of quite a pickle very elegantly, but was also an adventure I fully intend to regale our grandchildren with."

"Grandchildren?"

"Of course."

"But I thought you thought it was too soon for childr—" They had arrived at the restaurant, and the doorman popped open Capucine's door.

Jacques was already at the table, resplendent in an impeccably cut white linen suit, a Hermès silk square cascading from the breast pocket, a Turnbull & Asser blue-checked shirt open at the throat. He rose, took Capucine in his arms, kissed her cheeks, ran his hand down her back until he reached her Sig Sauer holstered at the back of her trousers.

"Ford's been restored to his flivver. Your *fesses* weren't this rewarding all summer long."

Alexandre glared. Just as he was about to open his mouth to remonstrate, the chef arrived with the maître d'hôtel and fawned over him. Alexandre responded like a puppy whose tummy was tickled, wriggling in pleasure. But beneath the sycophantic eyes, he retained his hardness. He would be fully capable of writing a scathing review if the food did not live up to his expectations.

"Where were you on vacation?" Alexandre asked the chef.

"La Ciotat, a stone's throw away from Marseilles. I had an epiphany of Midi cooking. I've brought the Mediterranean back with me."

Capucine gave Alexandre a sharp look.

"I would be honored if you could comment on my epiphany in your paper."

There was no escaping the tasting menu. The dishes arrived in an endless parade. All fish. The pièce de résistance was a *gelée de bouillabaisse* — a jellied version of the classic Marseilles fish stew. The pudding-like bouillabaisse had been made almost entirely with sardines and was served in enormous flat white plates. Rouille, the traditional garlicky-peppery orange paste that usually accompanied the dish, was served as polka dots in three colors meticulously placed across the tops: creamy white spots of garlic, golden dots of saffron, silver dabs of sardine.

The procession of dishes continued. All made of fish, all surrounded by highly complex mousses, all more titillating than delicious.

Dessert was the ne plus ultra. A perfect product of the laboratory. A flawless green sphere, which could have been apple skin had it not been so seamless. Both Capucine and Jacques were at a loss about how to attack it. Alexandre smiled the tight-lipped smile of a platoon leader about to spearhead a charge out of the trenches, raised his spoon, battered in the top of the orb. Capucine and Jacques leaned over, peering intently. No baby dinosaur emerged. It was an apple soufflé with a heart of ice cream flavored of Carambar, a popular children's caramel candy bar. Capucine finished the entire thing, something she never did with dessert.

As the meal had progressed, Alexandre had swelled. His gravitas, which had atrophied in the past two weeks, had been restored in the space of two hours. The maître d'hôtel arrived at the table and leaned over to stage-whisper in Alexandre's ear. "Chef wonders if you would enjoy coming to the kitchen to meet some of the staff. I also think," he said with a twinkling smile, "he may have prepared a little *surprise* that is not on the menu."

Jacques and Capucine watched Alexandre float off to the kitchen doors, followed by the maître d'. Jacques took a sip of wine.

"Corpulent Consort is like a pig restored to his pond of nitrogenous waste. He's finally recovered from his two weeks of culinary incertitude, a changed man. You, on the other hand . . ."

"What?"

"Seem to be even more troubled than when I pulled you out of the choucroute by pushing you into that dinghy."

Jacques took her hand. "I've always known that rubber was your thing." His braying

366

laugh was a far louder eructation than was acceptable in a three-star restaurant. Heads turned.

Capucine traced a complicated pattern on the starched tablecloth with her fingernail.

"I'm frustrated."

"That doesn't surprise me in the least. No one in the family thinks Portly Partner can possibly meet the demands of your celebrated libido."

Capucine tore off a sharply pointed end of a three-cereal roll that was still on her bread dish and threw it as hard as she could at Jacques. Disappointingly, the soft end made contact, not the pointed end, which would undoubtedly have drawn blood. Heads turned again.

"Let me guess. The wisdom of letting sleeping dogs lie has finally dawned on you. You've figured out who killed poor scruffy Nathalie, but you don't have any hard evidence. Both the powers that be and the hardest taskmaster of all, your inner voice of reason, tell you to drop the non-case. But, like the itch you were told not to scratch as a child, you just can't resist. Is that it?"

"Something like that."

"This is one time you might be advised to listen to that voice of reason."

"Why would you say that?"

"There are many more eddies and currents flowing through this tide than you're aware of."

"Trust me, Jacques, I may just be a humble flatfoot, not a well-placed spook like you, but I think I've been brought up to speed on all the little eddies at work here."

Jacques gave her a long, level look. "So you know that Nathalie Martin was a DST agent?"

"What!" Capucine said loudly enough to make heads turn and glare.

Jacques smiled his Cheshire cat grin at her.

"That can't be right," Capucine said. "We checked her out carefully. There's no doubt at all she was a bona fide boat bum."

Jacques took another sip of wine. "The DST, before it was merged into the magma of the administration's commonweal, had recruiting policies very much like the CIA's. They like to use stringers, people who are kept on very low levels of retainers and lie low, waiting to be called for odd jobs if the need arises. It's cheap and it's secure, even if it's not all that efficient."

Capucine said nothing.

"Almost invariably, these people are socially marginal," Jacques continued, "which is a plus because that makes them undetectable. Of course, their marginality makes them unreliable, and like in the CIA, there are endless cock-ups. They have no discipline and negligible training. Usually, the little training they have is very specific. You know, a little bit about a specific explosive or how to shoot a certain gun. Do you understand?"

"Of course I do. And what was Nathalie's training?"

"She knew how to shoot a Glock."

There was a long pause at the table.

"And had she ever used it?"

"Twice. With satisfactory results, apparently."

"And did she have her Glock with her on the boat?"

"Yes, she did."

"But the Italian police never found it."

"I have a very proprietary attitude about assets belonging to the French government, as you know."

Capucine could see Alexandre returning to the table, his expression of beatific joy cranked up a few notches.

"And what was her 'mission' on the boat?" Capucine asked with leaden quotation marks.

"That, *ma cousine,* is something even I

369

may not fully know. And even if I did, I doubt very much I would tell you."

CHAPTER 36

"You'd think there'd be an airport closer to Saint-Tropez than Marseilles," Garbe said, scraping the last of the pâté out of the tiny airline dish with his plastic knife. Capucine handed him her untouched luncheon tray.

"It's only forty-five miles away. We'll rent a car and be at the marina in less than an hour."

"And then what? We stand around all day and watch the forensics guys work? And our juge wanted not one, but two commissaires on hand? I'm goddamn glad I only have a hundred and twenty-three days of this bullshit before I haul my ass out of the force." In irritation he patted his empty left armpit, failing to reassure himself his Manurhin was there.

"I think her idea was to have me there so I could make sure they dismantle everything, right down to the water and gas tanks. And you had to be there because you're in charge of the case."

Garbe made a moue. It was not clear if it was at Capucine's comment or Air France's version of *blanquette de veau.*

"Right. I'm going to be a big help. I've never been on one of these boats in my life. And your basic forensics unit needs prodding to be thorough. What the hell. The good thought is that the day after tomorrow it will be less than a month. I can start counting down in weeks."

Diomede was easy enough to find in the almost empty maintenance area of the marina. Perched on stilted cradles, her deck was almost twenty feet off the ground. Men in filmy white jumpsuits scrambled up and down two willowy stepladders.

In the heat, Garbe had removed his suit jacket, which he held in a crooked index finger over his shoulder.

"Fuck this. No way in hell I'm going up there."

"I doubt either one of us would be welcome."

Capucine walked over to the boat and yelled up in the general direction of the deck. "How far along are you? Have you found anything you want to talk to us about?"

A man in his middle fifties, wearing half-frame reading glasses, peered over the side.

"You Commissaire Garbe?" he asked in a rolling Marseilles accent so thick *commissaire* came out as a four-syllable word.

"No. I'm Commissaire Le Tellier."

"Yeah. I forgot. The e-mail said there were going to be two of you. Obviously, we're finding stuff. We've been at it since before dawn this morning. What I don't know yet is if it has any relevance to your case. Why don't you two go find some lunch or something and come back in the late afternoon? Then I'll tell you what I ca—

"*Non, Jean, attention!* Don't use a blow-torch there. You'll melt the fiberglass. Cut it away with a hacksaw."

As they walked across the bone-dry cement lot, Capucine saw a small crane crawl toward *Diomede* and lift off a large stainless-steel canister, which had to be one of the two-hundred-gallon water tanks.

Driven by a sense of duty, they ate at a sad, empty little café in the marina service yard that provided a full view of *Diomede.* They both ordered the *gambas,* which turned out to be shrimp so oversize, they could have gotten into the ring with lobsters. The slightly metallic taste of frozen seafood cut through the unctuousness of a heavy garlic and herb sauce made thick with olive oil, but they were definitely welcome, particularly with an ice-cold bottle of Sancerre. Capucine smiled at the fact that she was sitting in one of the most famous areas of the Riviera, eating Brittany shrimp and drinking Loire Valley wine. Still, it was pleasant enough.

"So, are you going to stay in Paris after you retire?"

Garbe perked up. This was the top-of-mind subject.

"Nope. I have a little house in the *département* of Cantal, smack in the middle of the Auvergne."

"Are you a *Cantalou* by origin?"

"Lord, no. I'm a *Parigot.* I was born and raised in Paris. But I don't like people, and I do like the country. I bought my little place years ago. I'm doing my part for the republic. Cantal is the most depopulated region of France."

"And you're repopulating it?"

Garbe smiled. "*Si tu veux.* If you want. Fifteen years ago I bought eighteen acres, which are around a nice stone house, which is around a nice stone fireplace. It was cheap enough that I could afford the mortgage on a lieutenant's salary. The mortgage has been paid off for three years already. And now, in

374

exactly four months and one day, I'm going to move down there and be so far away from all this bullshit, it will seem like it never existed."

Capucine sensed he was warming up to a diatribe on his life philosophy, which she guessed was based on the fact that all you needed to beat the system was to be tough enough. But just as he got going, his lips tightened and he jerked his head in the direction of the café's window. The senior forensics technician was walking across the dusty cement toward them, a large plastic box in his hand.

The technician walked over to their table, pulled out a chair, asked the man behind the bar for a *demi* — a half-liter glass of beer.

"I think we've found what you asked us to look for, but we're still digging. Anyhow, since you came all the way down here, I reckoned I'd have a beer with you guys and tell you where we are."

How different the Provençal approach to life was than the Parisian one. In Paris the forensics unit would have been as secretive as a cabal of alchemists, would have remained utterly silent for at least a week, and would have communicated their findings in a dry, impenetrably complex memorandum.

The technician took a deep swig of his beer, put the plastic box on the table, hiked his eyebrows, and opened the lid. Putting his hand inside, he said, "Abracadabra," produced a plastic evidence bag, and waved it in front of them at eye level.

Capucine leaned forward and examined the bag. Actually, there were two bags. Inside the police-issue evidence bag was a commercial freezer bag, easily identifiable by its two-color sliding closure. The bag on the inside was mottled with shiny aluminum fingerprint powder, making it difficult to see what it contained.

Capucine held her hand out. The technician handed her the bag.

"Please, look but don't open it. We found this bag when we cut open one of the water tanks. It's been in water for a good bit of time, and the latent prints have been washed off and are not coming up with powder. I still need to get it under a high-power Luma-Lite and do some other little tricks we have back at the lab."

Close up, Capucine could see a luminescent jade juju so brightly colored, it could have been plastic. A dark strand, undoubtedly sweat-stained rawhide, could be clearly discerned passing through a round hole drilled in the pendant, which had also been dusted with aluminum powder.

Capucine handed back the bag and let the gesture ask the question.

"My guess was that someone put the little jade amulet in the bag, rolled it up, and shoved it down the deck opening of the water tank. Pretty good hiding place since there's no other opening to the tank. We cut open all the tanks on the boat — the other water tank, the fuel tank, and the holding tanks for the crappers. Nothing in any of them. Is this what you wanted?"

Capucine nodded. "The fingerprints may prove decisive."

"Good. Because just with the powder, there is a good set of latents. Two different people. When I get back to the shop, I'll see if the computer can ID them, and I'll get back to you on that tonight."

This definitely wasn't Paris. That was for sure. In Paris it would have taken a week.

"Did you find anything else?"

"There's a stainless-steel cable that runs from the point of the bow to the top of the mast. One of my guys sails a lot. He tells me it's called a forestay and helps hold the mast up and is used to fly the front sail, the jib. Anyway, on this particular boat there's a device you can use to wrap this jib around the forestay. We unfurled the sail and had a very careful look at the cable. There's a strand that's come unraveled, and it has what we think is blood on it. It's a long strand, and the bloodstains go up a good half an inch. Looks like someone was hanging on that cable and got quite a cut. We'll type the blood and get a DNA profile back at the lab."

"Did you guys find anything else?" Garbe asked.

"What do you think? It's a rental boat, so it's like a hotel room. People come and go. They clean them after each rental, I suppose. But that doesn't mean we aren't going to pick up traces of pretty much everyone who's been on the boat for at least the last six months or more. When I finally finish my report, which is bound to be at least fifty pages long, I'll send it to you. You can read it at night, and it will put you to sleep."

He called for another demi, presumably to dull the grim thought of having to dictate a fifty-page report.

When the beer came, the technician looked from one police officer to the other.

"I'll tell you one thing, though, that might interest you. There's a tiny little cabin in the front of the boat. My man, the one who's the big sailor, tells me that on big boats like that, there's always a bit of unus-

378

able space in the bow. It seems that the area is usually used to store sails, but sometimes they're turned into a small cabin for a teenager or a professional hand."

He paused to see if they understood. Capucine nodded. Garbe seemed to have floated off to the Auvergne.

"There's a bunk in there, all right. But the rest of the cabin is filled with a sail bag. My guy, the sailor, tells me it's something called a spinnaker. The way he describes it, it's a sort of parachute-like thing that can be used to pull the boat downwind. Apparently, it's considerably more complicated than that. He says they're optional extras for charters and not all that common. We checked the bag out. We have a portable Luma-Lite, which is nowhere near as effective as the big one we have back at the lab, but it can still show some stuff. There is a stain on this particular bag that looks very much like semen to me. Of course, that's just a guess, but we're taking the bag in to the lab. If it turns out to be semen, I'll give you a preliminary DNA breakdown when I send my report in tonight."

The technician downed the rest of his second beer and stood up.

"I have to get back. We'll be done in half an hour. A rough draft of my report will be on your computers before you get home, but it will take two weeks for the final boring tome to reach you."

He turned to leave and then swung back.

"You know, an administrative problem is going to crop up here. We've taken that boat apart pretty thoroughly, and we're sure as hell not going to put it back together. The owners are bound to complain. The Paris PJ will deal with the complaint, right?"

He slipped out the door, clicked it shut.

Garbe snapped himself back from the Auvergne. Capucine could see it took two jolts, and he wasn't all that happy to be back when he finally arrived.

"So does that give you what you need?" Garbe asked Capucine.

"It will, if the fingerprints and the DNA of the blood on the forestay check out."

"You know as well as I do they will. So we're going to be making an arrest?"

"As soon as the forensics report arrives."

"But we're arresting only the fall guy, right?"

"Fall guy? What fall guy? We're going to arrest the man who killed the victim. The perp." Capucine glared at him.

"And we're going forget about the loose ends, right?"

Capucine continued to glare at him.

"Let me ask you a question, Le Tellier," Garbe said. "You don't really think that the perp went to the trouble of shoving his little ornament into the water tank — and took the trouble to seal it in a plastic bag before he did — just so no one would find it, do you? Especially when it would be so easy to throw overboard."

"Of course not. Someone found it and hid it."

"And that someone would not be the same person who planted the shell casing that came from your gun, would it?"

"No, it wouldn't," Capucine said through clenched teeth. "But none of those two or more people committed any crime other than tampering with evidence. They certainly didn't kill anyone. And our job is to catch serious criminals and make sure they get the punishment they deserve."

"Punishment they deserve, eh. Well, I'll tell you one thing, Commissaire." He gave Capucine's title an ironic twist. "You and I are going to have to tune our violins very carefully, because if those 'two or more people' emerge in the court case, your perp is going to walk. You understand that, right?"

Capucine said nothing. Her jaw was so tightly clenched, the muscles stood out.

"My suggestion would be to say that the pendant was found somewhere at the front of the boat. There's a compartment that holds the anchor chain, isn't there?"

Capucine nodded.

"There you go. And you can tell your pal, the juge d'instruction, to make sure that forensics aren't put on the stand and that the defense never finds out about the shell casing." Garbe smiled innocently. "But, hey, don't get me wrong. With only a hundred and twenty-nine days to go, the last thing I need to do is open up a can of worms. So I'm right behind you on this one. Trust me on that."

Even before he had finished the sentence, Garbe's eyes lost their sharp focus and Capucine could see him transporting himself back to the Auvergne.

CHAPTER 37

Capucine slid her little Twingo into the no-parking funds delivery area in front of a Société Générale bank on the rue des Archives. It was 5:45 in the morning. The area was completely deserted. She stopped behind a nondescript gray Peugeot, which shouted out Police Judiciaire car pool. Garbe got out of the Peugeot and opened the door of Capucine's car with an extravagant smile. The smile was a first. He made a theatrical bow of welcome, revealing a heavy pistol in a sweat-darkened shoulder holster. He patted it affectionately.

"I'm guessing this is going to be my last arrest. One more goddamn thing I'll never have to do again."

They turned the corner and walked down the rue Sainte-Croix ·de la Bretonnerie. After seventy yards the street became so narrow that even a compact car would have a hard time squeezing through. Isabelle waited for them, leaning against the blue enameled door of a *porte cochère* recessed into a carved stone doorway. Capucine could see Momo a hundred yards down the street, leaning up against another doorway, a cigarette dangling from his mouth.

Garbe nodded in approval at the setup. Even though he had one leg out the door, he was still a flic at heart.

Capucine and Garbe had a desultory chat, frequently checking their watches. At exactly 5:57 a.m., they strode down the street. Momo joined them in front of a red-painted double door.

Isabelle pushed a small button nested in a chased brass frame. There was a rasping buzz, and the door popped open three inches. Momo pushed it fully open. As Garbe crossed the threshold, he reached under his suit jacket and popped the safety strap off his holster with an audible snap.

The door swung shut behind them, leaving them in a perfectly dark hallway, chilly and damp after the warm morning air outside. Two small, rectangular red lights shone out at them like the squinting eyes of a succubus. Momo pressed one of them, and the door popped open again.

"Merde," he said and pressed the other one. There was a loud clunk, and all the lights in the hallway and stairwell went on. They faced a set of ancient-looking bars running from floor to ceiling, with a small barred door in the middle.

"I've got my passkeys," Isabelle said, pulling out a large ring of keys.

Momo pursed his lips and shook his head. He went up to the door, grabbed a bar in each of his ham-size fists, and shook, testing for give. The muscles of his back bunched. He heaved. With a metallic ping, the door opened. Garbe nodded in approval again.

Without the slightest attempt at stealth, the four officers clumped up two flights of an ancient, once-elegant stairwell. Shabby as the building was, Capucine knew the apartments in that part of the Marais were very pricey.

Three floors up they arrived at a landing that had once been a delicate oak parquet but was now a jumble of badly repaired boards wobbling under their feet. The right-hand door was freshly painted and displayed a brand-new brass plaque engraved with the number ten. The paint on the left-hand door was peeling, and there was no number. Isabelle advanced to the right and stationed herself well off to one side. Capucine and Garbe fanned out and took positions a few feet to either side of the door. Garbe slipped his hand under his jacket but did not draw his pistol. Momo retreated four steps down the stairwell and flattened himself against the wall.

Garbe nodded. Isabelle stepped up and hammered loudly on the door with the heel of her fist. The sound rolled down the stairway. Nothing happened. Garbe nodded again. Isabelle hammered a second time. Capucine could hear a door opening on the floor below.

"Police! Ouvrez!" Garbe thundered in a deep bass. The door on the floor below clicked shut.

Nothing happened for several very long beats. Just as Isabelle was about to resume pounding, the door opened wide. Sleepy eyed, wearing a pair of jeans and a candy-pink T-shirt marked SAINT-TROPEZ in white, flowing letters, Serge opened the door.

Garbe's hand fell out of his jacket, and he stepped past Isabelle into the apartment. Serge recoiled, retreating from Garbe's advance.

"It's against the law for you to come in here before nine," Serge said, still retreating.

Garbe gave a bark of dry laughter. "That's searching, my friend, not arresting. We're not allowed to search your apartment between nine at night and six in the morning, but we can arrest you twenty-four-seven. And, anyway, it's after six." Garbe was clearly enjoying himself.

Capucine stepped into the apartment.

Serge's eyes saucered when he saw her.

"Capucine! What's going on? We're friends. We've known each other for years. I went to your wedding." The statement was so naïve, it was almost credible.

"But that didn't stop you from committing murder less than fifty feet away from me."

Serge's eyes opened even wider, but he said nothing. Both the commissaires expected more of a reaction. They both relaxed. Serge continued to inch backward, as if cowering. Then, in a lightning move, he feinted, slipped around the three officers, and darted out the door. No one gave chase.

They heard a shout and then a thud from the stairwell. Momo had caught him by the arm and had swung him against the wall. In a few seconds Serge appeared doubled over, walking on duck legs, his handcuffed hands lifted high above his back, the three links of chain connecting the cuffs enveloped in Momo's massive fist.

"Since you know the law so well, I won't have to tell you that resisting arrest is also a crime. If I wasn't in such a good mood, I'd be charging you with that, as well. But keep it up and I'll change my mind," Garbe said.

They took him to the Quai des Orfèvres and marched him up the stairs to La Crim', on the third floor of Escalier A. Isabelle and Momo held his arms, and Garbe followed behind. Capucine took the elevator. She wanted to let Garbe savor his moment unshared.

Isabelle and Momo had both worked at La Crim' for years before they left to follow Capucine to her commissariat, so they knew the procedures inside and out. They took Serge to a holding cell, removed his handcuffs, shoved him in, and found a desk to fill out the paperwork. Garbe and Capucine went off to breakfast at a corner café. It was not yet seven in the morning.

When they returned forty-five minutes later, they found that Serge had been transferred to one of the Quai's many interrogation rooms. In her days at La Crim', Capucine had always found the rooms medieval. Located in a sub-basement of the fort-like building, they were adjacent to the Seine and well below water level. They found the room. Garbe rapped on the damp steel door with his knuckles. A six-inch square judas creaked open and immediately shut again. A heavy bolt protested as it was pulled, and door opened with a rasp. Serge sat at a wooden table, in a cone of light from a shaded bulb hanging from the ceiling. Beyond the cone, the light progressively diminished to near obscurity at the peeling walls.

A uniformed officer stood behind Serge. Another lurked in a corner. Garbe gestured with his head that they were to leave.

"*Menottes?* Cuffs?" the officer asked.

Garbe shook his head.

The officer removed the cuffs and let them dangle from his finger. Both officers left the room, slamming the door shut with a clanging ring of finality. Much as Capucine detested the notion of so-called enhanced interrogations, she had to admit the mise-en-scène was as perfect as if created by a film director.

Serge massaged his wrists, easing the pain of the handcuffs. Two livid red rings were visible. The cuffs had been applied too tightly. They always were by the Police Judiciaire.

"Serge," Capucine said, "you've been arrested for the premeditated murder of Nathalie Martin."

Serge looked back at her with a self-assured smile. He was a long way away from being worried. They would ask him a few questions. His lawyer would arrive and have him released. He would have dinner in one of his bars that night. Over the coming months his lawyer would make it all go away. He put his hands in his pockets and crossed his legs under the table.

"Serge, let's talk about the events leading up to the crime. While you were waiting for us all to arrive at Port Grimaud, you had a little fling with Nathalie and shacked up in one of the two cabins with big beds. Isn't that right?"

"You got it. She was hot, over sixteen, far more than willing, and I'm not married. We used the cabin I gave you and Alexandre, but don't worry. I had Nathalie wash the sheets at a Laundromat before you slept on them." Serge was pleased with his cynical humor. "Was it your flic's second sense that told you that?"

"No. When we got there, your and Nathalie's body language spoke volumes. Also, when you gave us the tour of the boat and we peeked into her tiny cabin in the bow, there was none of her musky smell. It was obvious she had never slept there."

"Musky smell. Good way to put it. That

was her, all right. She was continually in heat.

"Things went well until we got to Bonifacio. Then Nathalie had a little dinnertime tryst with Dominique, and you found out about it."

Serge sat bolt upright on his stool. His face transformed into a Kabuki mask of rage. He clenched his fists hard enough to make the knuckles white.

"You're crazy. She'd never waste her time with a limp-wristed faggot like him."

"So you knew she'd had a fling, but you didn't know with whom."

"You're just guessing."

"When we went up to the old town to go shopping, you stayed behind and told us you'd meet us later. You went on the boat and heard Nathalie having sex."

"Nonsense. I was at a café on the port, having an apéro with the port captain. He's a longtime pal. He'll confirm that."

"We interviewed him. You two did have a drink. Then you wanted him to come examine your mooring. You told him you thought Florence had moored the boat too close to the dock, and you wanted the port captain to order you to move it away a foot or two."

Serge said nothing.

"The port captain refused and went home

to his dinner. You went down the quai and checked out the boat. When you finished with the stern lines, you went to the bow to examine that mooring line. That was when you heard Nathalie in the forepeak."

Serge said nothing but worked hard at keeping his face expressionless.

"That's why you killed her. Your jealousy took over. You couldn't stand the fact that she was sleeping with someone else. You stalked her. You lay in wait for her on the foredeck, and at the first opportunity, you put her over the side and let her drown."

He snorted a bravado laugh. "Conjecture. Not even conjecture. Guesswork. Hell, it's not even guesswork. It's just a wild stab in the dark."

Slowly, almost sadly, Capucine shook her head. "We have proof." Capucine paused to heighten the drama of the announcement. She paused a few beats too long.

"What proof?" Serge asked belligerently.

"Your jade amulet was found on the fore-deck. The thong had been broken, and Nathalie's clear fingerprints were superimposed on your hazy ones. It's conclusive that Nathalie wrenched the amulet off your neck."

For a brief split second Serge recoiled, his eyes dancing around the dim room, looking for a means of escape. Then he relaxed and assumed a sly look.

"She did rip it off my neck. Before you all arrived, we made love once or twice on the foredeck. Great stuff. You should try it sometime. Nathalie was a screamer. The second time we did it, she had a particularly intense orgasm." He smirked proudly. "She grabbed ahold of my amulet, and the thong broke. Voilà. That's how it got there."

Capucine gave him a mocking smile. "Of course. You made love in the crowded marina of Port Grimaud, in full view of all the people on boats only a few feet away. If there were any truth to that, you really would have had a few directives from a port captain. And the jade pendant just sat there, forgotten for two days even though the decks were thoroughly hosed down twice? No judges or juries are ever going to believe that one."

Serge deflated.

"And there's more. A long steel strand had come unraveled on the forestay. There was blood on the strand with DNA that matched Nathalie's. The blood was far enough up on the strand to indicate a deep cut. When Nathalie's body was recovered, there was a cut on the palm of her left hand consistent with the wire strand. The nature of the cut strongly suggests violence."

Serge's worry level skyrocketed. Despite the chill of the room, his brow was moist and his eyes quested for an escape route.

"Serge, listen to me. You have two choices here. Either you can cooperate with us and tell us your version of what happened or we will have no alternative but to have you remanded for premeditated murder. With the evidence there is no question you'd be convicted for the maximum penalty, life with no possibility of parole or remission for good behavior."

Serge panicked. He had never come close to thinking the consequences could be this severe. His breathing rate increased. His face became damp and pasty.

Garbe materialized from the shadows and eased gently in front of Capucine. He was reassuringly avuncular. His jacket was thrown over his left shoulder, hooked on an index finger. His stomach ballooned. He was a kindly, mature man anxious to help. He invited confidences.

Capucine retreated soundlessly into a dark corner of the room, realizing her role of bad cop had been shelved for the moment.

Garbe smiled protectively at Serge.

"Women are incapable of understanding men, don't you think?"

Serge didn't know what to say.

"I reckon it's because we have completely different equipment in our pants. Me, I completely understand why you had it in for that little bitch. I'd have had it in for her, too, if she'd cheated on me like that."

"But I didn't have it in for her. It was she who had it in for me."

"How do you mean?"

"Capucine is right. I did go on board that afternoon in Bonifacio. It's a thing I have. I like to stand on the dock and see how the boat is riding when it's moored. I like to check if the mooring lines are chafing. Good skippers do that, right?"

Garbe nodded encouragingly.

"So when I go up on the bow, I notice that the screen is pulled across the hatch into Nathalie's cabin. In the daytime. That's not normal. I wonder why. I try to open the hatch to have a look. But it's locked from inside. My first thought is that she's having a nap and I might join her."

Serge looked at Garbe with pleading eyes.

"You know, I thought it would be a lot more fun to spend dinnertime with her than in a restaurant, eating bad pizza. Who wouldn't, right?"

"Of course. Any man would."

"So I knocked. There was no answer. I

knocked again. After about three times I thought something was wrong and I really started pounding. I guess I was getting pissed off, too. So I say real loud, 'I'm going to get a screwdriver and open this thing.' See, there is a little screwdriver slot in the lock so you can open it from the outside. But I hear, 'No. Go away. I'm tired, and I want to sleep. Just let me be.'

"As I'm about to go, I think I hear whispering down there. I'm about to get seriously pissed off, but then I think, 'No, she's a little fucked up maybe, but she's a good kid at heart, and nobody would be stupid enough to screw two guys on the same boat.' I go up the stairs to the old town, but all the while I'm thinking and thinking. I just couldn't stop thinking about it. And when we all get back on the boat, Nathalie keeps avoiding me. She won't even look at me. Like I'd done something bad to her."

He stopped short.

"Look, I don't know why I'm telling you all this. You don't have a case here. I should just let my lawyer deal with the court."

"Look, my friend, let me tell you why you're telling me what you have to tell me. It's because you're not dumb. Commissaire Le Tellier is right. All she has to do is write up what she's got, take it to the juge d'instruction, and you'd find yourself in La Santé Prison, where you'd never get out. The only way you'd ever see the sky again is from the inside of a little exercise cage they have there in the courtyard, where you get to walk in little circles for half an hour a day."

Garbe paused for nearly fifteen seconds to let this sink in.

"But I like you. You seem to be a regular guy. I'd like to get my elbows up on a bar with you someday and have a beer or two."

Garbe paused again. There was no doubt his sense of timing was impeccable.

"In France we understand love. Judges understand love. You were legitimately enraged at this bitch. I can see why you wanted to slap her around. The bitch deserved it. So she fell overboard. The judge is probably going to see that as an accident."

Capucine was sure that Serge was never going to fall for a ruse so simple a child would see through it. But Garbe knew his business.

Serge put his face in his hands, the infallible sign that the suspect was about to confess. He wanted to confess. He needed to confess. He desperately wanted to reach out to someone and be helped, but he was still lacking the final quarter of an ounce of courage to do it.

Garbe put his large liver-spotted hand on Serge's shoulder.

"*Allez, vieux.* Come on, old boy. Let's get you out of this mess."

Serge sat up straight on the little stool and turned to face Garbe.

"It wasn't like that at all. I had to talk to her. I wasn't going to spend the next two weeks on a boat with someone who'd turn her back every time she saw me. Especially if it was a really hot girl I actually liked a lot. Do you understand?"

Serge looked pleadingly into Garbe's eyes to see if he was getting it.

Garbe nodded like an uncle.

"So what I did was to slide out of the little Plexiglas hatch in my cabin that night. It's an incredibly tight fit, and at one point I thought I'd got stuck, because I had my foulie pants on. So I pulled off the suspenders and wriggled out of the pants. Good thing I didn't have my jeans on under the foulies, or I'd probably still be stuck in that hatch." Serge laughed and quickly sobered. "That would probably be more fun than sitting here, though." He paused again, thought it over. "So, on deck I went forward and sat down with my back against the mast. I knew I'd be invisible there — it was a really dark night — and sooner or later Nathalie would come up to the bow to take a pee. I guess I must have fallen asleep — or passed out, probably. I'd had a hell of a lot to drink, I was so upset."

"Who wouldn't?"

"And then I got woken up by the rain. There weren't many drops, but they were so big, they almost hurt. And then there was this little flicker of lightning on the horizon, and I saw Nathalie. She was in a big hurry, ripping off her foulie jacket and climbing up on the bow pulpit like a monkey. Then she's hanging on to the forestay with one hand and pulling down her foulie pants with the other."

He stopped and smirked conspiratorially at Garbe. "Don't get me wrong, but it was quite a view in the flashes of lightning. She looked really hot like that, with her legs spread open while she was hanging way out over the bow of the boat."

Garbe leered back at him, man-to-man. "So what'd you do?"

"Nothing for a moment. I didn't know what to do. I wasn't sure what she was up to. Your average girl just sort of squats down and pees over the side. I figured maybe she was going to take a dump, but why wouldn't she use one of the heads below? So, anyway, nothing happens and she's kind of moaning up there, so I go up to her to see if she's okay.

" 'Get the hell away from me,' she says in this little voice when she recognizes me, and I say, 'Nathalie, we really need to talk. I like you a lot, and I have this feeling that I've annoyed you somehow.'

"And she gets really pissed off at me. I mean, *really* put out. She starts telling me I'm such a loser, I can't even see she's in serious pain. So I get in close and ask her what's wrong.

" 'Just go away,' she says, and I ask her if she want me to get her meds. Then she gets really nasty and starts saying things like, 'Loser, get the fuck away from me,' and stuff like that."

Serge was reliving the scene, his face contorted in anguish.

"So like an idiot, I keep trying to help her, you know, asking what's wrong and things like that. It was then that she said it. She goes, 'You fucking loser, when you were banging on my hatch like a total asshole this afternoon, I was getting boned by a guy. We were both trying so hard not to laugh, I thought we'd explode.'

"I didn't get it. So she goes on. 'And to get me to quiet down, this guy rolls me off

400

the bunk onto the spinnaker bag and pushes my face into it. And when he's got me half suffocated, he slides his bone up my ass. How do you like that, loser? While you're up there, knocking on the hatch like a little kid, this guy is butt fucking me. And he was pretty good at it, too. But he had a load like a horse, and now I've got a serious case of the runs. So just get out of here and let me take my crap.'

"It was at that point that I went berserk. I grabbed her ankles and started shaking her back and forth. She went crazy, too, and leaned forward to hit me, but all she managed to do was grab my amulet. I pushed her legs to get her off of me, and she went into the sea. Just like that."

He paused and looked down at the table-top for several long beats.

"It was an accident, I guess. I honestly don't know what I was trying to do. It just happened. That was all."

Capucine came up to the table. He looked up at her with innocent, childlike eyes.

"What's going to happen to me, Capucine?"

CHAPTER 38

"I congratulate you on your arrest of Serge. An absolutely brilliant deduction," Inès said over Capucine's office telephone.

"It wasn't exactly a deduc—"

"Actually, I was calling to invite you to dinner. To celebrate. Could you free yourself tonight? There's a wonderful restaurant around the corner from my apartment in the Fifteenth. It's where I take myself when I feel I deserve a reward."

Capucine demurred — she had planned on attending a restaurant opening bash with Alexandre — but acquiesced in the end. This was so unlike Inès, something had to be up.

The restaurant was fifties-style Japanese, so far off the beaten track that Capucine and Inès were the only customers. The walls were covered with looming black- and gold-foil wallpaper. A large fish tank in the middle of the room contained a single lonely koi daubed with bloodred splotches. An ageless Japanese waiter materialized in a well-pressed tuxedo. After greeting Inès by name, he led them to a corner table and handed them oversize tooled-leather menus listing a handful of Japanese cliché dishes.

"This is my favorite restaurant," Inès said. "You should bring Alexandre to give him a special treat."

A couple, sketched in varying shades of gray, arrived. The male looked like a mid- to low-level functionary, and the female like someone whose main activity was a daily visit to a Carrefour supermarket. They sat at a small table, not exchanging a word or even looking at each other.

"Let's order. I'm ravenous," Inès said. She beckoned the waiter over and asked for teriyaki. Capucine chose the *gyoza* — pan-fried dumplings — a safer bet. Cresting on her enthusiasm, Inès ordered a series of side dishes, *nikujaga,* or beef stew, *kakuni,* or stewed pork, and *nizakana,* braised fish. The waiter diligently scribbled Japanese ideograms on his pad and then hovered.

"Oh yes, the wine. Capucine, why don't you order that? You're the expert."

Capucine looked at the list of five or six wines on the last page of the menu and opted for the Sancerre, another safe bet.

Dinner started with miso soup, which hadn't been ordered. The Sancerre was tepid. Capucine was tempted to send her soup back and ask for a properly chilled bottle of wine but decided letting the evening find its own pace was the sagest course of action.

Inès took a sip of her soup — "so delicate" — and gave Capucine an earnest look.

"I had lunch today with Juge Léonville. He's very pleased with your arrest and the confession you obtained."

"It was all Garbe's work," Capucine said.

Inès seemed not to hear.

"He has asked me to consult on the preparation of the file that will go to the prosecutor." She paused, waiting, almost daring Capucine to say something. There was a long silence. The waiter arrived, assuming they had finished their soup. He lingered for a second, then vanished, leaving them to their miso.

"On one level, it's a very straightforward case, a crime of lustful passion. But on another there are, ahh, *nuances* that could prove troublesome." She again looked at Capucine, defying her to comment.

"And, in fact, there is even a third level. I was present and could even be construed as the intended victim. It's in everyone's interest, even Serge's, to obtain a speedy, reasoned conviction. Don't you agree?"

Capucine was spared answering by the arrival of the waiter with an enormous tray. Dishes were placed on the table with the speed of a croupier dealing cards. The waiter left wordlessly.

"Léonville — and I, for that matter — is of the opinion that Serge needs to be interviewed by him, not only because it is standard in such matters, but to make sure Serge understands where his best interests lie. We would like to arrange an interview with Léonville and myself acting as juges, and with you and — what's the man's name? — yes, Garbe, present, representing the police."

Inès attacked her teriyaki inexpertly with chopsticks, refusing to meet Capucine's eyes.

Later that night, Capucine sat alone in her kitchen, nibbling tinned foie gras on pieces of toasted baguette and sipping a half bottle of properly chilled Lupiac while waiting for Alexandre to come home.

Two days later, Capucine received a call from Inès.

"Léonville would like to interview Monnot" — Capucine noticed he was no longer

Serge in Inès's lexicon — "in his office tomorrow afternoon. He would like you and Garbe to be present. Of course, I'll be there, too."

When Capucine arrived, she discovered Serge in the hallway, on a long oak bench, handcuffed, sitting between two blue-uniformed prison warders. He wore a suit, clean but somewhat rumpled, and a wrinkled, tieless shirt. He was freshly shaved, his hair was neatly slicked down with water, but his eyes were as vacant as if he had been lobotomized. Catching sight of Capucine, he looked up at her in cowed expectancy. She smiled and walked through the door to Léonville's office.

Léonville sat behind his desk, with Inès facing him. Garbe sat in a corner, oblivious, clearly daydreaming about his retirement.

"Commissaire, I felicitate you on your arrest," Léonville said. "In fact, I congratulate you on your handling of the entire case. Your subtlety is matched only by your efficiency."

Inès beamed as if one of her pupils was being praised. Léonville pushed a button on his phone. "Okay, Céleste. Have the prisoner brought in."

The two warders escorted Serge into the room, loosely holding him by the upper arms. They sat him in a dark-wood, upright

406

armchair, while showing exaggerated respect to both juges. They removed Serge's handcuffs, retreated, presumably to stand guard in the outer office while waiting to be summoned to return their ward to prison.

Léonville's secretary entered the room, a laptop under her arm, and made to sit at a small table in the corner.

Léonville lifted a hand, palm outward. "Céleste, that won't be necessary." Wordlessly, the secretary left, closing the door behind her so softly, it made no noise at all.

Capucine was mildly surprised. The law required the juge d'instruction's examination of an indicted suspect to be noted and kept in the file. Still, the juge's powers were vast, and a stenographer clicking away at a keyboard was bound to create a certain amount of tension.

The interview took over two hours. Léonville assumed a tone of an older brother gently cajoling a younger sibling to tell about a minor, possibly even charming, peccadillo he had been too embarrassed to reveal to his parents.

Léonville took Serge through the incidents three times. Each time, Serge told his story without the slightest variation of the facts. However, with each telling, his affection for Nathalie became more and more evident. It was obvious he had fallen into a deep crush. Whether fueled by love or lust, his feelings for the girl were very real. At the third telling, his sense of regret and loss became palpable.

Léonville gave him a thin but friendly smile.

"You're very convincing. I'm persuaded the death was a tragic accident. Unfortunately, some sort of court decision will be required. I'm going to have the case sent to the Cour d'Assises. What do you think, Madame le Juge?" he asked Inès. She nodded.

Léonville returned his gaze to Serge. "It's a lower court than the Tribunal de Grande Instance and is used for less serious cases. The file I will deliver to the procureur will state the incident was involuntary homicide and will recommend every possible clemency."

Serge's shoulders dropped in relief.

Inès intervened. "But it is essential that you appear to be as cooperative as possible with the judges. The manifestation of your regret may even lead them to suspend your sentence altogether. Or if there is a jail sentence, it will be a very short one, and you'll be out in a matter of months. Do you understand?"

"Oui, madame," Serge answered meekly.

Once Serge had been escorted out of the office by the warders, Léonville turned to Inès.

"You were right. He's as hormonal as a teenager. He's also very charismatic. That's an important point. The judges should have no difficulty reaching a decision."

Inès turned to Capucine and smiled politely, even condescendingly. It was a smile of dismissal. Capucine rose, as did Garbe behind her. They walked down the hallway side by side.

"Drink?" Garbe asked. "I sure as hell need one, and I only have three weeks of this BS left."

They found a café and stood at the bar. Garbe ordered cognac and with his eyes invited Capucine to join him. He sank the double in one go and raised his index finger at the man behind the bar for another round.

"When I have to sit through crap like this, I wonder how I lasted my thirty-five years."

"What do you mean?"

"Christ, Le Tellier. You know the date for the court case is already set, right?"

"Yes."

"Have you been ordered to appear?"

"No."

"Well, I have."

"That's because you're in charge of the case and made the arrest."

Garbe blew air out of his lips and ordered a third cognac.

"And not because I have nothing to say about jade amulets or shell casings? But you might. Isn't that right, Commissaire?"

Capucine said nothing.

"Another drink?"

"Please."

The drinks came.

"Don't get me wrong, Le Tellier. The last thing I want is for this case to get remanded to a higher level of bullshit so they can make me work for another six months or more. But when the brown stuff is up to your neck and you're actually treading in it, it still turns your stomach. How many years you got left? The rate you're going, you're going to make *commissaire principal* or even *commissaire divisionnaire.* In jobs like that, I hear the *scheisse* comes right up to your eyeballs."

He threw a fifty-euro note on the bar and strode out without waiting for the change.

Capucine decided to be present at the trial, something she never did unless she was notified that she would be called as a witness. She was surprised to see that the case would be tried at the Tribunal de Grande Instance, after all, despite Léonville's promise. Of course, she said to herself as she walked through the imposing gilt and iron gates and up the massive stone steps to the imposing courthouse, *The ways of the magistrates are highly convoluted, and there may be some technicality that prevented a trial in the lower court.*

The courtroom, with its elaborately carved nineteenth-century oak paneling, was even more imposing than the exterior of the building.

Capucine was one of the first to arrive. She chose a seat on a bench almost at the back of the spectators' gallery. The room filled rapidly with spectators, who occupied all but the last two rows. There was a hush when ten magistrate's assistants arrived in judicial robes with starched white bibs. They lined up behind the raised semicircular dais, almost six feet above the level of the parquet below. Next arrived the nine jurors, dressed in somber street clothes, who took up position standing behind their chairs at either end of the dais. Finally, the three judges entered, resplendent in red and black robes, topped by medieval-looking velvet caps, and stood at the center of the dais, looking severely down at the spectators.

Despite the dramatis personae, the whole thing took less than half an hour, and most of that was stage setting. The presiding judge, identifiable by the extra gold trim on her cap, sat down, followed — with a loud rumbling of chairs and coughs — by everyone else at the dais. The presiding judge fussily arranged her robe, straightening her bib so the bloodred ribbon of the Legion of Honor and the cerulean-blue one of the Order of Merit were in clear view.

Serge was brought in by two gendarmes and seated on a small wooden dock at floor level. The gendarmes, at attention, sat behind him. He looked frightened and unsure of himself.

The presiding judge spoke to a man in judicial robes who stood on the parquet opposite the dock. Since time immemorial neither the prosecutor nor the defending attorney was given a seat. Instead, they roamed, gesticulating, during the entire trial.

"So, Monsieur le Procureur, now that we have heard the accusation, you may present your case."

Striding around the room, waving his arm for emphasis, the procureur read Serge's confession with dramatic pauses and a heightened inflection of key words. It was almost a caricature performance, but the bland statement couched in Police Judiciaire officialese came vibrantly alive. There was good reason that barristers and actors shared a club in London; it was the same métier. Behind the words, Serge came across as an arch villain, dominated by uncontrollable sexual appetites and rages.

The defense attorney opened his mouth to speak but was silenced by the raised hand of the presiding judge.

"Have the accused rise," she ordered.

Timidly, Serge stood up.

"Do you acknowledge that your confession is a true and accurate representation of the facts as they occurred and that you signed the document of your own free will, without coercion in any form?"

"I do, Madame le Juge."

"It's *Madame le Président,*" hissed the defense attorney, loudly enough to make a few of the spectators titter. The judge silenced them with a glance.

"And how do you plead?"

"I plead guilty, Madame le Président."

"*Je vous en prie, Maître,* you wanted to say something," the president said with a thin smile to the defense attorney.

"*Merci, Président.* The defense has no

reservations regarding the validity of either the confession or the plea, but it would like to be reassured about the bona fides of the jurisdictional issue."

"My dear colleague," the procureur said to the defense attorney, "how apropos of you to raise that issue. I was just about to call our first witness, *Capitaine de Vaisseau* Gilles de Bottin, of the SHOM, the Service Hydrographique et Océanographique de la Marine Nationale."

A lean and fit man in his early forties stepped onto the witness stand, a slightly raised podium surrounded by a semicircular wooden rail, directly in front of the judges' dais. The shoulder boards of his navy blue uniform bore five gold bands, signifying he held a rank equivalent to colonel in the army. He stood stiff and erect, almost at attention. The president looked down at him from her Olympian height.

"Capitaine de Vaisseau," she said, tapping a thick file on the dais, "the crime in this case occurred in the Strait of Bonifacio. I understand the dividing line between French and Italian waters runs more or less through the middle of that strait. Is that correct?"

"Oui, Madame le Président."

"And given that the body of the victim

was recovered on the beach of . . ." Purely for show, she put on a pair of half-glasses and consulted the file. "Isola Piana, a deserted island off the northeast coast of Sardinia, is it possible the incident occurred in Italian waters? Are you able to shed light on the matter?"

"I am, Madame le Président. In our view, the incident took place well within French waters. If I can abuse the patience of the court, perhaps I could be allowed to show a chart that will illustrate our conviction."

"Bien sûr, Capitaine. Proceed."

Four sailors in baggy white jumpers with tar-flap bibs over the back marched stiffly into the courtroom. One erected an easel at a forty-five-degree angle to the three judges, two others placed a large marine chart on it, and the fourth stood stiffly, holding a large plastic tube. The chart showed the area between the southern coast of Corsica and the northern coast of Sardinia. A long red line and a large black dot had been placed on the chart. The officer stepped out of the witness stand and placed his finger on the black dot.

"This is the position the boat gave when they called the Porto Cervo port captain's office." He pointed to a thick dotted line. "And this line is the course they were following. It stands to reason that the victim went overboard between ten and thirty minutes before the person who made the radio call noted the position on the boat's GPS. In other words, the incident happened at some point along this portion of the red line."

He looked up at the president, who said nothing.

The sailor popped open the long tube and pinned a large piece of clear plastic film over the chart. The film was covered with swirling blue and red arrows.

"These are the winds and currents of that particular evening. Currents in blue, winds in red."

The three judges leaned over the dais, examining the chart.

"We ran a computer simulation to model the course of the body."

The sailor affixed another sheet of film. There was a multitude of almost parallel lines leading to the southwest from the red line. The captain tapped his finger on the island where Nathalie's body was found.

"As you can see," he said, tracing a path back to the red line, "the victim went overboard precisely here. Fifty-eight point three nautical miles into French territorial waters."

The presiding judge made a note with a gold pen and then looked right and left at the two other judges. Both nodded.

"So there is no question that the incident occurred in French waters?"

"None whatsoever, Madame le Président."

The judge looked in the direction of the defense attorney.

"Does this exposition satisfy you, Maître?"

"Certainly, Président. What higher authority in these matters could exist than the Marine Nationale?"

The four sailors packed up their paraphernalia and left.

The president made a few more notes and then conferred in whispers with the judges on either side. There was a sense of expectancy in the room. She capped her pen with an audible click.

"*Très bien.* The case is clear. We will retire to chambers with the members of the jury and will return to pronounce sentence."

The three judges donned their caps and filed out, followed by the assistants and then the members of the jury. In the courtroom, the whispers of the spectators crescendoed like a rising wind into a chorus of outspoken comments. Capucine looked around the room. In the opposite corner she could see Inès staring at her lap, apparently reading something. The door opened a crack, and the procureur de la République de Paris slipped through, looking dapper in a trim lightweight brown suit, a blue-checked shirt, and a navy blue silk tie. Capucine recognized the hierarchical head of the Paris magistrature by sight. He sat in the row behind Inès. Capucine thought the two exchanged a complicit look.

The door behind the dais opened, and the troop of black robes and dark blue street clothes returned.

"The accused will rise," the president ordered.

Sure of himself, Serge rose, the hint of an expectant smile on his lips.

"Accused, we have deliberated this most heinous crime and are as dismayed as we are shocked. Your conduct reveals not only utter disregard for human life but also a disdain for womankind. It is abundantly clear that having bullied a defenseless, almost destitute woman, who worked long hours in your service, you took multiple sexual liberties with her. Because of your social and financial position in life, you felt it was your privilege to enjoy the freedom of her body." She paused to let this sink in to the court.

"And when you had taken your fill of

pleasure from that body and had grown bored with it, you were faced with, what was for you, the tediousness, for lack of a better word, of the chagrin of a servant on your luxurious vessel. You then engineered a confrontation in the middle of the night that resulted in the violent death of your lover, a woman who had served you faithfully with her nautical skill and" — she paused and lowered her voice dramatically — "her pulchritude." She paused again to let the court absorb her disdain.

"In my view, there is abundant evidence here of premeditated murder." She cast a sharp glance at the judge to her left, who wore no medals. "But the court is not in unanimous agreement in that regard. Therefore, we pronounce you guilty of willful homicide."

There was a murmur in the spectators' gallery, which the president stifled with a glance.

"The court sentences you to the maximum penalty allowable by law. Ten years' incarceration."

"No!" Serge shouted. "I've been tricked. This is unfair. I retract my confession. I retract my plea! I want a new trial!"

The two gendarmes grabbed his arms roughly. The murmuring in the spectators' gallery rolled like the breaking wave of a flock of birds taking off.

"Control yourself, monsieur," the president said, sneering at Serge. "The court is closed." She rose and left, followed by the two other judges and the covey of participants. Serge was handcuffed and led through a door behind the prisoners' dock.

In the hallway outside the courtroom, Capucine caught sight of Inès, who looked away from her and attempted to disappear into the crowd. Capucine rushed up and grabbed her upper arm. Inès pulled away, furious.

"You sold him down the river," Capucine said.

Inès shrugged her shoulders with Gallic indifference.

"Inès, Serge was a fool, not a criminal. But you offered him up like a sacrificial lamb for God knows what political tricks you have up your sleeve."

"Without sacrificial lambs the mechanics of the world would squeak to a stop like a machine without oil." She jerked away from Capucine, eyes glinting madly.

"What happened had to have happened. In any case, a miscreant is a miscreant, and I have no patience with them. There is one fewer of them loose on the streets, and that's to the good. Now that this nonsense is finally over, I need to get back to work." Inès shot Capucine a savage look. "I need to get back to work to salvage a case that I was already inches away from bringing to bay. A case in which I lost a precious opportunity because you let your senseless concerns and sensitivities stand in the way of justice. Now, let me go and do my job."

She gave Capucine an even more acid look. "And thank your lucky stars that you even have a job." She paused and shot a stream of chef's knives into Capucine's eyes. "Without my indulgence, it could have so easily been you in the van on the way to La Santé."

Chapter 39

Capucine bolted down the long marble staircase of the courthouse, her mind a vortex of resentment that she had been drafted into the very cabal of power brokers she had joined the Police Judiciaire to escape in the first place. But outside in the sun, her thoughts aligned themselves like a line of rising dominoes. There was only one culprit in this story, her. Serge's case was a no-brainer. All he had had to do was retain a mediatized defense lawyer. The lawyer would have had a field day overturning the case against Serge, painting a lurid tableau of police brutality while obtaining a confession under duress, portraying Nathalie as a gold-digging slag who frequently victimized yacht charterers, then charcoaling a sketch of a drunken quarrel on a wet deck, undoubtedly provoked by Nathalie, which resulted in a tragic accident. And if Serge had thought to mention Capucine's discovery of the jade pendant at any point in his interrogation, the defense lawyer could certainly have used it to create an artistic, soft-focus depth to his handiwork.

There was only one reason this miracle-working lawyer had not appeared and could not have. And that was her. Serge had believed Capucine was speaking through Inès when she bade him be as cooperative as possible and not rock the boat of justice in any way. As a result, Serge had not raised a finger to help himself and now would have his life scarred irreparably by a decadelong jail sentence.

Not only was her guilt overwhelming, but the very purpose of Capucine's life had been compromised. She didn't even know where to go. Certainly not to her brigade. Nor to her empty apartment. Nor anywhere.

She extracted her phone from her bag and pressed Alexandre's speed dial.

"Chérie!" Alexandre exclaimed happily.

"Buy me lunch."

"Right now? It's not even eleven."

"Right now."

"I know just the place."

They met at the outdoor terrace of the Louvre restaurant facing I. M. Pei's pyramid in the Cour Napoléon. The terrace was sparsely populated with tourists drinking café au lait and smirking at the herds of other tourists milling around the pyramid. Alexandre ordered a bottle of champagne.

"The court case didn't work out, did it?"

"He got ten years."

"Good Lord." There was a long pause. Alexandre studied the straight lines of tiny bubbles rising to the top of his flute. "How long before they let him out?"

"Not less than six. Probably eight or so."

Another long silence. Alexandre was visibly imagining the implications of going to jail in your thirties and coming out in your forties, saddled with the full stigma French society imposed on ex-convicts. Alexandre poured himself another glass.

Capucine let the impact of the court's decision lie heavy on the table. They stayed until three, lunching inside in the dramatically Rothkoed walls of the restaurant, then returning outside to the terrace for another bottle of champagne. The alcoholic buzz did little more than palliate the pain, but it was enough. She touched the speed-dial icon for her brigade.

"Commissaire, finally!" the receptionist said. "The Ministry of the Interior has called three times. *Conseiller* Bufo would like to invite you to tea in his office at four this afternoon. Shall I call and tell them you're coming?"

Capucine started to say no, but then decided, *Either you play the game or you don't.* The middle ground never worked.

She wondered what Bufo wanted. She'd met him once before. He was the cabinet member in charge of the country's various police forces and internal intelligence services. Their last meeting had been disastrous. She had been summoned with great pomp to be congratulated on her cleverness in solving a case as if she had specifically set out to shield a shady crony of the administration. Capucine had finally exploded when she was told she was to be decorated with the Légion d'honneur for her "service to the state," storming out of Bufo's office, the door resonating like a cannon blast.

Capucine didn't know what to expect. There had been no repercussions for insulting a dignitary in the stratosphere of the government, but on the other hand, she had never received the decoration, either.

She entered his enormous office with its gilt-trimmed paneling and automobile-size Louis XV desk, undoubtedly an original period piece. French windows overlooked the cool green garden of the Hôtel de Beauvau. One of them was ajar, and the pleasant scent of fresh-mowed grass filled the large room. Despite the sense of peace, Capucine approached Bufo's desk with trepidation.

Bufo's suety face beamed up at her, appraising. His pulpy lips simpered.

"Sit down, Commissaire, please do. This is the second time I've come across the brilliance of your work. And the second time I've summoned you to congratulate you. The last time we met, you refused a decoration. I was impressed with your humility."

His brow pleated into flabby folds, and the leer straightened out.

"Even though you refuse public accolades, I can assure you the government has every intention of persevering in rewarding you for your zeal."

The puddingy smile was back.

"I have personally dictated a note of commendation, which will appear in your file, over my signature, moving you up several notches in the promotion ranking."

Capucine groaned inwardly.

He paused and looked at Capucine flatly. She felt like a dragonfly alighting on the imagined safety of a lily pad, only to discover that a viscid toad already had its tongue out to flick her up.

"And I also made sure that your file makes no mention whatsoever of the fact that at

426

one point some dolt in your service might actually have had the preposterous idea that you could have been a suspect in the case." He laughed uproariously at the enormity of the dolt in question's stupidity, the fat on his protuberant stomach roiling like a sea calming down after a storm.

"And to what do I owe this?"

Bufo looked at her as if he did not understand the question. Eyebrows raised in innocence, he said, "Why, for purging the case of its extraneous complications and going straight for a pragmatic denouement."

"Extraneous complications?"

"Coyness is not generally viewed as an attribute in a policeman, Commissaire. Shell casings, jade amulets, things that had really nothing to do with the case." He smiled cynically at her, his flaccid lips squeezed into an obscene moue. "Commissaire, you fully deserve the early promotion you'll receive." He leaned over the table conspiratorially. "I wouldn't be at all surprised if you become the youngest commissaire divisionnaire in the Police Judiciaire."

He went on. Capucine didn't listen. She realized she was being conscripted into the ranks of senior police officers who were also government toadies. Her blood boiled. Bufo misunderstood her reaction.

"I can see you are concerned, Commissaire. Put your mind at rest. The shell casing from your gun is long gone, consigned to the oubliettes of the administration, from whence it will never return."

Capucine felt her hand strain to grab an ornate inkwell on the desk and hurl it into Bufo's flaccid face. At great expense she managed to construct a simulacrum of a smile. She rose.

"Monsieur le Conseiller, thank you for your time. This has been an extremely illuminating meeting."

Chapter 40

"They're here," the uniformed receptionist announced. "Capitaine Bourlon has the suspect in interrogation room A."

Capucine put her coffee down and walked down the hall to one of her two interrogation rooms. Both of the rooms had been redecorated in motel pastel blandness when Capucine had taken over the brigade. Capitaine Bourlon sat behind a vaguely Scandinavian blond-wood table; a uniformed brigadier stood in the far corner. Dominique sat on a hard-edged folding metal chair, chosen for its lack of comfort.

He attempted to stand up when he caught sight of Capucine, but the brigadier pushed him back down.

"Capucine," Dominique said. "What am I doing here? Am I under arrest?"

"Not for the moment," Capucine said. "You're about to be interviewed about your involvement in the murder of Nathalie

Martin."

"What are you talking about? You know I had nothing to do with that. I read in the paper that Serge had been convicted. This is ridiculous." His pitch rose.

"Let's start at the beginning. You had been having sex with Nathalie."

"Yeah, right, with my wife on board. Capucine, how do you dream these things up?"

"I dream them up from DNA analysis. There was semen on the spinnaker bag in Nathalie's cabin and trace deposits of semen in her anus. Both match your DNA perfectly." Capucine stared him down with a long stony look. She told herself she had become a convincing fibber. The police had no samples of Dominique's DNA. Of course, before the interview was over, a blood sample would be taken from Dominique, and Capucine had not the slightest doubt the match would be perfect.

"All right, okay, so I *did* have a little fling with her. She was available. And I definitely wasn't getting any from my soon to be ex-wife. All that skinny bitch cares about is her job. If you're not getting it at home, you get it where you can, right?" He stopped. His brows furrowed.

"Anyway, the fact that I was humping

some skank doesn't implicate me in her murder, now does it?" The words dribbled out of his mouth, damp with cynicism.

"It gives you a motive to kill her. The night she died, you were stalking her. You were hiding in her cabin, waiting for her to come off watch so you could have another go."

"Wh . . . why would you think that?"

"When I looked into her cabin while we were searching for her, I saw deep footprints impressed in her bed."

"That must have been Serge."

"No, he was passed out, sitting against the mast. It was you waiting for her."

"Look, this is all conjecture. There's no evidence of anything here. I shagged the girl. Big deal. Now I want to call my lawyer so he can get me out of here. I've had enough of this crap."

"This is a murder investigation. You have no right to have a lawyer at present. You'll be able to speak to your lawyer only after we indict you."

"Capucine, look. Please listen. I haven't done anything. You've got to believe me."

Capucine gave him her stoniest look. There was a very long silence.

"All right, I'll tell you. I *was* in Nathalie's cabin. I *was* waiting for her. Angélique had been on my back all day. You saw that. I was horny. I had it in for Angélique. I needed a good pop to calm me down. What's so bad about that?"

"Dominique, be very careful. Remember that lying to the police is a crime in and of itself." Capucine paused to let this sink in. "Did you see Serge kill Nathalie?"

"N—" There was a fifteen-second pause, and then in a tiny, almost inaudible voice, he said, "Yes." Another pause, then, in a slightly louder voice, he added, "Maybe. I'm not really sure what I saw. It was a very dark night. You remember, right? All of a sudden Nathalie appeared right above where I was standing. And she slips her foulie pants down, and I'm saying to myself, 'This is a great view' and 'Maybe I can talk her into coming down for a quickie.' But just as I'm about to open the hatch, I see someone walk up to her. I'm pretty sure it was Serge, but it was really dark. And I hear some talking, but I couldn't make out what they were saying through the hatch. Then I see whoever it was lean forward. I assumed he was trying to kiss her, and then I realized there was only one person up there. Nathalie had gone. That's the truth, Capucine. I swear it."

"What else did you see?"

"After a few seconds the person left my

field of view. Then, a few minutes later, someone came up and started yelling for Nathalie. I think that must have been you."

"And why didn't you mention this at the time? If you'd given the alarm right away, we might even have saved her."

"Come on, Capucine. How was I going to do that? Tell everyone on the boat that I was waiting in her cabin to shag her?"

Capucine looked at Capitaine Bourlon. "*Non-assistance à personne en danger.* Refusal to give assistance to a person in danger." They both knew the term so well, there was no need to articulate it. In France it was very serious.

Bourlon nodded.

"What?" Dominique asked sharply.

"Refusing assistance is a very serious business. It's going to have to go in the transcript of testimony, which you're going to sign when we finish."

"Now, wait just a minu—"

Capucine held up her hand to silence him.

"What did you do next?"

"Nothing. I figured everyone would come up on deck to look for Nathalie, so I just hung out and then went running around with the gang."

Capucine looked at Bourlon. "Finger-prints."

Bourlon nodded, stood up, and left the room. He reappeared almost instantly, followed by a uniformed officer carrying a long, flat metal box. Dominique recoiled in his chair.

"Don't worry. We're not going to hurt you. It's an electronic fingerprint reader. You won't even get your fingers dirty."

The officer rolled Dominique's fingers one by one over the long glass rectangle on the box's top. When he was finished, he looked at Capucine. "Commissaire, it won't take me longer than five minutes."

In fact, it took seven minutes for the officer to return and hand Capucine a file. "Eighteen points of comparison. Three more than needed." He left the room.

Capucine opened the file, flipped through the pages, and smiled a tight smile at Bourlon, who smiled thinly back.

Capucine looked stonily at Dominique and drummed on the file.

"Dominique, coupled with the crime you've already admitted, this is going to send you to prison for twenty years."

Dominique blanched.

"I want you to be perfectly honest with me. At some point earlier in the day you stole my pistol and used it to shoot at Nathalie that night."

"No, no, never. I'd never shoot anyone. Never."

"When the Italian police searched the boat, they found a shell casing in the scuppers of the bow area." She handed Dominique a page-size glossy photo. "This is the shell casing. It has your fingerprints on it. No court in the country would fail to believe that you shot at her. You certainly had the motive. You had just seen your lover kissing a rival."

"Capucine, wait. Wait. Please. Let me explain."

Capucine said nothing.

"I took your gun *after* Nathalie had gone overboard. *After.* Do you understand?"

"Why did you take it?"

There was a painful silence.

"Why did you take it?"

Dominique looked wildly around the room, scrabbling for a way out. He realized he had just painted himself into a corner.

"Look, Capucine, you've got to believe me. I didn't do it for myself. I . . . I did it because I was told to —" Dominique cut himself off. He realized his corner had become even tighter.

"Who told you to?"

Another long silence. More panicked searching of the walls.

"My uncle."

"Your uncle?"

"Well, he's not really my uncle. He's the husband of my mother's cousin. He's a very important man. He has a very senior job in a ministry. He knows I'm always broke because that horrible bitch wife of mine doesn't let me have any money, and every now and then he helps me out. He's a good guy."

"Which ministry?"

Dominique sagged in relief. They were going to talk about the uncle and not what had happened on the boat.

"The Ministry of the Interior."

"And what does he do there?"

"He's the personal assistant to a cabinet member. It's a very important position," Dominique said, the pride showing through.

"Which cabinet member?"

"A man called Bufo." This was great. The boat was going away from the story. Far away.

"And he told you to do this while you were in Nathalie's cabin in the middle of the ocean?"

Dominique laughed. Things were definitely coming back his way. He was getting off the hook.

"He texted me. On my BlackBerry."

Or maybe he wasn't all that off the hook.

"He texted you just like that?"

"No, you don't understand. A week before we left, there was a big Sunday lunch at my uncle's house in Versailles. I told them all about our trip, who was going, where we were going. Stuff like that. They have a huge place with a beautiful garden. I like to go there to paint."

Capucine stopped him with an open hand and then made a rolling gesture with her index finger to get him back to his narrative.

"So we talked about our trip to Corsica. A couple of days later, my uncle called me and told me to text him every day and tell him about the boat trip, especially all the stuff that happened. If I did that, he'd slip me five thousand euros when we got back. So while I was waiting for everyone to come on deck so I could get out of Nathalie's cabin, I did what I was supposed to do and texted him. He texted back and told me to find your gun, shoot it once, and stuff the shell into one of the holes in the scuppers. And that's exactly what I did.

"Remember, I hadn't really seen anything. I was just waiting for Nathalie, and all of a sudden she wasn't there anymore. So I hopped out of the cuddy and milled around with everyone else, coming and going, looking into all the cabins. I went into yours and found your gun in the top drawer of your chest of drawers. I took it and went up to the bow to shoot it off, like my uncle said. There was a lot of thunder, but I still didn't want to risk making too much noise, so I grabbed this jacket that was up there and wrapped it around the gun to silence it and catch the shell. You know, like they do in the movies. But as I was doing that, the goddamn gun went off all by itself."

The folly of leaving a bullet in the chamber, Capucine told herself.

Dominique mistook her silence for disapproval.

"It really did go off by itself. It really did. I'm not making this up. So I unwrapped the jacket and somehow managed to drop the shell. It disappeared. I have no idea where it went. So I wrapped the jacket around the gun and fired a second. That time I managed to hang on to the shell, which I stuffed into a hole in the scuppers, like I was supposed to."

He fell silent, exhausted with the effort of catharsis.

"Then what?"

"I stuck the jacket into the railing of the bow pulpit, put your pistol in my pocket, and went below. Everybody was listening to Serge on the radio, so I just ducked into your cabin and replaced your pistol. I swear, Capucine, that's all I did. You've got to believe me. I had nothing to do with Nathalie's death. You've got to believe me."

The uniformed receptionist stuck his head into the room and made a gesture with extended thumb and little finger, imitating a phone. Capucine had a call important enough to warrant an interruption of an interrogation. She went out into the hallway.

"Juge d'Instruction Maistre's secretary is on the phone. She asked me to disturb you. She said the juge will have a twenty-minute break between two meetings and she'd like to see you."

"When?" Capucine asked.

"In half an hour."

"Tell her I'll be there."

Capucine returned to the interrogation room and spoke to Capitaine Bourlon. "Put him in the detention cell. Something's come up. I'll be back in an hour. We can finish the interview then."

"Are you going to lock me up? But I told you I didn't do anything. I swear," Dominique said.

Capucine drove with the pulsing blue beacon on her dash and the siren wailing its *pam-pon-pam-pon.* There was no possibility of thought in the din.

In fifteen minutes Capucine was facing Inès across her desk.

"You called me the afternoon of Serge's conviction, but I wasn't able to take your call. I didn't want to leave you hanging. What was the matter?" Inès asked.

"An *état d'âme.* A state of mind. But I'm over it."

"Excellent. So you've filed the Nathalie case away?"

"Not at all. I've just arrested Dominique Berthier."

Under her foolish red frames, Inès's eyes smoldered.

"Dominique confessed that he fired the shots from my gun in an attempt to incriminate me for the murder of Nathalie. It seems he was acting under the instruction of a certain Monsieur Bufo, a big shot in the Ministry of the Interior."

"I know who Bufo is," Inès said. She glared at Capucine and traced patterns on the desk with her index finger. "And your plan?" Inès asked.

"Indict him. Have a procureur prosecute him. It's a serious crime. In fact, it's at least seven serious crimes. Among others, an attempt to incriminate someone, fabricating false evidence, several counts of lying to the police of two nations, and the pièce de résistance, refusal to assist a person in danger, who quite possibly died as a result of his indifference. He actually saw Nathalie go overboard. What would he get for all of that?"

"At least twenty years, if well prosecuted. But it won't go to court."

Her face like flint, Capucine said nothing.

"I suspected Bufo had one of his fat fingers in this," Inès said. "He wasn't named directly, but I had a hunch it might be him. I understand he doesn't like you. I don't know what you did to him, but apparently, he would be delighted to use you as a scapegoat."

"You seem far more informed than I am."

"*Instructed* is the right word. That's why the position is called a juge d'instruction." She smiled at her joke. "Sometimes I am instructed by the police, and sometimes by others." She continued to trace patterns on the desk.

"Capucine, you're being silly because you're angry. You're trying to go up against something you can't go up against. It's as foolish as throwing rocks at a herd of elephants. They won't even notice, but in the unlikely event they do, the consequences could be catastrophic."

"Elephants?"

"The denizens of the core of the power structure. They're as powerful and indestructible as elephants. And they take notice of little animals like you and me only when we can be of use."

"But you've devoted your life to bringing down these rogue elephants."

"Hardly. I only go after small game. I want results." She drummed the desk again, then smiled. "I know what you're thinking. I'm a hypocrite. But you're wrong. Sometimes the elephants actually help you."

"How were you helped?"

"Let's not waste time on something you'll read about in tomorrow's paper. Suffice it to say, I obtained a full dossier on Tottinguer. More than enough to prepare an unbeatable court case."

"From Bufo?"

"Good Lord, no. How naïve you can be, Capucine. I received it with the good graces of the senior partner of our largest law firm, who happens to be the biggest and possibly most powerful elephant of the herd."

"In exchange for what?"

"Nothing at all, really. I merely promised not to throw rocks. I promised not to be as foolish as you seem to want to be. You see, it really was a very good deal, don't you think?"

"I'm not sure I understand. I learned that Nathalie was an occasional operative for the DST. It turns out that Dominique is an outlier in Bufo's family. I assumed that this was all a plot to put you out of the way and have me blamed for it."

"You're absolutely right about that. And that's the way it would have happened if I didn't have a benefactor. A benefactor who acted in his own interest, not mine, but a benefactor nonetheless."

Capucine looked at her blankly, lost.

"Capucine, I have two words for you. Jade pendant. Does that answer your question?" Inès stood up. "I have an interview coming up. One I've been waiting a long time for. And one last thing before you go. Let me be perfectly clear. You have no case whatsoever against Dominique. No procureur in Paris would even look at the thing."

CHAPTER 41

Capucine stormed out of Inès's office, punched the elevator button incessantly until the elevator cab arrived, then accelerated her car in bursts, screeching to a stop when she was held up by traffic. At one point, after a stop so violent she skidded sideways, the driver of the car in front, a middle-aged man with a comb-over, shook his fist at her. Irate, Capucine clapped the blue police beacon on her dash and flipped on the siren, smirking as traffic scurried out of her way.

Back at her brigade, she ordered a perplexed Capitaine Bourlon to release Dominique, then stormed into her office and slammed the door. For fifteen minutes she drafted a terse resignation from the Police Judiciaire using a dented gold Waterman pen her grandfather had given her when she received her *bac.* The exercise calmed her. Her breathing returned to normal. She realized that the clerks in personnel would be oblivious to the nuances of her resignation letter. She tore it into minute pieces, scooped them into the palm of her hand, dropped the pieces into the wastebasket.

She extracted her phone and tapped Alexandre's speed-dial icon.

"Let's go out for dinner. I need cheering up. Where are you?"

"I'm at home, finishing up a piece. What a happy coincidence. I've booked at Le Grand Véfour. And your favorite cousin is coming along."

Capucine's breathing rate rose again. She felt like kicking the desk. It was always like this. Le Grand Véfour had lost its third star a few years before. With Alexandre on the premises, the staff would be all over him, lusting after the slightest scrap of high-powered praise they could get. She would be on show. Jacques would milk the situation for its comic potential. She should let the two of them go out, while she sat at home, in front of the TV, eating a frozen couscous meal from Carrefour. Capucine made an effort to control her breathing. *One. Two. Three. Four.*

"Why don't we go to Juvéniles instead?" Capucine said.

"The wine bar? It's a wonderful place, of

course, but wouldn't you rather have something a bit more exalted?"

"No. I've had my fill of the high and mighty. I want good, honest food and good, honest wine, prepared by people who understand both."

"You're on. That's an irresistible combination. Le Grand Véfour won't be happy with a canceled reservation, but into every life a little rain must fall."

They found Jacques already seated at a corner table, chatting with the owner of the restaurant, a voluble, portly, eternally baby-faced Scot, who had come to Paris twenty-five years earlier to write an article about wine and had wound up staying permanently.

One wall of the restaurant was lined with bottles stacked on their sides on dark-wood shelves. Unopened wooden wine crates were piled in front of the shelves. The feeling was that of a cheerfully discombobulated wine-shop. A chalkboard listed thirty or forty wines in a meticulous hand, but everyone knew these were only suggestions from among the hundreds of bottles available.

Over the years, the owner of the restaurant had become accepted as a genuine cognoscente in the French wine world. He categorically refused to serve Bordeaux, on the grounds that the entire region was priced far beyond its value and that the only viable buys were from the lesser known regions.

While Capucine was greeted by Jacques and the owner, Alexandre lingered, rooting through the current selection.

"You have a Coteaux du Languedoc that I've never come across before. How is it?" Alexandre asked when he arrived at the table.

Rather than reply, the owner held up his index finger authoritatively and then disappeared behind the bar, to return almost instantly with four glasses in one hand and a bottle in the other. With the legerdemain of a magician performing a card trick, he extracted the cork, put an inch of wine in his glass, took an explorative sip, nodded, and filled the other three. "Tell me what you think."

Capucine took a sip. It was smooth, mellow, unaggressive.

"Extraordinarily subtle and delicate," Alexandre said. "You're a genius. How do you find these treasures?"

"It's hard graft, but someone has to do it," the owner said with a laugh and a trace of Scots in his French. "Shall I bring a bottle?"

"Not just a bottle," Alexandre said. "I

want a whole case. The car is parked right out in front."

The restaurant filled quickly, and the owner wandered off to greet newcomers. The noise level rose steadily. Capucine, Alexandre, and Jacques breathed in the crowd, chatted desultorily, read the menu, then ordered from a pretty young Irish waitress. Goose foie gras with fig chutney for Alexandre and Jacques, and *jambon basque Ibaiona* — air-dried ham from Spain — and ripe cantaloupe melon for Capucine, to be followed by duck *gésier* confit salad for Capucine, a chicken tikka curry with cucumbers for Jacques, and haggis and mash for Alexandre.

The owner came up, poured the last of the Coteaux de Languedoc into their glasses, and asked if they wanted a second bottle.

A man sitting at the next table, imposing with his waxed handlebar mustache and flowing silver locks, butted in.

"I highly recommend the two thousand nine Domaine du Vissoux Fleurie Les Garants. It's powerful enough to balance with your dinners." He raised his glass to them.

Capucine breathed a sigh of relief. Table-to-table conversation was the norm at Juvéniles. There was going to be no discussion

448

of cases tonight.

But she was wrong. They chatted about nothing, drank a bottle of Les Garants with their dinner, then a second, then tasted two different Armagnacs. Despite the new French law, Juvéniles cast an unseeing eye on cigars, as long as they were Havana. Alexandre produced one from a leather case, lit it, offered the case to Jacques, who declined. Slowly the room emptied by half. The diners at either side of them were gone. They seemed to be enveloped in their own zone of privacy.

Jacques took Capucine's hand, kissed the tips of her fingers in a very un-cousinly gesture, and then raised his glass of Armagnac in salute. "So, cousine, you pulled off another one. You were very diligent in reading the signs from the sidelines."

Alexandre glowered at Jacques's kissing his wife's fingers. "What I've never really understood," Alexandre said, "is what was behind all this. We were taking a cruise with friends. How did so many of them turn into spies and murderers and criminals? It's like that Agatha Christie story on the Orient Express, where everyone turns out to be guilty."

"Cousin, I will take you up on your offer of a cigar," Jacques said.

He went through the irritating ritual of lighting up, puffing cautiously, scrutinizing the tip to make sure the nascent ash was even. After an interminable wait, Jacques spoke. "I can give you the background because my service is keeping its beady little eye on the situation," Jacques said.

He took another puff of the cigar and spent a long moment scrutinizing the ash. The owner of the restaurant headed over to chat but sensed the tension at the table and adjusted his path a few degrees to starboard, toward the bar, where he noisily prized open a wooden case of wine and began removing the bottles.

"It revolves around EADS, this Franco-German corporation created to merge French and German aviation and missile production and expand across the globe to become an aeronautical powerhouse."

Jacques took a deep puff on his cigar and eased into his tale.

"The plan was cooked up by consultants who are clever enough little elves but who are incapable of imagining that the people implementing their strategies don't behave like computer models. The seniors in the eleven companies that were merged, naturally enough, launched a cataclysmic battle for power. A battle, by the way, that is still far from resolved."

"So why is your agency so interested in this?" Alexandre asked.

"It's not rocket science," Jacques answered with the Cheshire cat grin. "Well, actually it is." He brayed an attenuated version of his earsplitting donkey laugh.

"Everyone knows about *le scandale* two summers ago, when large amounts of EADS stock was shorted only weeks before the announcement that the fabled double-decker transatlantic jet was going to miss its delivery date by over six months. Fortunes were made on the short sales. Our Inès was appointed to investigate but was unable to punch through the screen of anonymity. In short order everyone forgot about it all. Except terrier Inès, who has been barking away at the case ever since."

"Let me guess," Capucine said. "Conseiller Bufo was in charge of the police side of the inquiry."

" 'In charge' are big words to be used in this context. Let's just say 'involved.' But Bufo definitely deserves credit for his role in preventing any of the prime movers in the scandal from being named."

Jacques took a long puff on his cigar and watched the smoke rise to the ceiling. He leaned forward over the table. Capucine and

451

Alexandre leaned with him. Three school-children about to share a secret. "Bufo is a ministerial thug. He produces results but requires a good deal of direction. His puppeteer in the EADS case is none other than a lawyer you may have heard of, Etienne-Louis Lévêque. He's the spider at the center of the entire web. Or if you want a more *mondain* metaphor, a Richelieu, dressed not in ostentatious red, but in discreet bespoke Lanvin." He winked broadly at Alexandre.

"Bufo had two confederates on *Diomede*, Dominique keeping an eye on Nathalie, the sometimes DST agent, whose role presumably was to keep an eye on Inès and capitalize on any propitious situation that might arise. My surmise is that Lévêque placed his confederate on the boat, as well, to keep an eye on Bufo's confederates. It's a wonder we didn't stock up on eyedrops at every port of call."

"Jacques, how can you know these things? Dominique just confessed that this afternoon, and I tore up the procèsverbal."

Jacques said nothing and puffed a nimbus of smoke around his head.

"*Sapristi,* Jacques, enough sibling rivalry," Alexandre said, rapping on the table with his knuckles. "Just tell the damn story and be done with it."

The owner of the restaurant mistook the knuckle rapping for a request for more Armagnac and appeared with three tulip-shaped glasses. Embarrassed, Alexandre thanked him profusely. Everyone sipped. Jacques and Alexandre puffed.

"Think of it as one of those Italian operas with singers making unexpected entrances to sing a little aria. First, Nathalie wraps herself around the forestay, for reasons we won't go into in mixed company, and exits with Serge's help. Serge's jade amulet finds its way into the scuppers. Dominique pops out of Nathalie's cabin and fires a shot with Capucine's pistol, using Inès's jacket to muffle the sound. The shell casing goes astray and finds its way into the scuppers, as well. Frustrated, Dominique fires another round and manages to hang on to the shell casing, which he squeezes into its little hidey-hole. Pleased with himself, he melds into the clutch of people now milling around the deck."

Jacques looked up with an expectant smile, as if he were about to receive an accolade. Alexandre and Capucine stared at him expectantly.

"Well?" Alexandre asked in irritation.

"Hasn't Capucine told you?" Jacques asked.

"How could I have told him what I don't know? Did you find the casing all by yourself, or did someone give it to you? And what was that business with the jade amulet? What hidey-hole?"

"Isn't it obvious? Or are you insisting I betray confidences?"

Capucine made a moue, which evolved into a pout.

"Oh, all right, cousine. Aude investigated the foredeck. She gave me the shell casing. And, of course, I gave it to my favorite cousin."

"But what about the second shell casing, the one the Italian police found?" Alexandre asked.

"Now, that *is* interesting. I don't know, but I'll tell you my guess. There's a perforated steel strip that goes round the deck. It's there so you can clip various lines to it if the need arises. No need to explain to Tubby Hubby what a barber hauler is. The holes are small enough to catch a nine-millimeter shell, which is where I'll bet Dominique tucked the second shell. It would have been invisible there until the Italians got going with their lights."

Jacques puffed happily on his cigar.

"Jacques, there's a whole part of this story you're not telling," Capucine said. "What

454

about the jade amulet? Did Aude hide it? Why? You seemed awfully close to her. And what do you have to do with Lévêque, for that matter?"

Jacques took a deep puff on his cigar and let the smoke escape slowly through his sly grin.

"Me? Aude? We're just pawns in this tale. The important thing is that you seem to have friends in high places. Friends who have the instinct to know the precise moment you need to be extracted from the choucroute before something bad happens. I really can't say any more than that."

"Jacques, you're maddening."

"Actually, I have a question," Alexandre said. "Capucine told me that apparently Nathalie was a part-time hit man for the DST, unlikely as that may seem. Was she on the boat to rub someone out?" Alexandre crooned out the words "rub someone out" with relish.

Jacques said nothing but looked particularly enigmatic.

"Even I can guess that one," Capucine said. "Who else but Bufo? He must have decided to solve the Inès problem in his own way."

Jacques examined the smoke of his cigar rising to the ceiling.

"So," said Alexandre, "Inès's life was spared by Serge, the man she tricked into a confession so she could rob him of the last years of his youth. It's a story worthy of Maupassant."

"Isn't it?" Jacques said. "Right down to Serge's jade necklace."

"Jacques, you're impossible," Capucine said.

"Why? Because I know all your secrets?" Jacques stood up. "Walk with me. I have to meet some of my, ah, colleagues in the Palais Royal."

Alexandre went to the tiny counter to settle the bill.

"I have some news. I don't know if it's good or not, but it's definitely news." Jacques paused to see if Capucine would rise to the bait. She didn't. "A little piece of paper flitted across my desk this afternoon. It would appear that you are about to be promoted to commissaire principal." Jacques paused again, looking for a reaction. Again, there was none. "It won't be instanter. There's a bit of blather about your age, but there's also a *coup de pouce* — a little 'thumb nudge' — from Olympic heights. It will happen before the end of the year."

Capucine knew Jacques's little pieces of paper were never wrong. She would have to leave her brigade. There would be no more Isabelle. No more Momo. Just meetings. And even more meetings. Her shoulders drooped.

Alexandre joined them. "What's the matter? Are you two tiffing again?"

Neither Jacques nor Capucine answered. They moved out onto the narrow rue de Richelieu. Jacques led them to the left.

"Aren't we going the wrong way?" Capucine asked.

"No," Jacques said. "There's a little passage we can duck through right . . . here." He pushed open a black metal gate that looked like it might be the entrance to a building. After walking twenty feet, they found themselves in the immense, cavernous void of the Palais Royal. They strolled down a covered archway, past shops selling antique ball gowns, precious antiques, ancient medals and decorations.

Jacques tapped the glass storefront of one of the shops that sold medals. "It was either that or one of these." He pointed at the white, five-pointed cross hanging by the carmine ribbon of the Legion of Honor.

"I don't know which is worse." Capucine's eyes filled with liquid.

Jacques threaded his arm through hers and led her into the middle of the over-tended garden. The moon was full again. Alexandre followed behind, listening.

Of course you do. You're going to be needing lots more time at the hearth. And a ribbon would be no help at all for that.

"You're radiant in the moonlight," Jacques said.

"Isn't she?" Alexandre said from behind.

"I'd always heard about that but never thought it was really true."

"Jacques, does anyone keep any secrets from you?"

"Of course not. That's what I'm paid for."

He left them and sauntered down the garden. Capucine and Alexandre could just see the ruddy glow of his cigar when he puffed. At the end of the garden there might, or might not, have been two or three people waiting for him.

"So *that's* why you're having the guest bedroom repainted."

Capucine smiled up at him and said nothing.

The employees of Thorndike Press hope you have enjoyed this Large Print book. All our Thorndike, Wheeler, and Kennebec Large Print titles are designed for easy reading, and all our books are made to last. Other Thorndike Press Large Print books are available at your library, through selected bookstores, or directly from us.

For information about titles, please call:
    (800) 223-1244

or visit our Web site at:
    http://gale.cengage.com/thorndike

To share your comments, please write:
    Publisher
    Thorndike Press
    10 Water St., Suite 310
    Waterville, ME 04901